Heaven Inc. Urban Entertainment &

Angelic Script Publishing Presents...

Still
Thicker
Than Water

Takerra Allen

Cover Design:

Cover Concept: Takerra Allen and Sandra Mobley

Cover Model: Tara Cruz, Jill Espino, Kathy Lantigua

Cover Photography: Bhavash J

Edited by: Sandra 'Dee-Dee' Mobley and Takerra Allen

ISBN-10: 0-9844150-1-7

ISBN-13: 978-0-9844150-1-4

Printed in 2010

Printed in the USA

Acknowledgments

Alright, third time around. Really? Wow. Still brand new to this though, still growing and learning, and loving every minute of it. :-) Okay, enough. Let's get to it. Short & sweet. Yeah right, but I'll try. God. Seriously. To you be the glory. Mommy-do you see me down here? Are you smiling? I hope so. I never got a chance to tell you how perfect you were. How strong, and loving, and amazing you were. If I could live forever without you, or just one more day with you, it'd be the latter. I can't be selfish and I want you to rest in peace but I can't help how bad I MISS YOU. Daddy-you're my number one fan. I love you so much. Barry-you're my pumpkin, til death do us part. Baby aka Boobs-meow! Dee-dee-you know I couldn't do ANY of this without you. Seriously. Love you girl. Baby sister Leslie-so proud of you. Love you. Big sister N'neka-you're one of the most beautiful people I know. Adore you. Loving brothers-Corey, Billy, Malik, Landon, Tupac, Joe, I know I'm forever protected. Nana-you're the best. Been one of my best friends since I was like 2. :-) I love you. Aunt Leslie and Aunt Barbara, Ivan and June, love you all. All of my billions of cousins, aunts, uncles, etc. - we're thicker than water. Carol and Les Floyd-I know I'll always have another home with you. Alex-thank u 4 making my dad happy. :-) you're the best. Jaielyn, Trey, Naomi, Kamani, Chambray, Tanaia, Laila, Marcus, Jasmine, Malcolm, Brianna, Alexis, Ayesha, Greylin, Leilani-if you babies take anything from me I hope it's to follow your dreams, no matter what. The Mirandas and Romans-Puerto Rico! Love ya'll. Cover models-Tara, Jill, and Kathy. Thank you so much. Bhavash, thanks for the talent. All of the book vendors, stores, book clubs (whatsdastory, amazon, londa's, etc.), and reviewers that continue to show love-thank you from the bottom of my heart! I appreciate you all. All of the authors that show me love, love right back to you.
THIS BOOK IS DEDICATED TO MY FANS:
The Thicker than Water fans. The only reason that this book even exists is because YOU wanted it. This is YOUR book, I just wrote it. I hope you guys enjoy it, I hope it satisfies you. It would mean nothing if it was not everything you expected and more. I know every author says they have the best fans, and I'm sure I am sharing a few of you with them, but I think I truly have the most amazing supporters. I LOVE YOU.
Now turn the page and take a nice long sniff, you JUNKIES!
Anyone I forgot, I'm sorry. I'll catch you on the reprint, let me know. :-) Okay, it's about to start. Ssshhhh! Hope it's good. (crosses fingers)
Muahhhhhh! Xoxoxoxoxo

Chapter 1 - Life

There was something about today that made Sasha sick to her stomach.

Boom! Boom! Boom! "Let's go Sasha!"

Sasha took a deep breath, straightened her back, and went to unlock the bathroom stall door.

I can do this. And then it happened again, a sudden rush of vomit raced from her stomach to her mouth as she turned abruptly and exploded it into the toilet.

Boom! Boom! Boom! "Sasha, let me in! You know, you *are* getting married in exactly three minutes, bitch!" That was her annoying, country-ass cousin Cecile.

"Go away Cecile," Sasha mumbled, as she gripped the porcelain seat in the Buckhead Baptist Church.

"Move out of the way." Terri rudely pushed past the group of family members, who surrounded Sasha's hideaway stall. She began knocking firmly on the stall herself. "Sasha. Sasha, let me in."

When she received no response, she continued in true Terri fashion.

"Sasha, let me in this instant. It's your mother."

Like I don't know who she is.

"Sasha. Sasha," Terri repeated in a hushed voice.

Sasha unrolled the two-ply toilet paper and wiped the chunks from her lips as she made a comfortable seat on the stall floor. She could care less about the $8,000 Vera Wang dress that adorned her gorgeous body. She cradled her head in her hands, not paying any

1

mind to her flawless makeup that accentuated her flawless face. She could care less about her hair, this wedding, this day, this man, this life.

Why?

Ever since the surreal events that occurred two summers ago, Sasha often found herself asking that question. Why did her life take such an abrupt turn? Why did Kim have to die? Why did Neli have to ruin everything? And most of all, why did *he* have to break her heart?

Tears lined her face as she thought of Chauncey, the love of her life, the only man that she was sure would ever hold her heart, and the man that had cheated with one of her, used to be, best friends. *I guess Neli really did get the last laugh, huh? Chauncey and I are done, just like she wanted. My friends are gone, Kim is dead, Tatum is far away, my world is crumbled...hope the bitch rots in the nuthouse.*

Sasha could hear heels clicking toward her door and was sure it was someone else trying to convince her to emerge from the toilet, be a woman, take the shit on the chin and walk down the aisle. But the girl in her just couldn't bring herself to stand up and face the reality.

"Sasha," a sweet voice beckoned. Sasha looked down at the voice's feet and studied the Zanotti sandals that she had recently herself purchased. *Hmm.*

"Sash, it's me...Tatum." Sasha's ears perked at the delayed recognition of her best friend's voice. *Tatum made it.* "Open the door, girl."

Sasha didn't want to face the others, she could still see her mother's Prada heels and other less glamorous feet scattered around the door. She did however want to see Tatum, her girl, her best friend who had weathered the awful storm with her and still managed to remain by her side. She slowly unlatched the door and before anyone could get a word out, she pulled Tatum inside and closed it back.

Tatum chuckled, mouth opened, at Sasha's dramatic behavior but then embraced her fully in a long, warm hug.

"Ahh mama, I missed youuuu!" She squealed.

Sasha squeezed back harder and laughed, thrilled to see her partner in crime.

"Black bitch, how you been?" Sasha joked, still embracing her, and using the nickname they had used as girls. Sasha was the brown bitch, Kim used to be the yellow bitch, and Neli, formerly known as the white bitch, was now just the crazy bitch.

"I'm good, but what's up with you girl, locked in the stall like a little ass kid...Getting cold feet?"

Tatum had a feeling what was wrong with Sasha, but was confused as to how she had come this far, but was just now debating not following through.

"I don't know Tay...I don't know," Sasha answered truthfully, really not knowing. Tatum studied her friend with a look of uncertainty and brushed away the hair from Sasha's face with her left hand. She realized how beautiful she looked.

Her hair had grown out and was down in pretty curls, with a diamond tiara atop of her head. Her skin was perfection, and she had put on a little weight in her butt and thigh area, Atlanta was doing her physically well. But how was it mentally affecting her?

"Sasha, you know I know you better than anyone, and if you're not feeling it-" Tatum was cut off by Terri from outside of the stall.

"If you don't want to do it sweetie, we can call the whole thing off...just let me know now so I can cancel the band for the reception."

"Ma!" Sasha screamed, irritated that her mother had been eavesdropping on their conversation the whole time. Although her mother was ridiculously annoying in her prying, she did have a point, and was never shy about voicing it. Terri was no fan of Mike, and although Chauncey had brought more pain than pleasure, Terri was still on his team, cheering on the sidelines, and hoping that one day he and Sasha would be reunited.

3

Sasha leaned her head back and stared up at the ceiling, wondering what was holding her back. Mike was a good guy; he worked his way through medical school, was now a doctor, catered to Sasha head to foot, and took her and Chauncey's daughter, Aubrey, in as his own. Who wouldn't want to marry him? *Me.*

Tatum was still looking at Sasha with that look. That look that said, *just let me know what you wanna do?* Sasha knew Tatum was with her no matter what.

What am I thinking? Pass up on Mike, for what? For Chauncey? The man that's in jail, the man that I don't even know if I can trust? The man who clearly has no plans on leaving the street life alone any time soon? No, no way. I have to be smarter than that. I have a little girl to think about. Hell no!

"No, no, I'm fine. I'm doing it…Ma, you hear me, I'm doing it. So hang up the phone," she barked.

"I… I am not on the phone," Terri defensively answered, but then whispered into her cell, "Cancel that, wedding's back on."

Sasha rolled her eyes at her mother's assumption, and then took a deep breath and looked at Tatum with a smile.

"See, I'm fine. I just needed a moment…and I needed you," Sasha admitted, glad that her best friend was now there to hold her hand. Tatum looked at her with doubt.

"You sure?"

Sasha nodded vigorously.

"Yea, yea. Absolutely." She fingered her curls and adjusted her gown, and then she opened the bathroom door with true Sasha confidence. "Okay, let's go! Cecile, go tell the organist we're starting…. Ma, go get daddy… Tatum…" She looked at Tatum. "Hold my hand."

She rushed to the mirror and rinsed out her mouth, and then made sure her makeup was on point as a couple of people adjusted her gown. Then she turned around and faced the girls.

"Okay, now let's go get me married."

The melody of sweet violins began to play, as Sasha's one year-old daughter, Aubrey, walked down the aisle assisted by an older cousin. They were the flower girls. Followed by them, was the ring bearer, a little boy from Mike's family, and then the first bridesmaid, who was Sasha's old friend, Jayde.

Next was Sasha's cousin, Cecile, another bridesmaid, by her mother's choice. And last was Mike's best man, with Sasha's maid of honor, Tatum. Sasha heard the music change to the traditional bridal march, and her heart fluttered. Her father remained completely silent, but held a firm grip on her arm. *Thank god, because I don't think I can stand on my own.*

Sasha thought of the irony of her reflection, this was the very reason why she was getting married; she didn't think that she could stand on her own.

"You ready baby?" Her father asked her, but Sasha couldn't answer. She just looked at him with a smile as the doors opened wide.

The crowd stood at attention and focused on Sasha and her father as they began to slowly make their way down the aisle. Sasha held a plastered smile and studied the happy faces, grinning and snapping pictures. She felt like she was walking to her execution and she was hoping that her emotions weren't showing on her face. Halfway down the aisle, she felt as if she should finally look at Mike, maybe something that wasn't there, would suddenly exist in her when she saw his face. Maybe she could will herself to want him, need him, love him. The sad realization came about when she looked into his eyes and felt the need to run in the opposite direction.

He was looking at her with so much love, so much pride, so much adoration. The thought of her marrying him and depriving him of true requited love caused tears to form into her eyes, which people mistook for an overwhelming rush of emotion.

As she reached the altar, a sweat broke on her brow and she took a deep breath, hoping that she didn't have a repeat of the bathroom stall.

5

"Who gives this woman away?"
Don't daddy, don't say it.
"I do."
Her father and Mike exchanged Sasha with ease, as if she were money, and Sasha wondered why this was so easy for everyone else.
"Dearly beloved, we are gathered here today…"
Okay, okay, I can do this. Look at him, he's good looking… I mean, he is a little corny, and why the hell is his tie so tight? No, no… he's not corny, he's safe. Safe, reliable, gives me no trouble… Wait, what am I marrying, a man or a car? Oh god, Sasha stop it! Take his hands. Are they telling us to hold hands…? I think so. He's reaching for my hands. There, everyone is smiling, I must be doing the right thing. Why are his hands so clammy? …Look at him, he loves me. Look how happy he is. Concentrate Sasha, Concentrate…
"Marriage is the union of husband and wife in heart, body, and mind. It is intended for their mutual joy…" The pastor's voice subsided to a whisper, and then ceased.
What happened? Sasha wondered. *Is it over, am I supposed to say something now?*
She looked to Mike for some reassurance but was confused as to why he was not looking at her. Instead he, like everyone else, was focused on the aisle. Sasha turned, as if in slow motion, and swore that the breath left her body.
"Oh my god," she whispered.
Her heart raced, her head was light, and she had to reach out and hold onto the pastor's shoulder for support. It was him, and just like always, he commanded everyone's attention.
He was dressed in true street fashion, crisp jeans, fresh Air Force's, blinding jewelry, head full of waves, chocolate skin glowing, confident smile. He stood in the center of the aisle as if he belonged there and as everyone stared at him, he focused on Sasha.
"I tried to wait until the *'if anyone objects'* shit, but I figured I wouldn't waste anymore of your time…let's go kid."

Sasha held his gaze with tears in her eyes and stunned into silence. She hesitantly looked away at Mike and could see the rage radiating off of him. She looked back to Chauncey, who now held out his hand for her, as everyone studied Sasha wondering how she would handle the situation.

"Daddy!" Aubrey exclaimed, rushing up to him.

He picked her up and kissed her face lovingly and then looked back to Sasha.

"Come on princess, come on home. I got you…I'll never hurt you again."

"You sure?" The question escaped Sasha's lips before she even realized that she was talking.

"My word…I love you," he affectionately admitted.

"I love you, too."

Sasha's feet felt as if they were firmly planted into the ground but as she admitted her love for Chauncey, they began to take flight and she made her way to him. She lifted her gown and didn't even offer Mike an apology; she just rushed to her man, her love.

Chauncey pulled her close as she finally reached him, and looked deeply into her eyes. He held Aubrey with his right hand, as his left hand caressed Sasha's face. He leaned in to kiss her lips and Sasha braced herself for what she had been missing. She could feel his breath on her face as he went from inches away, to almost nose to nose with her. She could smell him, almost taste him, she closed her eyes and her heart melted, and then…and then…and then…

"Noooooooooo!!!" Sasha screamed, as she abruptly sat upright in her bed. "No, no, no!" She bawled, more quietly, when she noticed that Mike was still peacefully asleep next to her. Chauncey was gone. That was her reality. But in her dreams, she could still have him, or at least, she thought. Lately, it seemed that she couldn't even have that.

She looked down at her wedding ring on her finger, that barely sparkled in the dark, but she still knew that it was there. It was all a lie. She could hear the crickets chirping outside as she gently lifted herself out of bed, and treaded softly out of the room.

7

She crept into Aubrey's room and could see her sleeping serenely, clutching her worn out pink teddy bear. *We've got to get that thing out of here.*

Her baby, she was so beautiful, looking more and more like Chauncey every day. She blew her a silent kiss as she turned around and headed for the stairs.

She quietly made her way down the dark staircase and could see the moonlight illuminating the dimness of their home. As Sasha entered the living room, she took a seat on the couch, looking around at her beige living room in the night and thinking of how it reflected her present situation. Her life was now so beige. *Chauncey would never allow all of this beige. He would have made me throw some color, or at least some black up in here. Mmm, Chauncey.*

Her thoughts of him re-entered her head as she imagined him the way he appeared in her dream. Those thoughts then turned to ones of their old steamy nights, as Sasha thought of Chauncey's lips and tongue caressing her body. Mike didn't know how to do it like him; Mike didn't know how to do it at all.

Sasha's sex life was lacking and she was in desperate need. Sasha thought of how Chauncey used to throw her on the dining room table and eat her like dinner. She imagined Chauncey parting her legs and kissing her thighs as her fingers made her way down her white silk nightie and to her thighs, tracing her fingertips softly up and down, trying her best to emulate a tongue.

Then, she thought of him parting her second lips with his tongue and discovering her tender clit, gently sucking on it and flicking it, the way she loved. Her fingers tried to do these visions justice as she lay her head back on the couch and kicked her legs up on the table. *Oh,* she softly moaned.

You like that?

Yes...

Show me.

She moaned sultrily the way Chauncey liked it, and even said the dirty words lightly that he loved to hear.

Yes, right there daddy. Eat your pussy...this is your pussy. That's my girl.
She could hear him. She could feel him. And she wondered if whatever he was doing in his cell right now, could he taste her?
She could feel herself building up to an orgasm as she moved her fingers faster and faster.
"Oh Chauncey, oh yes...oh my god, yes," she cried in passion. Her face grew hot and her left leg began to shake as her hair lay against her wet forehead that was now sweating.
"Yes...yes..."
"Sasha!" Mike yelled, interrupting her one on one party, and cutting her orgasm short.
"Hu-huh?" She stammered, hoping that he hadn't heard her.
"You alright down there... You coming to bed?"
She took a deep breath to regain her composure, and pulled her nightie back down to her thighs. She *was* cumming, but now she figured that she was just coming...back to bed.
"Yes...yes I'm fine," she stuttered. "I'll be right up."
She could hear his heavy footsteps retreat from the stairs slowly back to the bedroom, and she wondered how she had missed hearing them in the first place. She also wondered how Mike had managed to keep her dissatisfied, even when he wasn't involved in the encounter.
Damn, she thought, standing up and making her way back to her bedroom. Back to reality.

Chapter 2 - Truth

*The past couple of years have been so crazy. I never knew we
would end up like this.*
*For starters, my best friend Sasha, and her baby's father
Chauncey, are apart now. And they were like the hood's Bonnie
and Clyde, Newark's own Beyonce and Jay. She's married now, to
some square dude, Mike, living down in Atlanta, and Chauncey's
locked down doing a bid. And it's such a shame.*
*Chauncey was like a big brother to me, he grew up with my own
brother Chris, and they even worked for the same man...for my
man, Respect. Or Ree, as I like to call him.*
*See Ree, he's like the alpha man, he's got it all; swagger, boss
status, intellect...and my heart. But, my brother got caught up and
snitched on him and Ree had to go on the run. Now, my brother's
dead. And Kim's dead... Kim, our sister, our girl, damn.*
*See she was the life of the party, and I miss her so much.
Sometimes I even miss Neli...Nah, maybe I just miss the way the
four of us used to be.*
*Neli, she was our other friend, and she's in the damn crazy house
now, but really, she deserves more. I don't care if she don't have it
all, the way she set it all up, fucking Chauncey behind Sasha's
back, trying to get Sasha killed, and even having Kim murdered, I
could never forgive her! I'm kinda glad Chauncey beat her the way
that he did, even though that's what got him locked up.*
*Damn, see what I mean, it's been crazy for everyone. And me, now
here I am...But where am I?*
"Where am I?" Tatum questioned aloud. She stared at the cursor
on the computer screen for a couple of seconds before she became
frustrated and slammed the laptop closed. This was the third time

10

this week that she had attempted to put her thoughts on paper, hoping that it would help get her book started. After all of the drama that occurred two summers ago, writing her dream book went from being a fantasy to a checkpoint on her must do list. In addition to forgetting *him.*

Tatum had way too much shit on her mind.

She got up from her computer desk and walked over to her bed, picking up a throw blanket and wrapping it around her shoulders. As she made her way to the thermostat to turn the heat up, she wondered what the weather was like in Jamaica.

"It damn sure aint 48 degrees," she whispered, turning her heat up to the max.

She never did have the courage to pick up and follow Ree to Jamaica, even though she had contemplated heavy on it. She hadn't heard from him, or even had a sign of him, since he had sent the mysterious postcard in the summer of '08.

Now, here it was, a year and a half later, and he was still in her thoughts.

It gets better every day though. I get over him a little more every day.

Tatum felt like she had made the best decision, not wanting to live her life on the run, and bank her whole future on a postcard. *I don't care what Sasha says, sending a postcard does not equal, 'I love you, come to Jamaica, and spend the rest of your life with me.'*

But no matter how much she tried to convince herself, she knew that he had wanted her to come.

Had? But would he still? Tatum wondered, laying her head back against the wall, getting lost in her thoughts.

Just then, her phone began vibrating on her computer desk as she walked over and answered, not recognizing the number.

"Hello," Tatum greeted, sounding more like a question.

"Heyyy bitch, what it do?"

Tatum smirked.

"What it do? Okay, Atlanta overload…Whose number is this?"

Sasha paused briefly before answering.

11

"Oh… it's mine. We got a new house number."

Tatum laughed.

"Oh I see, you mean Chauncey been blowing yall shit up so much that Mike finally decided stop playing 'yes m'am' to you, put his foot down, and change that bitch up."

"Yeah, well, something like that," Sasha chuckled, watching Mike drink orange juice straight from the carton as it spilled onto his shirt. It was the little things that disgusted Sasha.

"Oh…he's around," Tatum guessed, noticing Sasha's short replies.

"Yeah…but about the other thing, I don't get it?" Sasha spoke in code.

"What you mean?" Tatum asked, slipping on some cozy socks. Her apartment still wasn't heating up.

Sasha watched as Mike made his way out of the kitchen, wiping his shirt with his hand, and out onto the deck where his photo studio was located. It was a hobby that he had recently taken up and Sasha was not allowed in it, not that she cared anyway. Once he closed the sliding door, Sasha continued.

"Okay, he's gone now. But yeah, I don't get it," she whispered. "How can he get mad about Chauncey calling here, Aubrey is Chauncey's daughter too. He has a right to talk to her… I don't get how he can be mad at that."

Tatum rolled her eyes at Sasha's naivety.

"I can. Shit, Chauncey be buggin', calling all day, all night. And all times of the night at that. Aubrey doesn't even be up…how does he do that anyway?" Tatum pondered, wondering how Chauncey managed all of these special privileges in jail.

"You know what it is," Sasha drawled in her country accent, thinking of how many connections Chauncey had. "But I guess you're right. That's why I let Mike change it. We were arguing so much about it, he kept bitching so I told him to just do it. Chaunc gon' have to just hit the cell when he wanna talk to Aubrey."

"They can do that?" Tatum questioned.

"Chauncey can," was Sasha's simple answer.

There was a brief silence as Tatum thought of how evident Sasha's love for Chauncey was. If Mike couldn't see it, it meant he just didn't want to.

Tatum had to change the subject though, talking about Chauncey made Tatum think of Ree, being that they were so close. Chauncey was Ree's number one, the next in line when Ree was still heavy in Jersey's drug game. Tatum changed the topic.

"Wait, why didn't you call the house?"

"Oh, it was off," Sasha responded, sounding distant.

Shit, Tatum thought. *I gotta pay that bill.* She wanted to change the subject again before Sasha offered her any money. She wasn't doing badly to where she needed any handouts. Yeah, money was tight without her brother helping with the rent, but her hair clients kept her able to pay her bills and still manage to be fly. Things still, were just not as easy as they used to be and she found it now more difficult to stay on top of everything.

Damn, when Ree was around. That's all she could think. She didn't want for anything with him. But his wealth wasn't even what attracted her. She was in love with him. *Oh well.*

Tatum now knew she had to get off of the phone matter.

"Well, I know Chauncey's gonna be pissed when he tries to call."

It seemed that Sasha perked at the mention of Chauncey.

"Yeah, I know..." Sasha paused and then continued. "You know Tatum, I think I wanna visit you."

Tatum smirked, and twisted her mouth to the side.

"You wanna come see me, huh? When?"

"Tomorrow!" Sasha exclaimed. "I'm gonna come see you tomorrow, if I can get a flight."

Tatum shook her head from side to side and laughed to herself. She knew that Sasha wanted to visit Chauncey ASAP because he would be hot when he tried to call the house and it was disconnected.

"Yeah well, you know you're welcome, but don't expect a party bitch. This visit's short notice as hell and I got shit to do," Tatum joked.

"Oh please Tay, I'm taking you for a spa treatment. We're gonna get facials and massages, and you get to see your goddaughter, and…we can bring you your extra special, crazy huge Christmas gift. You know you need a facial too, you probably look like shit," Sasha laughed.

Tatum sucked her teeth and went to the mirror, wondering what this gift was that Sasha was doting over. Tatum studied her long black curly hair and mocha complexion in the reflection. She looked gorgeous, but felt she could use a treatment.

"Fuck you girl, I look good," she murmured. "But wait, Christmas is weeks away...and you got this big gift already for me? You mean Miss Procrastinator did her Christmas shopping already?"

Sasha rolled her eyes playfully and giggled.

"Haha, but it's *Mrs.* Procrastinator now, I'm a married woman, remember?" She remarked sarcastically. "And yes, that's what good, suburban families do." She and Tatum shared a laugh.

"Whatever!" Tatum exclaimed, getting excited about seeing her friend. "Just call me when you get your flight info."

Sasha agreed, and the girls ended their conversation. Tatum decided to lie down and rest her eyes for a moment.

A couple of hours later, a loud knock at the door awoke Tatum from her nap. She reached over and looked at the clock, and saw that it was after 5 pm and dark out. *Damn, where did the time go?* She slowly rose out of her bed and walked to the door.

"Coming," she muttered, barely audible.

The banging on the door became more intense and louder and Tatum felt herself catching an instant attitude, as she made her way through the dark hallway to the front door.

"I said I was coming, damn," she snapped, finally snatching the door open. She rolled her eyes seeing that it was only Nikki, her brother's ex, and the mother of her nieces. She had Tatum's two nieces - Chanel and Tangee, all bundled up in their matching pink Northface coats, with McDonald's bags in their hands. Tatum brightened seeing the girls.

14

"Hey mamas, did you guys have fun?"
They nodded and made their way into the house past her, desperate for heat and their fast food fixes.
"Bye girls! Love you!" Nikki screamed after them, but they were already inside. "Damn Tay, what took you so long to come to the door? You know I got my six o'clock meeting today."
Nikki was a recovering cocaine addict, who unbeknownst to Tatum and the girls, had been clean for the past year and getting her life in order. She had recently been granted unsupervised visits with Chanel and Tangee, which Tatum was no huge fan of.
"Well, I guess you better get going then," Tatum quipped nonchalantly.
"Yeah, I guess...bye Tay," Nikki added, double stepping down the stairs and back to her 1988 Subaru in a rush. She was trying desperately to get back in Tatum's good graces after abandoning her children for mostly all of their lives, but Tatum was making that extremely difficult to do.
Tatum watched with contempt as Nikki pulled off, and then she shut her door on the cold December weather. She was happy the girls were back home so that they could enjoy some quality time together, and so that she could finally take her mind off of other things.

Chapter 3 - Anticipation

"Okay so, can you answer me this one question Sasha...Why the fuck, do you have so many outfits for two days?"
Sasha turned around with a fake attitude but then busted out laughing. She was standing in her walk in closet, packing her Louis Vuitton duffel bag, and her childhood friend Jayde, was sitting on her bed giving her the 21 question session.
"Actually it's for three days, and I don't know, I'm not sure what the weather is like in Jersey," Sasha defended with a serious face, but not making eye contact as she tossed another pair of jeans into the bag.
Jayde rolled her eyes and took her nail file out of her purse, not believing a single word Sasha was saying. As she filed her nails, she continued her accusations.
"Yeah, whatever. All you gotta say is I wanna make sure I look good when I go see my baby daddy, Jayde. That's all."
"I told you I'm not going to see him," Sasha said in a hushed whisper. "And stop being so loud before Mike hears you."
Jayde sucked her teeth.
"Mike, Smike, whatever. I don't care if that little mothafucka hears me! Aint like he gonna do shit, he's softer than cotton, Sash," Jayde chuckled.
Sasha studied Jayde, sitting there perched up like the Queen of England, and she wanted to defend Mike, but she knew Jayde was telling the truth. And if the truth needed to be told, Jayde would do the honors. She didn't bite her tongue for anyone, and standing at 5 feet 10 inches with bold emerald green eyes, long flowing jet-black hair, and the best body that her money could and had bought her,

16

people were either intimidated by her height, her beauty, or both. And she used it to her advantage.

Sasha had known Jayde since she was younger, when she used to live in Atlanta as a girl. Their parents had been close and they had grown up together. They had lost touch when Sasha moved to Jersey, but when she came back to the South, she was happy to link back up with Jayde. It was good to have a friend close by with Tatum being so far away.

And Jayde was the friend to have. While Sasha had gone off to college and fell in love, gotten pregnant and lived the hood fairytale, Jayde had stayed in Atlanta and mixed and mingled with the Georgia elite, and built a stone wall of connections and friends that could get you anything, anywhere, and anytime. She was something like the it-girl in Atlanta, and the Real Housewives didn't have shit on her! If people thought Sasha was bad with her self-adoration and extra dose of confidence, then they wouldn't want to meet Jayde. She was a bad bitch.

"Hello ladies," Mike greeted them cheerily, entering the room and holding Aubrey, just as Jayde had finished dissing him.

"Hey babe," Sasha responded holding up two sweaters and trying to decide which one to bring. She threw both onto the bed and then she walked over to Aubrey.

"Hey mommy's girl, hey baby girl," she cooed at Aubrey, who giggled.

"Hi Mommy," she replied adorably.

"I said hello, Jayde," Mike restated.

"Hello Mike," Jayde said sarcastically with extra joy. She then smiled at Aubrey and reached out her arms. "Hey mama, hey girl... Come to Auntie Jayde."

As Mike handed off Aubrey he looked down at Sasha's bag and got a lump in his throat and his stomach twisted in worry.

"Going somewhere, babe?"

Sasha played it cool making her way back to the closet.

"Oh, yea... Tatum asked me to come up and visit her this weekend, being that we won't see each other on Christmas. So I'm gonna go up there."

Jayde shook her head from side to side as she sat Aubrey on her lap facing her. She didn't understand what the big deal was, and why Sasha felt the need to lie about visiting Chauncey; lying to Mike, to Tatum, to Jayde, and to herself.

Mike hated her going there but he knew there was nothing he could do. He knew she was going to visit Chauncey and he tried to be okay with it, but he wasn't. Every time she would go he would call her constantly and when she returned, he would drill her for weeks about what she did.

"That's all, you just going to see Tatum? You not going to the jail?" He put it out there.

Sasha knew she could just fess up, but she didn't.

"No. Unh-unh, I just went not too long ago, remember?"

"Yeah, I know. That's what I was going to say," Mike answered, matter of factly. "So, how long you're going for?"

Sasha sighed. *Here goes the interview.*

"Um, just the weekend."

She went to her shoeboxes and retrieved a couple of pairs of stiletto-heeled boots.

Mike studied his beautiful wife in her cut off shorts and wife beater tank top. She was gorgeous with a body of a goddess, and he was very possessive now that he had finally gotten her. He had waited for years for Chauncey to mess up, while he played the friend role, and he did not want him to ever get another chance of winning her back.

"Oh, okay. Well, I'm not working this weekend. I can come with you," he suggested, making his way closer to her.

Sasha turned and looked at him.

"Babe, you're a doctor. You're always on call. You can't just leave for a whole weekend."

She dismissed his notion before he could get any further with it.

Mike felt as if he was getting the brush off and he didn't like it.

"Well, babe, I have vacation days…I can put them in and then I won't be on call."
Jayde rolled her eyes and continued playing peek-a-boo with Aubrey as Sasha tried to zip her bag closed.
"Yeah…well…it's kinda gonna be a girls' weekend. We'll be doing things for just the girls. Can you hold this while I zip?"
She wanted to change the subject, he was so clingy.
Mike struggled to hold the bag closed and pressed on.
"What kind of things for the girls…and maybe if you didn't pack… so many clothes… it would close more easily."
Jayde had heard enough. She grabbed Aubrey's hands and whispered to her loud enough for everyone to hear.
"Maybe if Uncle Mikey didn't pester mommy so much… and didn't have his head so far up mommy's ass, then maybe mommy wouldn't need a girls' weekend, right? Right Bri-Bri?" Aubrey laughed, as Sasha held in her own laughter.
"Jayde!" She yelled as Mike just cut his eyes at her.
"You know what Jayde, you should put all of that energy you use trying to pry into Sasha's life, and find a man of your own…. and I am not Uncle Mike…I'm daddy. Say daddy," he urged Aubrey.
Jayde looked at Sasha like he was crazy and Sasha stopped fumbling with her bag and stood alert with her hand on her hip. She hated when he did that.
"Stop Mike," Sasha ordered, upset.
"Stop what?" He feigned like he was shocked, but he knew Sasha was mad, and why.
Sasha walked over and picked up Aubrey.
"Stop telling her to call you *that*. You're going to confuse her."
Mike laughed obnoxiously.
"Confuse her? How… she doesn't have a father! You're acting like she sees two different men, everyday, and she doesn't know who her father is. He's in jail."
He laughed again like he had said the funniest thing in the world.
Sasha was becoming angrier by the minute.

19

"That's right, in jail. Not dead, Mike!" Sasha could feel tears welling in her eyes and didn't know why. "And even if he were, *he* is her father, and will always be…you can't replace him, Mike."

Mike's face dropped instantly and he just stood there, staring at her as his temper surged and his heart broke. He knew her last statement was not just in reference to Aubrey.

Sasha held his stern gaze, but then blinked away her tears and put Aubrey down. Mike wanted to say something but just nodded and made his way to the door without a single word spoken.

Jayde bit on her bottom lip not sure of what to say for once, but glad that Sasha had stood up for herself, and for her daughter's father. As Sasha went back to her packing, now searching for her toiletries bag, she started thinking of how Mike had just walked out without even defending himself against her hurtful comment. Another thing that disgusted her about him.

"So what's up after this…you wanna go grab dinner?" Sasha asked Jayde, desperate to get out of that house. Even though it was a spacious, two-story home, it suddenly felt cramped. She turned around and looked at Jayde when she didn't get an answer.

Jayde went into her purse and pulled out her phone with a blank look on her face, as if she were thinking of a response.

"Helloooo…earth to Jayde."

"Oh, um… No, I can't girl…I've got some business to take care of."

Jayde could tell Sasha was skeptical of her answer so she tried to lighten the mood. She stood up and walked over to Sasha with a big grin.

"Buttt, when you get back from seeing 'yo baby daddy' we can go over to Justin's, and eat a whole bunch of Soul Food that aint no good for us and talk about your *Jersey* experience."

Sasha chuckled at Jayde, momentarily forgetting the delayed and obvious excuse that she had come up with.

"First of all, you know you aint gonna eat a whole bunch of nothing, with your perfect body-obsessed ass…and since you want to be so secretive," Sasha paused and playfully pushed Jayde. "I want Sylvia's, not Justin's...on you."

Jayde grabbed her purse and slid on her Dior shades, after walking over and giving Aubrey a kiss. Aubrey was now playing with her mommy's lip-gloss in her toiletries bag, lost in her own little world.

"You got it babe," Jayde told her, blowing Sasha a kiss and making her way to the door.

Sasha stood for a moment wondering what was up with that about Jayde. It seemed that since they had reconnected, there was something that she kept hidden from Sasha.

Maybe she got a little jump off that she don't want nobody to know about...yeah, that's probably it, Sasha figured, as she looked down at her things.

She pushed the thought out of her head and looked at her daughter, smiling and knowing that packing her up wouldn't be half as much work. Then she took a deep breath and braced herself for her trip back to Newark, NJ. *Here I come.*

Chapter 4 - Allure

"Oh my god, pollution!" Sasha screamed dramatically. "And look, dirty snow! Northfaces!"
Tatum cracked up laughing at her crazy friend who was running around the front of Newark Airport, in the cold night air, acting like a kid in a candy store.
"Damn, I missed Jersey!"
"Bitch, it has not even been that long," Tatum reminded her, putting Aubrey into the car seat and walking around to the driver's side of her Honda Civic EX sedan.
Sasha got into the passenger seat and looked around the car.
"What happened to the truck?" She asked, admiring the new car. It was nice, but Tatum had loved her truck.
"Ah, I don't know. I wanted a change...plus the gas on that thing."
Sasha cut her off.
"Say no more." And they both laughed.
"It's nice though, this a '08?"
"Nah, '07...hey Aubrey!" Tatum cooed, turning around in her seat and looking at her goddaughter.
"Hi Auntie," she answered, smiling wide. She was only three months from being two years old, but spoke so clearly. Sasha spent a lot of time with her and Tatum believed that was why she was so developed.
Aubrey sat, looking cute with her two curly pom-pom ponytails and big brown eyes. Chanel and Tangee were knocked out in the backseat next to her. "You hungry?"
Sasha buckled her seatbelt and answered hastily.
"Heck yeah!"

"I was talking to your daughter," Tatum laughed at Sasha's spoiled ass. "But what you want, mama?"

"Mmmm, I want a, no two, dirty dogs. Yummmm," Sasha proclaimed, rubbing her stomach as Tatum scrunched up her face. Tatum had seen enough of the street vendor hot dogs for a lifetime, but Sasha had been feigning for them.

"Oh come on, don't judge me," Sasha pouted. "I haven't had them in so long."

Tatum smiled at her, so glad that she was here, even if it was just for the weekend. This was her best friend, and she hated to admit it, but she had been lonely.

"Okay, okay, no judgment," Tatum said, turning up the radio and exiting the airport, heading for Broad Street. It was just like old times.

Back in Atlanta

Jayde's stiletto heels clicked across the marble floor, as she strategically lit candles around her luxurious condo located in the Buckhead section of Atlanta. Her home was located inside of the elegant Sovereign Tower, which curved high along the Georgia skyline, and sat its residents on top of the city as if royalty. Jayde owned two of them, and had recently revamped them, knocking down the walls and turning her two, into one, mega condo.

She wore a long, black, sheer slip-nightie, which hugged her artificial, yet perfect, ass and breasts. Her hair was pulled back into a long ponytail, displaying her striking green eyes. She moved around her dimly lit living space as the sounds of Trey Songz newest CD blared from her theater speaker system. As she lit the last candle, there was a knock on the door.

"Come in," she demanded. She glided over to her bar and poured a glass of Nuvo, keeping her back turned to the door, and her guest. "You want a drink?"

"Not that pink shit," he barked, trying to sound hard. However Jayde's hypnotizing, bare ass that showed through her see-thru gown, made it hard for him to maintain his composure. He looked around at the spacious place and wondered how much it ran her. And he wondered why it was so damn dark; the only light seemed to be coming from the candles.

She could see him still standing through the glass of the bar, but she remained with her back turned to him.

"Well the pink shit is what we have, so that will have to do. Have a seat."

She poured another cup and strutted over to him as he nervously took a seat on her snow-white suede sofa. Jayde was like a predator of the jungle, and he was her prey, for the night.

"You got that for me?" She asked, handing him the drink and taking a seat on the couch next to him. Her presence was so strong and demanding, yet her body and face were so soft.

"Uh, yeah," he mumbled, trying not to focus on her perfect nipples on display through her gown. He reached into his inside jacket pocket, and took out a folded manila envelope. As he went to hand it to her, his elbow knocked the drink over on to the table.

"Aw, shit!" He muttered, embarrassed. Jayde giggled.

"Relax… it's all there?"

She was referring to the money he had handed off.

He nodded as he got up to retrieve something to clean the mess.

"You got some paper towels, or someth-" But Jayde cut him off by standing up and placing a hand on his chest, forcing him back down to the couch.

"Sssshhh, don't worry about that, sweetie."

She stood in front of him as he sat back down, looking up at her. Her pussy was directly in front of his face and he could see even in the dark, through the sheer gown, that it was completely bald and waxed.

She thumbed through the envelope and assessed the bills inside. *Ten G's, ten stacks of ten, all there.*

"Good boy."

24

He sat there wondering what else she could want. The money was on point, everything was all good. Instantly the thoughts of his girlfriend and newborn baby entered his mind. He started to get up again, adjusting his jacket.

"Well, thank you. I definitely don't play around with money; you don't have to worry about that."

Jayde looked at him as he spoke and subtly licked her lips. His deep voice was sexy and his smooth brown complexion and shy, yet thugged-out, demeanor, had her wanting to take advantage of him. He could see the fire in her eyes.

"So if that's it, I think I better head out-"

Jayde pressed her lips against his forcefully and shoved her tongue down his throat, pushing her body up against his. He moaned and slowly wrapped his arms around her but then immediately pulled back and lightly pushed her away.

"I can't," he whispered, out of breath. "I got a girl, I got a baby."

Jayde didn't crack a smile or show a bit of emotion.

"Congratulations," she spoke evenly. "Do you like your job?"

"Huh?"

She stepped closer to him.

"I said…do you like your job? You like being able to support that *girl* and that *baby*?"

He stared into her venomous eyes and had an idea where this was going. Word around town was that she was crazy, but he had no clue. He nodded.

"Yeah…yeah, of course."

Jayde stroked his smooth cheek with her hand; he didn't seem a day over twenty.

"Good…I treat you good, right?"

He definitely knew what time it was.

"Absolutely."

She nodded coolly and placed her hands on his shoulders, pushing him slowly down onto the couch. She slid the spaghetti straps off of her arms and slowly wiggled out of her gown. Her goddess-like nakedness had his full attention.

"You be good to me baby, and I'll be good to you."

Thoughts ran through his mind, but he knew none of if mattered. Just looking at Jayde, he presumed that he would never get an opportunity to fuck anybody that looked as good as her again. He wondered what it was that made her want to put niggas in compromising situations to get off, knowing that she could probably get any man she wanted just by asking. *It must be a power thing.*

He thought of his girl as Jayde thrusted at him to lie down on the couch. And he briefly thought of all of the money he had recently started making since dealing with Jayde. He wouldn't be thinking for long however, as she pushed herself up to mount his face, pressing her wetness against his mouth. With some hesitation, he gently protruded her with his tongue and flicked it back and forth on her clit, lightly at first. But as she gradually began to move around sexily and moan, he could feel lust taking over him and he palmed her ass cheeks, spreading her further and really going face first into her. She rode his tongue with rhythm and ease working herself, and him, into a frenzy.

"Mmmmmm, yes baby. Ooh, just like that..."

She tasted good, and smelled like flowers, vanilla, and rich bitch shit.

"Oh, right there."

The more she seemed into it, the harder, and faster he lapped at her, and the harder his dick became.

"Ohhh, yes...ooh you gonna be my favorite," she moaned, engulfed in the pleasure of his tongue. He wrapped his lips around her clit and sucked gently as she grabbed the arm of the couch and arched her back.

This bitch is wild.

He wondered how often she did shit like this. He would like to think that he was so irresistible that she just had to have him, but the way she talked let him know this was not the case. It didn't matter though; he was full blown into it and couldn't wait to fuck her.

Damn, if only daddy could see his little princess now, he mused.
Jayde continued to ride his face on the brink of her orgasm and felt
no guilt doing so. Her motto was clear as day.
*It's always business. And just because it's pleasure, doesn't make
it personal.*
Her body tensed, and she knew her blissful moment was near, as
her head became clouded and light. She bucked and moaned and
when she felt her nut rising, she grabbed his head and pushed him
deeper into her. He them palmed her ass harder and licked her
more intensely.
Jayde released her juices powerfully onto those perfect lips she had
been eying.
"Oh! Yes! Yes! Fuckkkk!" She screamed.
After a few seconds of recuperation, she slowly dismounted him
and stood up.
He sat up, with glossy lips and watched her ideal body, ready to
give her the dick.
She picked up her drink off of the table and took a sip, without
turning around. With her back still to her young conquest, she took
a deep breath and then simply muttered,
"Now, get the fuck out."

"September."
"Get the fuck outta here!"
"I'm serious!" Sasha laughed. "September…September is the last
time that I even *seen* his dick."
Tatum dropped her jaw in shock and laughed again.
"Damnnnnn."
"I know, tell me about it."
The girls were in Tatum's living room, drinking wine, and catching
up. Tatum was on the floor by the coffee table, and Sasha was
seated on the couch. Aubrey, Chanel, and Tangee were sleeping in
the bedroom and Sasha had scarfed her hot dogs down long ago.
Now the topics were of adult content, her and Mike's sexless
marriage.

"But wait," Tatum questioned. "I mean, how do you do it…like how can you just say fuck it, I'm not gonna give him none?"

Tatum and Sasha continued laughing as Sasha got back with her.

"Unh, unh, hold up…Hmm, I don't know Tay. How do *you* do it?" Sasha smirked. "You aint give nobody the draws since…well… you know."

Tatum's laughter subsided slowly and Sasha realized she had touched on a sore topic. She felt bad about bringing Ree up; she knew he was kind of an unspoken subject. Especially seeing that every time he was brought up, Sasha and Tatum got into it about what she should have done.

'That's different," was Tatum's only answer. She paused, deep in thought, before continuing. "I don't have a husband. And, I don't know…I'm just not feeling anybody else right now."

Sasha giggled to lighten the mood.

"Well, I'm just not feeling my husband, right now."

That caused the girls to share another laugh.

"Yeah, well then maybe you should've thought a little more before you married the punk," Tatum quipped, pouring another glass.

Sasha took a sip of her third glass and knew she had to say it. Tatum was right about her and Mike, but she was wrong about something else.

"Yeah, well maybe you should've thought a little *less*."

Tatum cut her eyes at her friend; she knew she was going to do this again.

"Sash, don't start with me, okay?"

"I'm not…but seriously Tay, I can't help it if I feel like you should've gone to Jamaica. Like seriously, what's the point of being miserable?"

Tatum loved Sasha but Tatum was also the type of person that if you said something to her that she didn't want to hear, she would tell you something right back that you didn't want to hear.

"You're right."

"I'm right?" Sasha was shocked.

"Yup...you're right," Tatum agreed. "Same way that I can't help feeling like if you were going to be miserable in your *marriage*, then you might as well have just forgiven Chauncey."

The words forced Sasha into silence.

"That's different," she finally mumbled.

"Oh, really? How?" Tatum needed to know.

"Well, first of all. Chauncey was dead wrong...and besides that. Mike is better for me. Chauncey is and will always be in the streets. Ree gave it up."

Tatum laughed.

"Not by choice! Sasha, he's a fugitive, c'mon."

"A fugitive that you still love."

They locked eyes for a minute and then Tatum looked away, not wanting to talk about it anymore.

"Sash, can we just change the subject, please."

Sasha nodded and smiled sympathetically at her friend. They were both feeling the same pain, but Sasha felt that she didn't want Tatum to make the same mistake that she had made. She didn't want Tatum to put mind over heart, too.

"Yeah, we can change it, Tay. But just answer me this one question, okay?"

Tatum sat up and folded her hands on the table. She knew she would probably have to agree to get Sasha to shut up.

"Okay, what?"

"If you could do it again, would you do it differently?"

Tatum stared at her friend and really didn't know the answer. The answer was somewhere in her gut, but she didn't want to admit it. Her stubbornness wouldn't let her. So she sufficed for a meek, "I don't know."

Sasha nodded and took the last sip of her wine.

"Subject officially changed," Sasha promised. She thought of how she couldn't wait to give Tatum her gift.

Her thoughts, and Tatum's as well, were broken by a new video on MTV Jams.

29

"Ooh turn that up, that's the new Young Money video," Sasha said, snapping her fingers and singing along with the hook. *"I can make your Bedrock, I-I-I, I can make your bedrock girllll."*
Tatum turned it up and sang it too as the female rapper of the group performed her part of the song. Both Tatum and Sasha smirked and looked at each other. Then they realized that they were thinking on the same page and laughed out loud.
"You think so, too?" Tatum asked, surprised.
"Oh my god, yes. The first time I saw her I was like, wow... that's Kim all day," Sasha replied, thinking of their beautiful and lively friend.
Tatum laughed, but then looked down and felt tears building up from her chest.
"Damn, I miss that girl."
She looked up at Sasha after a long silence and saw that the tears were cascading down her face. She went and sat next to her on the couch and rubbed her shoulder.
"It's okay mama, I know…it's fucked up."
Sasha breathed deep, trying to calm herself, but the tears kept coming.
"I just feel…" She paused and sighed. "I just feel like sometimes, that…that it's my fault. If Neli would have never-"
But Tatum cut her off.
"Nah-unh Sash, Neli was crazy. It had nothing to do with you."
"It had everything to do with me Tay!" Sasha became upset and more distraught. "It was me that Neli wanted to hurt. It was my man that she wanted, and Kim was just a pawn caught up in the middle of all of that shit. It's my fault."
Tatum shook her head at her friend. Even in her pain, Sasha still felt that it was all about her. Tatum knew she couldn't help it.
"Sasha, listen to me…Neli, was sick. She *is* sick. She needs to be locked up forever. You don't know what was going through that girl's mind."
Sasha nodded, trying to hear Tatum, but she couldn't help her feelings of guilt. Tatum tried to bring life back into the room.

"Anyway, Kim would not want us sitting up here, crying and shit, on our girls' night in…and she definitely wouldn't want you blaming yourself Sash."

Sasha forced a smile and nodded again.

"You're right Tay," she finally admitted. Then she added as if it had just come to her mind. "You know what, Tay?"

"What?" Tatum asked.

"I think I'm gonna take Aubrey to see Chauncey tomorrow."

Tatum couldn't maintain her amusement.

"Oh, really…you think?" She mused sarcastically. Sasha grabbed a pillow off of the couch and hit her with it, laughing along.

"Oh, shut up, black bitch."

The girls laughed and drank and talked, until they both passed out in the living room, just like old times.

Chapter 5 - Disclosure

The next morning, Sasha woke up early to head out to Rahway where Chauncey was housed. She dressed Aubrey extra cute and talked to her the whole time excitedly.

"We're going to see daddy...you're gonna look sooo pretty for daddy."

Aubrey was desperately sleepy, so she just looked at her happy mother like she was crazy.

By the time they headed out, Aubrey was dressed in a baby, mango-colored, Juicy tracksuit and matching Juicy faux fur coat.

And Sasha opted for all black, from her thigh high Prada OTK riding boots to her skintight black jeans and black cashmere sweater. Her caramel skin glowed, her makeup was flawless, and her now shoulder-length black hair, was bone straight. She had butterflies in her stomach and she couldn't wait to see Chauncey. She wanted them to look perfect to him.

As they made their way out of Tatum's apartment complex, quietly enough not to wake Tatum or the girls, Sasha got a strange sensation. It was like a feeling of déjàvu' mixed with alarm. She made her way to Tatum's car with Aubrey in her arms, and looked around at the quiet and empty development. The sun was just rising and there was an eerie calmness. *Maybe I'm just nervous.*

She opened the back door and placed Aubrey into the car seat and as she buckled her in, she felt someone standing behind her. She stood up frightened and turned abruptly, bumping her head on the ceiling of the car.

"Ouch!"

However, when she turned around, there was no one there. There was no one even outside.

The realization calmed and freaked her out all in one. She hurried and strapped Aubrey in, and then trotted around the back of the car and got into the driver's seat, locking the doors, and looking around again.

Damn, I'm bugging. I'm bugging, right?

She peaked at Aubrey who was looking back at her cool as a breeze and she began to calm again, thinking of the trip they were about to make.

Yeah, I must be bugging.

"Okay Bri-Bri, we're going to see daddy."

"Mills."

Sasha stood up quickly and grabbed Aubrey. The older, black heavyset guard looked Sasha up and down. She was fine as wine to him.

"You here for Chauncey Mills?"

"Yes," she agreed, even though they went through this every time. It was as if the guard was so upset that he couldn't get a woman like Sasha himself, that he took it out on her every time she came to visit, giving her a hard time. Truth be told, he hated that the criminals that they housed, seemed to have everything, even in their darkest hour. *A woman like that should be with a man like me,* he figured.

"Get in line," he simply ordered.

Sasha stood in line for another fifteen minutes as everyone, guards and guests, studied her in awe. Finally, the doors were opened, and she and Aubrey were able to make their way to a small white table amongst many, and wait for Chauncey to come out. Aubrey had dozed back off sitting up in a chair next to Sasha.

Sasha sat there in anticipation, with her arm around her sleeping daughter and prayed that they looked perfect.

I wonder if he's gonna think I got fat, she wondered, even though the only thing that had gotten fatter on her was her ass.

At last, the long line of inmates made their way to the gymnasium-looking room. Sasha searched the numerous black faces for the one

33

she would recognize and she briefly wondered why so many of our good, strong, black men had to be locked down. There were young ones, old ones, dark ones, light ones, any and every kind a sister could want. And then as if on cue, there was the one that she wanted. He smiled at her and smoothly made his way over and Sasha's tummy did somersaults.

"Look at you, baby girl," he greeted her with his deep baritone, as she stood up and embraced him in a warm hug. He held on a little too long, and she allowed him, because she had secretly wished for him to.

"Hey Chauncey," she drawled in her sweet southern talk. "You look good."

And good he looked. His body was on point, and even through the plain, off-cut beige apparel, you could see that this time locked down had done him justice. His arms, his chest, his stance, it was all on point. This was a real man, Sasha thought to herself. His hands slowly traced her curves as his eyes traveled down her body, and he bit his bottom lip. *Damn!*

She looked like something out of one of his late night dreams.

"I aint fucking with you though, for real," he flirted, finally taking his hands back to himself respectively. She giggled bashfully and bent down to pick a sleeping Aubrey up out of the seat, as his eyes were glued to her ass.

"Wake up mama, look who it is."

Aubrey slowly opened her eyes and brightened at the sight of her father. It didn't matter how long she went without seeing him, they had a strong connection that Sasha adored and envied simultaneously. Aubrey took one look at Chauncey and then at Sasha who was still holding her, and went into diva act.

"Daddy," she whimpered, with outstretched arms. Chauncey smiled wide and felt a surge of emotion, but kept his game face on. Aubrey melted his heart.

"Come here, princess."

"Hey," Sasha whined, playfully punching him in the arm. She remembered when that was her name, she missed those days.

34

He looked up from Aubrey at Sasha and smiled with his eyes. Then he motioned for them to sit while still holding Aubrey in his arms.

Once they were seated comfortably, Chauncey looked deeply and warmly into Sasha's eyes and she felt like he was looking straight through her, he still had that power over her.

"What's up with the phone?" He asked, already knowing the answer.

Sasha sighed deep and looked down before answering. She stumbled on her words.

"Chauncey...Mike...I don't know. You call all the time."

"All the time," Aubrey mimicked cutely, and Sasha laughed nervously. Chauncey chuckled at his daughter but then became serious.

"Oh, so now I got a limit? I got a limit on when I can call my own daughter and my own..." He paused. "And you. Fuck this dude think he is?"

Sasha didn't want him to be upset, so she tried to mend the situation.

"Chauncey look, he's just a little insecure when it comes to you...to us, and what we used to have. Look, can you just call the cell until he calms down a little, for me?" She asked sweetly, tilting her head to the side and looking at him with pretty brown eyes. "He'll be over it soon."

Chauncey ran his tongue on the inside of his cheek, really fuming but willing to put his anger on hold. He would be dealing with Mike soon enough. He looked at Sasha again, tuning into her.

"So what's up with you...what you been up to?"

She shrugged and smirked.

"Nothing much, getting ready for the holidays. My parents are coming down."

"Oh yeah?" Chauncey asked. "You cooking?"

He remembered her banging ass Soul Food holiday dinners; just the thought seemed like heaven compared to what he would probably be eating.

35

"Yeah, I'm cooking a little something. I feel like I just cooked for Thanksgiving, but I know my dad is gonna wanna eat, and my mom can't burn like me... But all this food is making me fat," Sasha quipped and Chauncey chuckled.

"C'mon ma, go 'head with that. I mean, your ass got a little fatter... but that's a good thing," he joked, shooting her a wink.

"Shut up!" Sasha screamed at him.

"Nah, for real tho'...stand up."

Sasha looked at him like he was crazy.

"I'm serious, stand up...do a little turn for me." When Sasha hesitated, Aubrey chimed in.

"Stand up, mommy."

Sasha looked at her shocked and amused.

"Well thank you little girl, whose side are you on?" Sasha laughed and then nervously stood up, placing her hands on her hips.

"Happy now?"

Chauncey grinned broadly.

"Now turn around...come on, just turn around."

Sasha turned slowly, giggling the whole time, and Chauncey took in her impressive shape. He didn't think it was possible for her to get any badder, but she had managed to. She sat back down, looking around and making sure no one was looking at her like she was crazy.

"Damn, ATL doing it like that?" Chauncey asked as they both laughed. "Good looking on that, that was my Christmas present," he added.

She waved her hand at his blatant admiration, trying her hardest not to blush.

"Whatever...but what you got for me?" She knew her flirting with Chauncey was dancing on the line, but she couldn't help it. Just sitting across from him had her panties on soak. He raised his eyebrows at her but then responded.

"I got something for you...I got something for both of ya'll."

"Really?" Sasha asked, not expecting that.

He nodded and stood up, handing her Aubrey. When he sat back down, he slowly lifted up his right sleeve.

"I got this last week."

Sasha looked on and felt tears coming to her eyes but she tried to hold them back.

"Chauncey," she whispered in disbelief.

He had gotten her and Aubrey's faces tattooed on his arm, from a picture that she had recently sent him of the two of them together.

"I can't believe you did that," she added, truly not being able to believe it.

He rolled his sleeve back down and shrugged. "Why not? That's my baby girl right there..." He smiled at Aubrey, and then looked at Sasha with love. "And you gave her to me."

Sasha felt choked up so she looked down to break the intensity of the moment.

"Wow."

They talked for a few more minutes and mostly Chauncey used the time to talk with Aubrey as she told him all about what Santa was bringing her. By the time the visit was over, Sasha had fallen right back into her comfort zone with Chauncey, like she always did when she came.

"Alright Chaunc," she said, getting up to leave. "I don't know what week I'm coming back next month, but just call the cell."

Chauncey nodded and hugged them goodbye, and then kissed them both on their foreheads.

"Or maybe I'll be home by then."

Sasha's world came to a screeching halt and she instantly felt like she would pass out.

"Huh?" Was all she managed to say. Chauncey snickered, knowing that she was probably in shock.

"Mills!" The guard called to him. "Let's go!"

"They granted me parole, my early release date is scheduled for next month, if all goes well," he added, nonchalantly.

Sasha shook her head from side to side astonished.

"What? ...How would you...? When were you gonna tell..."
He smiled and walked away, shouting behind him.
"Keep ya fingers crossed, baby girl...daddy's coming home!"
She wasn't sure if that was meant for her or Aubrey, or both. All she knew was that the news of Chauncey possibly being paroled was something that she didn't know if she could handle.
As she finally made her way out of the jail, her mind ran wild.
Of course she wanted him to come home, right? Be a father to Aubrey? But there was a small part of her that enjoyed him being locked away, and that was the part that knew that it helped control her desire to be with him.
Oh my god, oh my fucking god.
Climbing into Tatum's car all Sasha could wonder was if Chauncey came home, how much self control would she really have?
Damn, this nigga...
And then she pulled off.

After all day and night of Sasha and Tatum going on and on about Chauncey's revelation, even during their spa treatment, and then a breakfast at IHOP the next morning, Tatum was dropping Sasha and Aubrey back at the airport.
"Damn girl, these trips be too short," Tatum said, hugging Sasha. She didn't want her to leave.
"I know," Sasha whined, pouting her lips. "Maybe you can come down to the A soon, though?"
Tatum nodded.
"I just gotta get some shit straight up here, and I will."
Sasha nodded and smiled and then heard her flight boarding.
"Alright girl, I'll call you." Sasha gave Tatum another long hug. She grabbed Aubrey's hand and turned to make her way to the terminal, waving at Tatum.
"Bye brown bitch, who knows when I'm gonna see you again!" Tatum shouted.
Sasha turned around and smirked.

"Sooner than you think!"
Tatum scrunched her face in confusion, she was sure she wouldn't be seeing her for at least another month.
"What you mean?" She yelled out to Sasha but she just waved her hand and disappeared into the terminal.
Sooner than I think? Tatum questioned to herself, wondering what the hell Sasha was up to. *Oh, boy.*

Chapter 6 - Devotion

A Week Later

Sasha sat on her living room couch, eating Oreo cookies and watching Mike and Aubrey decorate the Christmas tree. Aubrey was so excited and she was walking all over Mike, placing every single decoration at the same level as her height, which was the bottom of the tree.

"Mike, yall gotta spread 'em out," Sasha laughed. "You two got the tree looking extra country."

Mike giggled.

"Oh yea?" He turned to Aubrey who was placing a snowman ornament on the same branch as a silver ball. "Well, tell Mommy she needs to get her lazy bones up, and help us." He laughed and Sasha rolled her eyes.

"I'm tired," she defended and they shared another laugh.

They continued to bask in the Christmas delight, and Sasha's thoughts turned to Chauncey. She wondered what he was doing right now, and she wondered if the events would have played out differently, would this have been them?

"You know...," she started at Mike. She figured now was as good a time as any, and she didn't want any surprises coming his way. "Uhm, Chauncey may be getting paroled soon."

Mike was silent and continued to search for a spot for the ornament in his hand. After thirty seconds of silence, Sasha probed.

"Did you hear me? I said-"

"I heard you, Sasha," he snapped.

She sighed, and turned and looked out of the window into the darkness.

"Well, I just figured I'd let you know. I guess it's a good thing."

"A good thing for who?" Mike questioned, looking at her intensely. Sasha swallowed hard.

"A good thing for Aubrey, of course."

Mike took a break from the tree and made his way over to the mini bar where he had a cup of coffee and Kahlua.

"And how do you know this, anyway?"

Shit, Sasha thought to herself. She had lied to him about her trip to Jersey. And that's the thing about lies, they always force more lies even when you promise to never tell another one.

"He told Tatum."

Mike shook his head in disbelief.

"How does this guy damn near kill a girl, and only serve two years and some change, and is even considered for parole?"

Sasha was surprised by Mike's lack of understanding, or was she?

"You think he deserves to be locked up?" Sasha asked, thinking of all of the evil Neli had done. Mike was fuming.

"I think he got what he deserved!" He raised his voice and Aubrey's attention was brought to their argument.

"Daddy don't got dessert...daddy got me... and mommy... on his arm."

Sasha's eyebrows raised in bewilderment as she tried to stop Aubrey. This little girl didn't know what a secret was.

"No baby, Mike said Daddy got what he *deserved*. Not *dessert*. Deserve means-"

"What's she talking about Sasha?" Mike cut her off, wondering what Chauncey had done. He had heard Aubrey clear as day and knew in his gut that Sasha was lying to him about visiting him.

"She's talking about the apple pie that I'm supposed to make, but I told you Bri-Bri, tomorrow."

Mike looked at her with little patience.

"Sasha, you know what I mean...about *him* and his arm."

Sasha shrugged and then feigned as if she had just remembered something.

"Oh, you know what...I think she's talking about something else Tatum had told her...I think Chauncey had gotten a tattoo of

41

Aubrey or something." She stood up and made her way over to the tree. "But okay babe, I'm ready to help you guys, if you want?"

Mike took a deep breath and sipped on his coffee. Chauncey was a piece of shit. The thought of him being out of jail and in their lives made his skin crawl, but what could he do about it?

At least that mothafucka will be in Newark, far away from us. She can send the kid up there to see him and I'll just stay on her so much that she won't even want to go with her. Maybe with the kid with her father, we can work on one of our own? A boy... Yeah, I've got nothing to worry about.

And Mike had no idea how wrong he really was.

"Shit," Tatum mumbled, dropping her keys as she tried to open her front door. She had two handfuls of bags from Toys R' Us, Walmart, The Children's Place, and Macy's that contained all of her last minute Christmas gifts for the girls.

Finally getting up the steps and opening the door, she dropped the bags as Chanel and Tangee came running.

"Oohhh," Tangee screamed, just knowing the contents of the bag were for her.

"Nah-unh, no peaking. Or I'm gonna tell Santa to not even stop here next week," Tatum warned.

Chanel, the oldest, rolled her eyes.

"There *is* no Santa, Auntie Tatum."

Tatum looked at her wide-eyed, not wanting Tangee's world to be crushed. Even though Tangee was nine years old, she still believed somewhat. Chanel had outgrown the phase.

"Oh, I forgot, you're *eleven* now...you're grown right? It's okay, I'll tell Santa just to bring Tangee all of the goodies, right Tang?"

Tangee laughed and Chanel tilted her head to the side in her getting grown, preteen behavior. She just wanted a Wii game and a new Ipod, she didn't care if it came from Santa, Tatum, or Jesus himself.

Keisha, Tatum's friend from the hair shop, came strolling out of the living room.

"You all set?" She asked.

"Yup, just about. Thanks Keish for staying with them."

"No problem," Keisha waved off, buttoning her coat. "Bye girls...if I don't see yall next week, Merry Christmas!"

"Merry Christmas," they responded in unison as Keisha walked out of the door.

"Bye Tay," she shouted back.

"Later Keisha."

Tatum brought the bags into the living room and plopped down on the couch.

"Ya'll go, get outta here," she laughed at the girls who were hovering around. "Go get the decorations so we can finish doing the tree."

They happily made their way off, as Tatum picked up the mail she had placed on the table before she left. She sighed deep, looking at the big pile of bills.

"Alright, bring it," she said, bracing herself.

She thumbed through envelopes. *Bill, bill, bill...what the fuck is this?*

Tatum looked at the papers with furrowed eyebrows, wondering what was going on. It didn't take but thirty seconds for her blood to go from calm to boiling.

Nichole Samuel vs. Tatum Mosley...No this bitch didn't!

Tatum slammed the papers down and picked up the phone, mis-dialing the numbers twice out of anger before getting it right.

Sasha answered on the first ring.

"Hey Tay, what's up?" Sasha was happy that Tatum was putting a break in between the Chauncey/parole conversation.

"Sash, you are not gonna believe this shit! That *bitch* is taking me to court for custody of the girls!" Tatum had tears in her eyes and her heart was in her throat.

Sasha was just as upset.

"What! That's crazy...she just came back into their lives, they barely know her. And your adoption is final!"

"Well apparently, according to these papers, the adoption can be overturned because she didn't agree to it…they're saying we didn't go through the proper procedures to locate her ass. But you can't find nobody that don't wanna be found!"

Tatum could feel her hands shaking and she was ready to hit somebody, anybody.

"Girl, trust me…this can't happen. Tay, it's okay….I'll call my dad, he'll get the best lawyer on the case, she can't do this."

Tatum sighed and tried to surge her temper. She was glad that she had a friend like Sasha who could remain calm and rational when she was irate and well, irrational.

"Thanks Sash, but girl, I can't afford that. This is the last thing I needed right now... Shit."

Tatum ran her hand through her hair in despair.

There was a long silence, and then Sasha spoke.

"Tatum, I'll take care of it. I know how much this means to you, mama…Don't worry about the money."

"Sash, I can't let you foot that," Tatum argued but Sasha cut her off.

"Unh-unh girl, enough. It's done. Now new subject, don't even worry about it."

Tatum forced a smile through her worry and felt her concerns being lifted. Sasha was right; a good lawyer will shut this whole situation down. She was so lucky to have her.

"Thanks girl."

They talked for about twenty more minutes, and when Tatum seemed to be completely calmed, Sasha went in.

"So, since you know now that I would do absolutely anything for my bestest friend, I need you to do something, too."

Tatum looked at the phone like Sasha was crazy.

"What?" She asked warily.

"I want you to… open your gift," Sasha said anxiously with giddiness.

"Oh… okay girl. You scared me."

Tatum breathed a sigh of relief and took the cordless over to the bare tree that Chanel and Tangee were standing next to.

She grabbed the red envelope and opened it delicately, she was sure that it was money inside of this card.

"It better not be some sentimental stuff up in here either, getting all soft and shit and making me cry," Tatum joked, opening the card.

What she saw inside prevented her from reading the words.

"Sasha, what is this?"

Sasha sucked her teeth and rolled her eyes.

"Duh Tay, *plane tickets.*"

"Bitch, I know what it is. But what *is* it?" Tatum could feel her heart fluttering and she was scared to look at the destination.

Sasha spoke slowly, choosing her words carefully.

"Well...you know how I said I would do *anything* for my bestest friend? ...well, I need you to do this for me. I need you to come on vacation with me."

Tatum closed her eyes and then finally opened them and read the tickets.

No, god no.

Sasha continued to speak.

"I just really need a break, you know Tay? I think this will be good for both of us."

"Bullshit," Tatum barked. "Jamaica, Sasha!" She took a seat on the couch and closed her eyes. "I can't Sash. I'm...I'm scared," she finally admitted.

There was a silence and Sasha felt bad, but she was sticking to her guns.

"I know. But Tay, it's just a visit, a long weekend. It's not forever... and I don't know, you can't be scared for the rest of your life. Plus, you owe me, and it's paid for already. We leave the day after Christmas."

Tatum shook her head and protested in her mind, but she knew there was no debating it. She owed Sasha way more than Jamaica for the favor she was doing for her, still she couldn't fight the fear in her heart. *Jamaica's a big place...maybe I won't even see him.*

Tatum knew that she wasn't over Ree, and she wasn't sure if she was prepared for even the slight chance that she would see him again. It was easier this way, with him being there and her being here. It made her feel like it was impossible for them to be together. And although she wasn't sure what the real problem was, Tatum was scared of the love that she felt for him.

It's just a couple of days...it's only a couple of days.

But in the back of her mind, Tatum couldn't help but wonder what Jamaica had in store.

"Good afternoon Mr. Knights."

"Hello ladies."

"Hi Mr. Knights, how are you?" Another beautiful woman greeted.

"I'm well...how are you Megan?"

"Better now," she smiled. Another woman intervened.

"Hello Mr. Knights, can I get you anything?"

"No, I'm fine sweetheart."

"That you are," she whispered to another woman, as they both giggled.

From left to right, Ree was serenaded with greetings and advances from gorgeous women of all ages, shapes, and colors.

Employees, guests, potential guests, departing guests, they all loved him.

"Ehllo Mistah Knights, dah weadah lookah quite right tahday, no?"

A leggy, model-type, native of the island questioned, as she strutted through the lobby in her string bikini and high heeled sandals. She smiled seductively at him and Ree couldn't help but give her his brief, but undivided attention. As he glanced up from his paperwork, he gave her the once over approvingly.

"Indeed," he answered with a smirk and then focused back on the sales reports in his hands.

He continued to make his way through the lobby, his walk and powerful swagger demanding attention. His stance, broad shoulders and sculpted tattooed arms, chiseled handsome face, and dark eyes, couldn't help but reveal his thug appeal. But other new elements told a different story, like the slight glow in his brown skin and the new calm in his face. It told a story of Jamaica treating Ree extremely well. In fact, he wasn't even Respect, or Ree, anymore, at least not to them. He was Sean Knights. Respect was left back in the states.

The hotel business had not only been profitable to him, but had also added a sense of stability to his life. He never had to look over his shoulder or worry about anything, because besides the fact that he was legit now, the people of Jamaica loved and respected him so much. They would go to great lengths to protect him and his family, they were like Jamaica's royalty, and that brought him a sense of peace.

Still, the side of Ree that craved adventure, excitement, the side that ran the streets, and ran them well, found it a little difficult to still, after all of this time, become adjusted.

He reached the main desk, and sat the papers down as the front desk clerk checked in a couple. Ree looked at them quickly, and had to do a double take, the woman had a familiar smile. A smile, like her. He glanced at her for a couple of seconds, lost in his thoughts. When she grinned wider, completely captivated by him, he realized that he was staring. He shook his head lightly, to shake his reminiscent thoughts of Tatum away.

"My apologies… It's just for a second, you reminded me of someone." He spoke to the woman, but still acknowledged her husband, or boyfriend in respect. The woman was hypnotized. Everything about Ree, from his handsome face, muscular build, his sexy dreads that he wore pulled back, his appealing lips, his dark eyes, confident yet nonchalant demeanor, all of it made her melt. She took it all in.

"Oh please, it's fine…no problem," she smiled, as her man looked at her with raised eyebrows. She was flirting as if he weren't there.

"Enjoy your stay," Ree coolly added to them both, making his way to the back office.

Tatum, I'm not coming back, and I want you to come with me...
...I can't......

Ree found himself thinking back to the last time they were together. Standing there in her hallway, watching the tears fall from her beautiful eyes, Tatum had played on his mind for a while after that day. And it seemed that it hadn't been too long ago that she had stopped occupying his thoughts. But one smile had just sent the memories flooding back.

"Aw man," Ree mumbled to himself, running his hands over his face. His thinking was interrupted.

"Hello son," his father addressed him, entering the office.

"Pop," Ree acknowledged back.

"Getting ready for the holiday rush?" His father questioned, making his way over to the mini-bar in Ree's office. His father had developed a habit for drinking heavily, and Ree wondered if it had anything to do with the absence of Ree's mother. Like Tatum, Ree had lost his mother at a young age, but the difference was that poor Tatum had lost both of her parents, in a car accident, at the same time. Knowing her, you would never be aware that she had that pain inside, and Ree commended her for that.

"Yup," he answered. "Sales reports estimate some good numbers. Reservations are looking good."

His father cut in.

"Yeah, you'll double those numbers by the way. Make sure you're properly staffed...are you staffed enough?"

Ree sat down with a confident smirk on his face and kicked his feet up on his cherry wood desk.

"Now Pop, I thought I was the one running this 'ere thing? ...You want it back?" Ree quipped. "I can always provide the people of Jamaica with, eh, other services," he suggested slyly, while lighting the tip of his blunt.

"Yeah Sean, we all know what kind of services you would love to *provide*. Have the whole damn island riding the white pony."

Ree chuckled at his father's outdated terminology referring to cocaine use and he shrugged.

"Yeah well, just let me handle business. I'm good at it," Ree assured him.

His father gulped down the glass of scotch as if it were water.

"Ah!" He said in satisfaction, and then added to Ree. "Just make sure you're prepared, son."

Ree nodded confidently, as he inhaled the premium weed smoke, but he had no idea that he was not prepared in the least for what was to come.

"I got it all under control."

-Interlude-

Christmas Eve

Somewhere in an Atlanta suburban home, Sasha soaked in a hot steamy bubble bath. She cried softly as the classic Otis Redding song drifted from her speakers...

This is my lover's prayer
I hope it'll reach out to you my love
This is my lover's prayer
And I hope you can understand it my love
My life is such a weary thing
But it may be old pressure bringing rain
You keep me wanting, waiting, and wishing
When I know deep down I'm not the blame...

While somewhere in a lonely cell in Rahway, Chauncey lay staring at the ceiling, playing the very same song...

What you gonna do tonight
When you need some loving arms to hold you tight?

49

Tell me, what you gonna do tonight
When you need my heavy voice to tell you goodnight?
Honey but, you can't let that be no problem,
You've got to come on home and help me solve 'em
Then I won't be missing you
And honey, my lover's prayer will be all over, oh now...

Ironically in Jamaica, Respect took a sip of his Hennessey Black and closed his eyes to the same tune as he sat by the pool of his estate. He briefly thought of the girl with the smile from earlier that day, and then he thought of Tatum...

What can the matter be, now?
It can't be that serious we can't talk it over
Living in this misery
Darling, you can't make my life all over...

And back in Newark, NJ, Tatum sat on her living room sofa singing the last verse to the universal track that seemed to touch right on her heart. Otis' voice echoing off of the walls...

Honey but, you don't let that be no problem
Just come on home and help me solve 'em
Then, I won't be missing you, I won't be missing you
And my lover's prayer would be all over
It got to be all over...

All lost in their thoughts, consumed by their minds, the song seemed to sing four tales of four people, at one time...

Don't keep my life going round in so many circles
This is my lover's prayer, come on, come on home
This is my lover's prayer, I'm singing out to you
And I hope it will reach ya, I hope it gets to you...

Chapter 7 – Thirst

The day after Christmas

"I can't, I can't do this."
Tatum gripped and then released the handle on her Gucci roll away luggage bag. She walked to the other side of the hallway and stared at the bag as if it were going to talk back to her.
"What are you talking about…you know you wanna go," she murmured to herself, slowly walking back over and taking hold of the bag again.
She had went shopping, purchased the brand new and perfect everything, down to the toothbrush, gotten her hair trimmed and conditioned with a clear gloss rinse, had her teeth whitened, nails and toes done, and even under went the ever so scary, Brazilian wax, all in preparation for this trip. She was nervous, she was skeptical, but she knew she was at a moment in her life where she was ready to do something drastic, exciting, and do basically what she really deep down inside wanted to do. She was going to Jamaica.
"Wait, am I really?"
It was already 9 am. Tatum was supposed to catch a 10:30 am flight, meeting Sasha by 3 pm in Jamaica for check in.
How mad would she be if I just said 'fuck it' and chickened out?
Tatum mused to herself, as her doorbell startled her out of the question.
"Who is it?" Tatum yelled.
"Car service," a muffled voice responded, sounding like a woman with a bad English accent.

Tatum furrowed her eyebrows in confusion and then looked through the peephole apprehensively.

She laughed in amazement as she opened the door.

"So what, you didn't trust me to meet you there, bitch?"

Sasha was standing there with a wide smile in Chanel shades and a floppy straw hat, looking festive and island bound.

"Exactly!" She shot back. "But I also thought that it would be way more fun if we all went together…are you excited? Tatum, I'm so excited!"

Tatum looked at the black Maybach parked in front of her door and then back at Sasha.

"Yeah, I'm excited…and nervous," she admitted. She tried to squint and look inside of the tinted windows. "Who's we?"

As if on cue, the door opened and Jayde slid out in a tiny black mini-dress with her cell phone glued to her ear.

Her face was serious, but when she looked up at Tatum, she softened with a warm smile.

"Hi Tatum, I'm Jayde…good to finally put a face to the name."

"Likewise," Tatum responded, but Jayde had already started back her intense conversation. She popped the trunk, took out her car charger, and returned to the backseat, as Sasha and Tatum stood at the top of the steps.

"Ya'll do know it's still winter, right? We not in Jamaica, yet."

Tatum was referring to Sasha and Jayde's tropical apparel, while Tatum opted for a more casual BCBG tracksuit.

Sasha smirked.

"We know, but we'll be there before you know it. I have another surprise for you, boo…can't wait…? Okay, I'll tell you…we're flying on a jet. A private jet!"

Tatum looked at Sasha wide-eyed, while Jayde rolled down the window.

"Come on ladies. Let's get a move on…my pilot's waiting on us!"

"Her pilot?" Tatum questioned, grabbing her luggage and carefully locking her door. She debated whether she should call and check on the girls one more time before she left, but she figured it would be okay. She would call them first thing when she landed.

This was the first time they would be with their mother for more than a 24 hour period, but they both had cell phones pre-programmed with both hers and Keisha's numbers just in case.

They made their way to the car and settled in, and the driver took off.

Jayde stayed on the phone for the first ten minutes or so. She spoke minimally with words like "I don't care", "Just do it", and "Make it happen". Tatum made a note to herself to later ask Sasha exactly what Jayde did for a living.

Finally, she ended her call and breathed a sigh of relief. She smiled and poured herself a glass of champagne, offering some to Sasha and Tatum.

"What the hell, why not," Tatum said, taking a glass, as Jayde lifted her own and the girls followed suit in a toast.

Jayde cleared her throat before she spoke.

"Here's to Jamaica...and to finding Tatum's man!"

She winked at Tatum and Tatum gave Sasha a look. The look meant that Sasha talked too damn much.

"I don't know about ya'll, but I am so souped!" Sasha started, changing the subject. "I could use a little fun, and sun, and a break away from Mike's ass... My parents are still down in Georgia visiting my aunt, so they took Aubrey over there with them. I don't have to worry about anything, except my damn self!"

She took a sip of her champagne and snapped her manicured fingers, ready to get the party started.

Tatum nodded and looked around at the fly ass Maybach and all of its luxury.

"I know right, I could definitely use this getaway. And ya'll done went all out! Maybach, private jet, champagne... what's next?"

Tatum giggled and took another sip, enjoying the diva treatment.

"Well, I hope you don't mind," Jayde said. "It's just when Sasha told me that you guys were going, I insisted ya'll use the jet... No sense in changing flights, being around all those noisy ass people, when we can get there in three hours flat on the G5, ya know? The Maybach though, that was her idea, she wanted to do something special for you."

"Yes, I wanted to make this your *fantasy* weekend," Sasha sang, batting her eyelashes. Tatum laughed.

"You are so dramatic, oh my god."

"Aint she though?" Jayde agreed. "Always has been, ever since diapers."

Tatum glanced at Jayde with a chuckle. She wasn't sure if she was trying to rub in Tatum's face that she knew Sasha longer, or if the arrogant, self-absorbed persona was just her.

"Speaking of fantasy," Jayde continued. Her green eyes sparkling and her red lipstick shining. "What's your favorite car, Tatum?"

"That's easy," Sasha spoke first.

"Aston Martin, DB9, convertible," they spoke in unison.

Jayde nodded her head impressed and laughed at the friends.

"Okay, okay good choice. Let me see if I can make this happen."

She grabbed her phone again and dialed a number quickly. After a few seconds, she spoke.

"Miguel…Jayde…Uh-huh, great…Listen, I need a favor…DB9… Aston Martin…When I land…Three nights, four days…Oh no, that's not an issue…"

She took the phone from her ear for a second and turned to Tatum.

"Black or silver?"

Tatum was stunned, mouth agape, but regained her composure.

"Um, silver."

Jayde did a thumbs up and mouthed the words 'good choice'. As she wrapped up the conversation, Tatum looked at Sasha like *'what the fuck?'*

Sasha then leaned in and whispered.

"Her father was rich, she owns businesses."

Tatum shrugged and took another sip of her champagne. She figured to herself that Jayde may not be so bad after all.

Jamaica I'm coming, and I'm coming in a muthafuckin' Aston Mar, shutting it down!

54

"What the hell do you mean no reservations?"

"Like I say, Mrs....?" The clerk asked Sasha, forgetting her last name.

"Seals... Bernstein," she corrected, remembering that she was a married woman.

"Yes, Mrs. Bernstein. We do not have any reservations for you, are you sure that you called Botanical Bay Resorts?" She asked in her native accent.

"Yes, I'm sure," Sasha snapped, and Tatum nudged her.

"Botanical Bay? We're not staying at Paradise Breezes?"

Tatum was a little disappointed that they were not staying at Ree's resort, the one he had sent the postcard from.

"I couldn't find it," Sasha whispered.

Tatum sighed and calmed her nerves a little. She figured she could stop twiddling her thumbs and looking around nervously now that she knew that they were not at his resort.

"This is the bullshit," Jayde mumbled. "This is why I don't stay at resorts when I come here."

"Wait, you've been here?" Tatum asked, surprised that she hadn't mentioned it in the car or on the plane.

"Just a couple of times...Excuse me, may I talk to your manager?" Jayde turned her attention to the clerk. "You are not accommodating, at all."

The young Jamaican girl caught an instant attitude from the Amazon, beautiful bitch named Jayde's, condescending tone.

"How am I not accommodating... you don't have a reservation, therefore, I cannot accommodate you."

Jayde leaned onto the desk, glad that her long hair was already pulled back into a bun, in case it came to blows.

"No, you worthless, minimum-wage, island-trash servant... there *were* reservations. And you can, and will, accommodate me and my friends in a *room*. Especially, when her credit card has already been charged by your fucking establishment. Now get your damn manager, bitch!"

The girl could see the fire dancing in Jayde's eyes and was slightly frightened. She was happy when she received some assistance.

"Maybe I can be of some service... that'll be all Elsa. You can help the next customer," a beautiful mocha-colored woman said to the clerk. She was averaged height, with tight black curls that hung down her back, pretty dark brown eyes, and a radiant smile. Her skin glowed and she had an exotic look that let on that she may have been an island girl.

"Are you the manager?" Jayde asked with a dose of irritation.

"I am... I apologize in advance for any confusion there may have been. Hopefully, I can assist you better." Her island accent was smooth and she took her time when she spoke. Sasha stepped back up to the desk with her credit card and online print out. She read the woman's name tag.

"Trinity? ... Hello Trinity. We're having a little dilemma. I made these reservations months ago, my card has been charged and everything. However, we're being told that we don't have rooms."

Trinity gave a disappointed look and took Sasha's information from her hands. She hated when these types of problems occurred, especially around the busy holiday season.

"M apologies Mrs. ...Bernstein," she said reading the credit card. "Just give me one moment, and I will get this situation resolved immediately. Get you ladies squared away, no worries."

Trinity disappeared behind the desk after giving a reassuring smile to her three gorgeous guests. The original clerk, who was ear hustling the whole time, sucked her teeth. She was jealous of the three women since the moment she had laid eyes on them. If it wasn't Jayde's green eyes and tall model height, it was Sasha's strikingly beautiful face and designer labels, or Tatum's long gorgeous hair, hypnotizing smile, and seemingly perfect voluptuous body. They were all equally beautiful.

Jayde felt her envious vibes and took it as a proposition to insult.

"The manager was nice...Now why the first bitch couldn't be as *accommodating*... Fucking monkey."

56

Tatum looked at the clerk, who had obviously heard the comment and she repressed her giggles. She did resemble a monkey, or some sort of primate.

"Aw man, this is gonna be a trip," Tatum laughed, as Sasha and Jayde snickered.

Jayde could be a little over the top, but Tatum had to admit, the girl seemed to be entertaining.

The pretty hotel manager returned with a smile, Sasha's card, and three room keys. They were sure that they were now all settled. She handed Sasha the things.

"Now ladies, I've got good news, and I've got 'not so good' news."

Jayde rolled her eyes and was ready to pull out her phone and make some calls. Trinity could see her frustration and she continued.

"The bad, well, 'not so good' news is that the rooms are all booked due to the unexpected holiday rush."

Sasha sighed and Tatum pursed her lips and ran her hand through her hair. Maybe this trip was a 'not so good' idea.

"The good news however, is that I can place you ladies in the top Presidential Penthouse Suite – living room, dining room, kitchen, sauna, Jacuzzi, four bedrooms, wrap around balcony, private elevator-"

"Perfect!" Sasha screamed excitedly, cutting Trinity off. Jayde hung up her phone and Tatum smiled wide thinking of how luxurious this trip seemed to be playing out. All of the good signs were making her a tad less nervous about possibly seeing him again, although she tried not to think too much about it. Just the thoughts had her stomach doing somersaults on the plane ride over. Trinity beamed, happy to have pleased the guests. She knew that the owner would be equally pleased with her work.

"Great. The suite will be of no extra charge, just the original price you were going to pay for your original reservation. And once again, I apologize for any inconvenience. Enjoy your stay."

The girls took their keys and thanked the manager, heading towards the nearby elevators. Jayde shot one last nasty look at the original clerk and dangled her suite key in her face.

"Cut it out Jayde," Sasha laughed.

Once they were a distance away, Trinity turned to Elsa.

"Elsa, I am very disappointed in the way you handled those guests. I know you are aware of how important customer satisfaction is."

Before Trinity could get any deeper into her lecture, the desk phone rang and she answered sweetly.

"Botanical Bay Hotel, how may I help you?"

There was a brief silence as someone spoke on the other end and then Trinity answered.

"Oh no, I'm sorry. We were formerly Paradise Breezes, we just recently became Botanical Bay... No problem... Take care."

Trinity hung up the phone and sighed. She knew the name change would cause confusion and she made it a point to answer the phone 'Botanical Bay formerly Paradise Breezes' from now on. She turned back to Elsa.

"Now, what was I saying?"

Elsa looked at her blankly before responding.

"Your man's here."

Trinity felt the butterflies before she even knew if he was there. She turned slowly and her heart skipped a beat as she saw him heading in their direction. She blushed and faced Elsa again.

"Elsa, please. For the last time, that is my boss."

Ree approached the desk smoothly and both ladies admired him.

"Hello Elsa... Trinity."

"Mr. Knights," Trinity simply replied as Elsa smiled nervously.

Trinity held eye contact with Ree but spoke to Elsa.

"Um, Elsa, can you refill the mint bowls?"

Elsa frowned.

"But they're not even empty."

Trinity gave her a stern look and Elsa sucked her teeth and made her way to the back.

"Her boss...whatever," she mumbled.

When she was out of view, Trinity slowly approached Ree with a slightly seductive walk. She bit her bottom lip and grinned.

He was leaning coolly against the desk looking ever so sexy. She loved his power, his confidence, his ruggedness.

"Hey you," she whispered.

"Hey yourself," he responded, leisurely wrapping his strong arms around her tiny waist, once she had finally made her way to him. "How's everything going, any problems?"

She wrapped her arms around his neck and pressed against him, trying her best to get a rise out of him.

"No, not really... Oh wait, we *did* have one issue with some ladies' reservations. Buttt I upgraded them to the penthouse, no charge, and made them very happy."

Ree nodded approvingly. He knew the value of happy customers, from his previous business.

"Good girl." He moved around her so that her back was now to him. Then he kissed her lightly on the neck, tickling her with his goatee and sending sexual shocks through her body.

"Why don't you throw in a couple of spa packages for them too, make sure they return."

His voice was so smooth and deep in her ear. Trinity closed her eyes and breathed heavy. Her nipples hardened and her female juices poured.

"Yes, Sean," she obliged. She could hear Elsa returning and Ree took a few steps away from her. She tried to peck him on the lips before Elsa reached the desk but he coyly moved his face. That was one thing that irked her, he never liked to kiss her on the mouth. He tapped her on the behind as the phone rang, and she answered with a broad smile, forgetting the kiss diss.

"Good afternoon Botanical Bay, formerly Paradise Breezes, how may I help you?"

Ree gave her a wink and made his way to the back as Trinity watched him leave, still creaming. *Damn, I wanna have his babies!*

"Now, are you gonna be okay out there?"

"Yes."

"Remember what I said, one day at a time…baby steps."

"I know."

"You take care of yourself. I don't wanna see you back in here now."

"You won't!"

The sun gleamed bright as the iron-gate opened and revealed the gorgeous outside. Things like fresh air, sunny days, freedom, things that were once just a craving, were instantly very new, but very real.

With all of these precious elements as surroundings, ironically the first thought of the moment seemed to be a less obvious one. *Sasha.*

"Come on, that's the past now…we're focused on the future."

Why am I even thinking about her?

Neli took a deep breath and looked around the outside of the facility. Her cab was supposed to be waiting out there for her at 4pm. sharp. She lifted the sleeve of her pea coat jacket to check the time on her watch.

The fading, but still visible scars on her wrist were reminders of her past. Reminders that no matter how much she may try to focus on the future and leave her old ways behind, she would never forget the damage she had done; to others, and to herself.

"Quarter after, what the fuck?" She could feel herself already becoming frustrated, she wanted out and far away from that place. She looked up and could now see the cab slowly approaching.

"Thank god."

Today is the day, it's the beginning of the rest of my life. I can start life new, find myself, develop myself, and make myself into a better person… I can channel positive energy back into the world, try to right some of the wrong that I've done…I know I've ruined many lives and I know I'm probably going to hell for some of, well most of the things I've done. I'm not proud of myself, at all… I hurt people, people that didn't deserve it, Sasha. Chris… People that I genuinely cared about, Kim. Tatum... People that I loved dearly...Chauncey... I know I will never be able to repair the damage that I've done, but I can try my best to live positively, at least so I can feel like I've changed... So I can feel like this has worked... So I can feel like I can sleep at night...

"Hey honey, you getting in or what?" The cab driver barked in a thick African accent.

"Oh, I'm sorry." Neli didn't realize that she had just been standing there dazed out. She picked up her duffle bag and climbed into the backseat. Closing the door once she was inside.

But yea, where was I? Oh yeah, turning over a new leaf. Baby steps... Starting over... Finding a purpose to my life. But first, there's something I have to do...

"Honey, please, where to? I don't have all day. Why you keep zoning out?"

"Oh, I'm sorry, again. Um..." *Where to? Where to? Are you gonna do it? Yes...I have to.* "Um...Yes...Newark. Newark Airport, please." And the cab pulled off. *Baby steps.*

Chapter 8 – Illusions

"Oh my god, this shit is so fly!" Sasha screamed, running from the last bedroom.

"No, ya'll gotta see the sauna, that bitch is niceeee," Jayde contested flopping down onto the white sectional couch.

Tatum went to the large glass windows and pulled back the heavy drapes, letting the sun in and admiring the perfect view of the ocean.

"This whole damn suite is banging, I can fit my whole apartment in here," Tatum added, lost in her thoughts. Those thoughts were telling her that this, beautiful place, beautiful island, could have been her home. And she blew it.

"What you thinking about over there Pocahontas?"

Jayde had given her the nickname on the plane ride over, telling Tatum that she had figured she was Indian instead of Trinidadian.

Tatum turned from the window with a smirk and shrugged, and Sasha put her hands on her hips.

"You thinking about how we gonna find Ree on this big ol' island...don't worry Tay, we'll find him. If it's fate, destiny, everything that's meant to be-"

"Aaah, aah, aaaahhh, shut it up with all that fate and destiny bull!" Tatum joked, laughing at Sasha while Jayde giggled as well. "I'm thinking about how I need to change out of this hot ass sweat suit, pronto." Sasha waved her hand like whatever, and Tatum unzipped her jacket and made her way to the first bedroom, where she had placed her belongings.

But seriously, would she find him on this island? Was it meant to be? Was it fate? *Is it my destiny?*

"Where you going, boss?" The Jamaican hotel bellhop asked Ree, holding the elevator door opened for him.

"Ah, Trinity and Elsa got swamped at the desk wit' a fuckin' mob of people...so I gotta do the honors of dropping these packages off to some customers... Penthouse suite, please."

"Right away, boss."

The bellhop allowed the elevator to close and pressed the top button labeled 'P'.

"So they got you doing the common folk duty I see...getting your hands dirty?"

The bellhop laughed at his own joke and Ree chuckled, as the elevator continued to ascend. He had no idea just how dirty Ree's hands had gotten over the years. Many people of Jamaica, like Rodney, knew and loved Respect's family dearly for the money, jobs, and opportunities that they had provided to the most poverty stricken sections of Jamaica. But with those opportunities came the means to the ends, the violence, the drugs, the murder. From hit man to drug lord, Ree had done so much dirt, that it was impossible for him to ever be completely clean, not in this lifetime anyway.

"Yeah, something like that...how's it going with you, Rodney? How's the wife, kids?"

Ree had hired Rodney as a bellhop when he was fresh released from a Jamaican prison. Rodney had spent over a year in the prison for a crime he did not commit, all because of some dirty officer who was after Rodney's wife. To make matters worse, Rodney was accused of assaulting the officer, and therefore beaten and starved for weeks at a time. His wife was raped in front of his children, and Rodney was forced to hear the horror stories of the event from the officer's very mouth. It wasn't until Ree's father heard of the news and decided to intervene. With Ree's father being an incredibly powerful man in Jamaica, the problems for Rodney, let's just say, disappeared. Rodney was released from prison, he was pardoned, the officer was never heard from again, and Rodney was given the job at the hotel. He was forever grateful to Ree and his father for it.

"Things are good, I cannot complain at all. The wife, kids, all well."

Ree stood with his hands behind his back, slightly behind Rodney, and watched the numbers climb. He looked at Rodney out of the corner of his eye.

"How's money?"

Rodney paused and then spoke.

"Money is fine Mr. Knights, I am much honored to work for you."

Ree nodded but knew that Rodney was too hard a worker and too modest to admit when he needed something. Elsa had already let on that he was waiting on the next paycheck to buy his son some shoes and some groceries.

"Rodney, be honest. If there is something you need, the kids, anything. Let me know… A closed mouth don't get fed."

Rodney swallowed hard, scared to take the moment. His boss was a kind man, but Rodney was old school and unlike the other workers who did not know, Ree's reputation had preceded him with the old school island natives as being a very deadly man. His family was hungry though, he had to take his chances.

"I guess, if it is possible," he stuttered. "An advance, just a few dollars, from my check...I will pay back-"

The doors opened as they reached the penthouse floor.

"No advance Rodney." Rodney was immediately ashamed and embarrassed. "You come to my office, after your shift. I will have some money for you… You're a good man Rodney, a better man than me," Ree added.

Rodney could not contain his joy.

"Oh mah gudness, thank you Mr. Knights! You are a good man, de' best man, eva!" Rodney's native tongue progressed the more excited he became. "God bless you! Ah yes, thank de' lawd!"

Ree chuckled and walked off the elevator as Rodney continued to rave until the elevator closed again.

Ree thought of what it must be like to love so strong, that you would humble yourself to another man to ask for help to provide for the ones that you love. He was always taught that one who did such was not a man at all, but he now knew that a man like Rodney, was exactly what a man was. The best of men in fact, and that is why he felt Rodney to be a better man than him.

He made his way down the hall and as he approached the suite door, a tall and strikingly beautiful woman emerged from the room carrying an ice bucket.

Damn, Ree thought, but the thoughts did not show on his face.

"Mrs. Bernstein?" He asked smoothly. He was not familiar with Sasha's new last name.

"I wish I were, but she's right inside...shall I get her for you?"

Shit! This muthafucka is fine!

Jayde's primal animal instincts were on full gear and she wanted to ravage Respect. Everything about this man screamed power, and power made her horny. She squeezed her thighs together, unbeknownst to her, and bit her bottom lip to fight the urge to cum on herself.

"Nah, that's not necessary...just take these. For the inconvenience earlier." He looked down from her green eyes, briefly taking in her almost impossibly perfect physique as he handed her the envelope of spa packages. She was sexy, but something about her screamed poison.

Jayde looked down at the envelope and then up at the god who stood before her.

"Thank you...and who are you, are you the owner or something?"

Ree could see the hope in her eyes and he caught her checking out his diamond bezel watch, scanning him for wealth. He chuckled and was instantly amused, but completely turned off.

"Nah sweetheart, I'm just the bellhop." He turned to walk away and then added, "Enjoy."

Jayde shook her head from side to side and watched him leave. Damn, he was fine. But broke she did not do. She made her way in the opposite direction of the elevator towards the ice machine.

Oh well.

"Where were you?" Sasha asked, as Jayde made her way back into the room.

"I went to get ice," she answered matter of factly.

"Ice for what… And isn't there ice in the fridge?"

"No mommie dearest, the ice trays in the fridge are empty…and ice… for this."

Jayde pulled out a bottle of Nuvo from her bag with a grin, and made her way to the small kitchen.

Tatum then emerged from the bedroom with an aqua sundress on and her wavy hair, long and loose. Now she fit in.

"Damn, well pour one for me," she added, taking a seat on the tall stool.

"Ya'll are drinking this early, we are about to go to dinner in an hour, we can drink then."

Sasha had the whole trip mapped out but Jayde and Tatum combined would be able to shake her plans up a bit. She needed to let loose as well, she just didn't know it yet.

"Relax bitch, didn't you tell me this was a vacation," Tatum teased.

Jayde watched Sasha and Tatum interact and smiled lightly, wondering what it was like. They were the kind of rare friends that had a rare closeness, you could see it. And as she looked at Tatum, she realized that she had a rare beauty.

With all of Jayde's nipping and tucking and her gorgeous eyes and height and with Sasha's full lips, and almond eyes, and flawless, well put together look, Tatum seemed to effortlessly have that natural, I just wake up in the morning and look like this, Ivory soap, don't take much at all, kind of beauty. Jayde poured the drinks.

"Anyway, enough about the drinks, and by the way, you're having one too," Jayde said as she poured Sasha's as well. "But oh my god, I just saw the sexiest, finest, Jamaican brotha I have ever seen in my life! I mean, damn, I wanted to fuck him right there on the hallway floor, that's how fine he was." Jayde fanned herself just thinking about Respect.

"For real?" Sasha asked.

"Wow," Tatum added.

"For real," Jayde reiterated. "The boy had swag for days, but guess what?"

They both looked at her waiting, knowing that she would answer the rhetorical question herself. And she did.

"He was a fucking bellhop, a doorman."

Jayde took a big gulp of her drink and shook her head in disappointment, still in disbelief. She thought her shit was on point and she wondered how he could have afforded the 2010 Millenary Collection Audemars Piguet watch on his salary. *Shit must've been a replica.*

"Oh well I know he's out, for you," Sasha cracked.

"Aw, well maybe not, it's just for fun right? Aint like you marrying him or anything." Tatum was less materialistic, not realizing that Jayde was standing here creaming over *her* man.

Jayde tittered.

"Honey, we don't have fun with the help."

"At least Jayde doesn't," Sasha concurred, getting up from her stool. "I gotta call my baby."

She went to her phone and left Jayde and Tatum in their discussion.

After a few rings, her mother picked up.

"Ma, let me speak to Bri-Bri."

"Hello to you too Sasha, how are you? Me, your only mother, I'm fine...hold on." Sasha rolled her eyes as she heard her mother call for Aubrey. And they wondered why she was so dramatic.

"Mommy," Aubrey murmured.

"Hey pretty girl, what cha doing?" Sasha cooed in a sweet voice. Aubrey giggled at her mother's voice and they small talked for a minute or so before Aubrey returned the phone to Terri, Sasha's mother.

"Did you speak to Chauncey?" Was the first thing that Terri asked when she was back on the phone.

"No, why?" Sasha asked.

"Because, he called here wondering why he couldn't reach you, and I had to tell him that you went off to Jamaica. How could you not even let him know, Sasha?"

Sasha breathed deep.

"Ma, let him know how? And I don't have to let him know anything, Chauncey is not my husband!"

"Well he should be," Terri snapped back. "Do you know that *husband* of yours dropped Aubrey off, and didn't even say goodbye to her? I'm telling you Sasha, when you're not around he is totally different. I don't trust him."

Sasha sucked her teeth.

"Ma, you don't trust *me*, that don't mean anything."

"I do trust you. I love you, you're my child."

Sasha was shocked that her mother said that she loved her but she still wasn't letting her off.

"Yeah, well trust and love are two different things.... I love Chauncey, but I don't trust him. And you love me, but you don't trust me…you love me, but you don't like me," Sasha quipped to her mother. All Terri could respond with was a simple "Sasha, hush."

The ladies chit-chatted for a few more minutes before Sasha ended the call and returned to the kitchen.

"How's Aubrey?" Tatum asked, who had just hung up from checking on her nieces.

"She's fine…where's Jayde?"

"Oh, she said she had to make a call."

"Oh okay, I'm gonna ask her if she's ready to head out…I'm hungry, what about you?" Sasha asked Tatum.

"Starving."

Sasha laughed and went toward the room on the other side of the suite that Jayde had taken. As she got close to the cracked door, she could hear Jayde talking hushed and harshly.

"Nigga, did I ask you for your fucking life story? I don't give a fuck what happened, I want my money… every last fucking penny, you hear me?" There was a silence as Sasha stood frozen, listening. She had never heard Jayde so demanding, so angry, so…scary.

"I'm out of town for a few days, but when I get back, shit better be straight, or else…"

Or else what? Sasha wondered. Jayde disconnected the call and Sasha stood still for a couple of seconds and then walked in the room as if she hadn't been there all along.

"Hey girl, you ready to eat?" She noticed Jayde had an angry grimace on her face and was rigid. "You okay?"

Jayde turned to Sasha and then snapped out of her anger.

"Oh, yeah girl I'm okay. Just…business. Yeah, let's go eat."

Jayde walked past Sasha and out of the room, and Sasha slowly followed. She was still a little skeptical but figured she wouldn't be too concerned. This was her vacation, shit, and she had her own problems that she would try to party away this weekend. Jayde was a grown ass woman, and whatever she was involved in, that was her business. *To each her own, and to me, mines... Let's Eat!*

Chapter 9 - Destiny

"First of all, when you're on vacation, you're supposed to try new things," Sasha defended.

"Tripe, yuck! It just looks nasty." Tatum turned up her nose as she decided on the roasted fish.

"The lady said it's a Jamaican delicacy," Sasha reminded them. Jayde shook her head.

"No, *that*, is a Jamaican delicacy," she said pointing at a Taye Diggs look a like. "Come here Langston, come give Stella her groove back, baby."

The girls cracked up laughing.

"Please Jayde, you are not even old enough to be Stella," Tatum chuckled. "Stella was what, 40?"

Jayde grinned and sipped her wine.

"No, I'm not 40, but I'm not 23 and 24 like you two," she admitted. Tatum was shocked and Jayde continued.

"I used to babysit Sasha when she was about 4 or 5 years old, Pocahontas."

Sasha smirked, knowing that Tatum was surprised by Jayde's revelation.

"Well, how old *are* you?" Tatum asked, growing tired of the mystery.

"Thirty-four," Jayde answered proudly.

"Wow," Tatum responded, mouth open. "You look good, girl! I mean that's not old, but you don't look a day over 21."

"Thank you mama, I owe it all to Dr. Perricone, and Dr. Martinez... shit, and Dr. 90210, Dr. Spock, Dr. Giggles... man, I got so many doctors, it don't make any sense," Jayde joked.

Sasha choked on her wine, giggling, and Tatum laughed loud feeling tipsy from the champagne, Nuvo, wine train they had been on.

Ree turned around from the bar instinctively, but made no recognition as he scanned the restaurant. *Damn, don't tell me I'm hearing things.*

He figured it was just a coincidence, or maybe it was in his mind. The smile, the laugh, maybe they weren't like hers at all. Maybe he just wanted them to be.

But that laugh, that was so much like the sweet laugh that Tatum had when she thought something was really funny, and she couldn't hold back. She'd laugh loud like that and her eyes would squint up, and her mouth would be open wide, showing all of her pretty teeth, and it would make everyone else around her laugh too. Like the time at the pool in Disneyworld. Ree chuckled at the memory.

"Hey, you okay? Are you here?" Trinity playfully asked Ree. He focused back on her.

"Of course," he lied.

"You wanna order some food?" She asked. She wished that she could cook for him but it was a skill that she did not possess, no matter how hard she tried.

"Nah, I gotta get back to work." He downed the rest of his drink and stood up.

Trinity leaned into him, hoping for a kiss and when he puckered his lips, she smiled. And he planted a soft one, right on her forehead. He turned to walk away.

"Hey!" She shouted to him. He turned and faced her, waiting for what she had to say.

"Why don't you kiss me next time on the lips, Mr. Knights?"

She said it in a joking manner, but was really serious. He tilted his head to the side and looked at her.

"You talking crazy," was all he replied with a sexy smile, and with that, he headed out of the restaurant. He thought back to a night he and Tatum had lay in bed, kissing until their lips were sore.

71

Ree... have you ever kissed anyone the way you kiss me... ... ...
Never... ...
Good...promise me you never will... ... ...
I won't... ...
Promise? ... ...
Promise... ...

And he hadn't.

The next day, the girls decided to take advantage of the free spa packages that they were given.
"I can't believe you forgot to tell us about these," Sasha said to Jayde, as they all headed downstairs on the elevator. They had spent all night after dinner at the hotel lounge, and now were looking forward to winding down with a little relaxation time, followed by some sightseeing and shopping. At least that's what was on the Sasha itinerary.
"Girl, after seeing that fine ass bellhop, I forgot what the hell the conversation between us was even about."
Tatum remained quiet, half hung over, and half thinking of Ree. She couldn't help but feel like she was so close to him, yet so far. She wondered if she should go searching for him or leave it alone.
How mad would I be at myself if I leave Jamaica without seeing 'what if'?
The doors opened to the main floor, and as they were coming out, Rodney was coming in.
"Excuse me, can you tell us which way is the spa?" Sasha asked him. He smiled warmly at the ladies and pointed straight ahead.
"Right that way lovely ladies, you can not miss it."
They thanked him and he went to get onto the elevator.
"One more thing," Jayde said. "Where's the other bellhop?"
"The other bellhop?" Rodney asked, confused.
Jayde nodded, she couldn't stop thinking of how fine he was.

"Yeah, you know. The one who brought us these." She held up the envelopes. "Brown skinned, his hair was like-"

"Okay, that's enough, thank you," Sasha said to Rodney, pulling Jayde away. "We're going to the spa Jayde, not to find the bellboy."

Jayde pouted and crossed her arms.

"Aw c'mon, I just wanted to see if I could make his little broke ass day, that's all." She laughed and Tatum and Sasha chuckled as the girls made their way across the lobby.

Once they reached the spa, they were blown away. It was completely decorated in white, with white calla lilies in vases and white bowls with white chocolates inside. There were white leather chairs and white marble floors. They approached the young girl at the register.

"Hello ladies, how are you this afternoon? May I get you ladies a package menu?"

Tatum handed her the envelope.

"Hello, we received these yesterday."

The woman looked at them and looked back at the girls.

"Great, you guys get a fabulous treatment today. A full body massage, spa pedicure, and manicure."

"Do we get a facial too? If not, can I purchase one separately?" Jayde asked, but was cut off by another voice.

"You can most definitely get a facial, no charge."

The girls turned and found Trinity standing there, looking radiant. They all exchanged hellos and Trinity turned to the worker.

"Can you please get my friends some towels and robes...and you know what, get one for me too, I think I may join you ladies."

The girls all giggled.

"Rough day?" Tatum asked.

"Already," Trinity agreed. "This season is so busy. I'll be happy when everyone goes home and everything goes back to normal...well, everyone except you guys," she joked. The girls shared another laugh as the worker brought them towels.

"By the way, thank you for this," Sasha said, excited about getting her favorite thing, a massage.

"No problem…it was actually my man's idea." She blushed just thinking about Ree.

"Some man, the way you blushing," Tatum teased. "Let him know that we said thank you, as well."

Trinity beamed.

"Girl, you have no idea, he is, whew," she laughed. "But will do. Okay ladies, let's go get changed and pampered."

After the girls were dressed in their robes, they emerged from the locker room and found the female masseuse waiting. She was surprised to see Trinity with them.

"Ms. Trinity, you get treatment today, too?"

"I am, Mildred. I am treating myself. Ladies, this is Mildred, and she is a miracle worker."

The girls said hello and introduced themselves and Mildred focused on Tatum.

"Ms. Trinity, this is your sister? You two look alike."

The girls laughed and Sasha and Jayde looked for the resemblance, and there was one. Both ladies had long curly black hair, mocha dark brown complexions, and wide bright smiles, but Tatum was prettier by far. And her face was much softer.

"No, she is not. But I will take that as a compliment," Trinity smiled.

The girls were split up; Sasha and Trinity were to start with massages, and Jayde and Tatum with facials. They were on their way to their rooms when Trinity asked the girl who performed the facials, if she would do hers as well.

"I'm not sure if I have time for both and I would much rather get my facial first."

The girl looked confused, not sure of what to do.

"I can only do two at a time," was all she could say in her light voice. She didn't want to get in trouble.

Trinity laughed.

"Sweetie, I'm the manager." But Tatum intervened.

"No, it's okay. I'll get my massage first. I'd rather do that...we can switch."

Tatum saw that unlike the massage room, the room for the facials had both girls in the room together. And although Jayde was cool, she would much rather have Sasha to talk to during facials. She and Trinity agreed to switch.

Tatum entered the massage room and took off her robe. She wrapped the towel around her and laid face down as she was accustomed to doing. The room was quiet and she wished that she had Sasha to talk with her during massages as well. She pulled all of her hair forward and let it hang toward the floor as she tried her best to zone out. Her thoughts immediately went to Ree.

I can't believe I'm here. It took me over two years to muster up the courage, but I'm here. I have to find him. I have to see him. I miss him...

Tatum continued to zone out as she waited for Mildred to come in and work those miracles on her.

Meanwhile, at the front of the spa, Ree entered in search of Trinity. He had thought of the way he had been treating her, keeping her at a distance, the way she had brought up the whole kissing situation, everything.

Then he thought of how he had asked Tatum to come with him, how she had turned him down, and then how she had never come even after he reached out to her again. He had been so sure that he had succeeded in getting Tatum out of his system, but for some reason, she recently had crept up in his mind again. She was the only woman that Ree had ever felt strong enough about to even consider it being love, but that was over two years ago, and it was time to let that go.

He wanted to make it up to Trinity for the way he had dipped out on her the night before. He greeted the girl at the register and asked if she had seen Trinity. Before she could respond, Mildred walked up.

"Hello Mr. Knights. Ms. Trinity is one of my rooms, prepping for a massage... Room 207."

Ree winked and smiled.

"Thank you, Mildred." Even Mildred couldn't help but to swoon at his charm as he made his way down the hall.

"Ms. Trinity is a very lucky woman."

"Indeed," the other girl agreed.

Tatum was halfway into a sleep when she finally heard the door open and Mildred enter the room. She heard the footsteps as she approached but couldn't bring herself to say anything, she was fully relaxed. She kept her eyes closed and anticipated her massage as her mind kept her in peaceful thoughts of Ree.

Finally, Tatum felt a pair of strong hands working on her back and she exhaled.

Ree was instantly aroused at the sight of Trinity's smooth back exposed and a small towel only covering her bottom half. He rubbed his strong hands over her smooth skin and noticed that she felt extra soft today. He leaned down to her, and she smelled so good, so much like…*damn, there goes my mind again,* he thought.

"You smell so good," he whispered, in his deep baritone and kissed her lightly on the back. He inhaled her scent and it was like an aphrodisiac to him. It awakened his senses in a way that they hadn't been in a long time. "Damn," he whispered, working her over with his hands.

Tatum's heart raced and she was sure that she was dreaming. *But it feels so real.* None of her dreams of him had ever been this palpable. She could feel him, hear him clear as day, smell him. She parted her lips and submitted to the ecstasy. It felt so real that she wanted to cry, and she could feel every nerve on her body coming to life and her juices began to form.

Ree licked the spine of her back slowly and Tatum moaned in pleasure. He could feel his dick harden as he inhaled her intoxicating scent and rubbed her smoothness. They both were in the brink of passion. Tatum, sure that she was in a sensual dream. And Ree, feeling as if he was reminiscing of another time.

"I missed you," she cried, half conscious.

76

Ree stopped, instantly. He closed his eyes and tried to rationalize. *It can't be...It just.* He backed away and stared at her; she was still facing down but suddenly looking like someone else. He was scared to say the name, scared that he just may be going crazy. But he wouldn't have to.

The instant halt on her dream caused Tatum to slowly open her eyes. *What just happened? Did Mildred even come in the room yet?* She turned over slowly and the breath left her body. Their eyes met, and the world stopped. After a few moments of staring, the silence was broken.

"Tatum?" He barely managed to get out. Nothing in him could believe it, but it had to be real. She was here, and every emotion he could possibly feel went through him at once.

"Destiny?" She found herself asking lightly to herself, still in a state of shock.

Ree studied her as if she wasn't real, completely in awe of her, and he ran his hands over his face to regain his composure.

"What...When...What are you doing here?" He asked this as if her being there had thrown a monkey wrench in his new life. Tatum wasn't sure if it was a good monkey wrench, or a bad one.

She awkwardly moved around to cover her body with the towel as she stood up. She wasn't sure how a minute ago she was ready to make love to him in her dream and now here in reality, she was nervous and embarrassed. She held her towel with one hand and used the other to run through her hair.

"Um...I don't know...Sasha wanted to come... and get away...and I figured...I mean I just thought since you..." She paused, flustered, and looked at him. She swallowed hard and then smiled lightly, taking in everything about him that she was crazy about, everything that she loved. It was him. "Are you even happy to see me?" She was still real and upfront, and he loved it.

He smiled as he looked at her. She was even more beautiful than he remembered. Over the time he had forgotten little things, like the small beauty mark on her cheek, or the sparkle in her eyes, and the way her skin glowed. All of these things now all at once, combined with her essence and her beauty, let it be known, no one could hold a candle to her.

"You have no idea," he assured her. He went to make his way over to her and the door flew open, stopping him in his tracks.

"Oh my god, I am so sorry, baby. Mildred told me she sent you to the wrong room." Trinity stood there embarrassed for Tatum, and for Ree. And Mildred stood behind her.

"I'm so sorry Mr. Knights... I had no idea Ms. Trinity was not here."

Trinity walked over to where Ree stood and the reality came crashing down on Tatum like a ton of bricks. The kisses on her back, the sweet words, his hands, his tongue, it was all for *her*.

It was all my man's idea... Trinity had said earlier. *Her* man...

Tatum stared at Ree for a few long seconds and he looked as if he wanted to say something, but wasn't sure of what. As if he knew how hurt and embarrassed Tatum could be, and he was hurt for her. Well, he had no idea.

Tatum blinked away tears and looked down at the ground. She was mortified. Ree spoke her name.

"Tatum."

Trinity looked up at him curiously.

"You guys know each other, Sean?" She asked, sensing that there was something in the air, and definitely something in the way that he said her name. He answered her but kept his focus on Tatum, who just looked down.

"Yeah...we know each other from the states."

Trinity was taken aback and by this time Sasha and Jayde had made their way to the door.

"Ree?" Sasha questioned, shocked.

"Bellboy?" Jayde asked, confused.

Trinity intertwined her arm into his, a simple but territorial gesture. A message to Tatum that Ree paid no mind to.

"Oh, wow. Well, these are the ladies that had problems with their reservations yesterday... It's a small world, right baby?"

Tatum couldn't take anymore. Maybe hearing that he had moved on would have been a little easier to deal with.

But seeing it right in front of her, with all of the pet names and love gestures, was like torture. She finally mustered up the strength to say…

"I think I need to put my clothes on."

She stormed out of the room with tears in her eyes, without so much as a glance at Ree or his Tatum stunt double, and she made her way to the locker room with Sasha and Jayde hot on her trail. Ree called out her name one more time, but she didn't respond. She didn't even turn around.

Mildred turned around and left as well, but Trinity remained. She stared at Ree as he just looked straight ahead blankly.

She didn't want to let on, but she was terrified.

"Sean… is everything okay?" She finally asked him.

After a few seconds he looked at her and nodded coolly.

"Yeah…yeah everything's fine."

And then he walked out of the room and left her standing there alone. No hug, no wink, no smile, and definitely no kiss.

"No, I don't give a fuck! I am getting the fuck out of here… Jayde, if you don't want me to hate you forever, I would appreciate it if you got on that little magic phone of yours, called up one of your jet friends, and got me a flight off of this fucking island!"

Tatum was pissed. She was storming around the suite, throwing things into her bag with tears streaming down her cheeks. This was not apart of the plan. He was supposed to be like her, unable to move on. I mean yeah, he could've fucked around, but a serious relationship, that was not even in his character, unless it was with Tatum. Anybody else shouldn't have even been able to get that close. *Oh my god, he kisses her!*

Tatum thought of the way that he kissed her back, he had to kiss her lips twice as good. And it tore her apart, as much as she wished that it didn't.

Jayde was still in shock that Tatum's man, the infamous Ree, was the bellboy that she had met. She snapped out of her thoughts.

"Okay, now look, calm down sweetie...so, he's got a bitch, so what, right? Just put your shit down and move her out the house...take back what's yours."

Sasha sat on the couch stupefied. She couldn't believe their reunion had played out like this. She wanted to console Tatum, but she wasn't sure of what to say. Although it was worded all wrong, Jayde did have a point.

"Are you even sure that it's that serious?" Sasha asked Tatum, finally saying something.

Tatum took a break from her tirade and answered.

"Yes, I'm sure."

Sasha stood up and walked to her.

"But how, how do you know?"

Tatum was visibly upset by the question.

'I just know!" She shot back.

"How?" Sasha asked again, not feeling like that was good enough.

"Because I know!" Tatum repeated. "I just know...I know...I know...him."

Her tears came down as she stated it again.

"I know *him*." She knew the way that he was with Trinity, was nothing light. Ree was not one to play games or waste his time with purposeless relationships. If she had his time, she meant something.

Sasha wrapped her arms around her friend and rubbed her back and Tatum wiped her face with her hands. She couldn't believe that she was crying.

"Are you sure you want to leave?" Sasha asked.

Before Tatum could answer, a knock on the door interrupted. Jayde figured she would be the one to answer, being that the friends were having a one on one.

She opened the door and Ree stood on the other side, serious as ever.

"Tatum here?"

Jayde opened the door wider so that he could look in, and Tatum and Ree made eye contact. They both stood there staring at one another, and Sasha was the one to initiate conversation.

"Ree, come in…Um, Jayde…why don't we let them talk?"

Sasha and Jayde made their way to Jayde's room which was the furthest away as Ree came in, closed the door, and walked over to Tatum. His aura was so dominant; it was hard for Tatum not to swoon. There was an awkward silence as both of them tried to figure out what to say. Ree spoke first.

"You know, about the room incident, and the massage thing…I'm sorry about that, Tatum. I know that whole situation was uncomfortable."

Tatum shook her head nonchalantly.

"You don't have to apologize Ree, you thought I was somebody else…right? So why are you sorry?" She hated that her words came out angry but she couldn't help it.

"That's not fair, Tatum…and I wouldn't exactly say that."

He thought of how lost he was, feeling her, smelling her, imagining that it was her, only to find that it really was her. It was never Trinity, even if it really would have been Trinity, it still wouldn't have been her, not to Ree.

Tatum chuckled, not buying it.

"Well, what *were* you thinking, then?"

Ree shrugged.

"I don't know, what were *you* thinking? I know you weren't thinking that it was me."

Tatum was stuck and had no response. Ree could see her frustration and didn't want to go any further with this argument.

"Look, it was an…unusual way for us to meet again, but it happened. And now, you're here…and I'm here…and I'm happy. We have a lot of catching up to do, and some things to discuss."

Tatum heard him talking and it all sounded so good, but the sharp pain of someone else having him still stung her. He continued.

"I have a very important business dinner tonight, I couldn't miss it if I wanted to…and trust me, I want to…" He paused and looked at her yearningly. "So I would love, no I would be very honored, if you would please have lunch with me tomorrow, Miss Lady?"

The name he called her took her back, but looking around at the present took her here. She couldn't look him in the eyes.

"I...I wont be here tomorrow...I'm leaving."

His face collapsed into sorrow and anger and he stared at her waiting for her to look at him. When he realized that she wouldn't, he called her name.

"Tatum... Tatum, look at me." She turned her head so that he couldn't see the tears coming on and he called her again.

"Look at me, Tatum."

She finally did and her heart melted. He stared her straight in the eyes.

"Don't do this shit. Don't run from me." He was so demanding. His words echoed in her head as Sasha came out of the bedroom, interrupting his intense warning.

"Excuse us for a moment," she said, grabbing Tatum and dragging her into the bathroom.

Once inside and door closed, Sasha let her have it.

"Now, I done heard enough."

Tatum was shocked, both by Sasha's tone, and her open admission to eavesdropping. Tatum looked at her like she was crazy.

"Yup, that's right, I've been listening... And I can't believe you, bitch! That man has done nothing wrong, and I know it hurts that he hasn't been a complete angel, or celibate, like you, but from what I can tell, that chick don't mean nothing! Now if you don't cut out your temper tantrum, and go to lunch with him tomorrow...I don't know what Imma do." Tatum sucked her teeth and shook her head in disbelief as Sasha added on.

"No, I take that back, I know exactly what I'm gonna do....I wont get you that lawyer," she threatened.

"You wouldn't do that," Tatum said in disbelief.

"Try me."

Tatum couldn't believe this person who was imitating the sweet Sasha.

"Sash, that's not funny, that is a serious situation!"

"And so is this…" Sasha countered. "Now go out there, and say yes."

Sasha looked at her sternly, and then made her way out of the bathroom, and back into the room with Jayde, without another word.

Tatum stood in the bathroom a little while longer in shock, wondering what had just happened. She didn't know what had come over Sasha, she didn't know why she was so upset with her, and she didn't know why she was taking it to the extreme of posing threats.

But if she knew one thing, the one thing she knew, was that she was going to lunch with Ree tomorrow. And deep down inside, she thanked Sasha for it.

Chapter 10 - Obsession

The bedroom's tall, glass, double-doors opened extensively, allowed the cool island breeze to creep into Ree's lavish estate. He sat in his favorite spot, right in the doorway, deep in contemplation - no drink, no music, no television, no distraction. He was aware, but paid little attention to the fact that Trinity was gracefully prancing around the room, staring at him, dying for him to say something, anything to her. She knew something was up and could literally feel him pulling further and further from her.

Ree couldn't get the whole situation with Tatum out of his mind. He couldn't believe that after two years, she was there, just minutes away from him. He reflected on when she had come out of the bathroom with Sasha, and had a sudden change of heart, agreeing to meet him the next day. He was relieved, and grateful, but he was confused at the now present uneasiness between them. As if they were strangers, just getting to know each other. He figured the time and circumstances had formed a wedge between them. And even as he had made his way out of her suite, with no little more said between them besides the time and place to meet, he still couldn't deny the growing feeling of simplicity and comfort having her around him again had provided. His father had even noticed a change in him, but he had chalked it up as simply being a good day.

"So, remember how I was telling you that my mother wanted to meet you?" Trinity started, trying her best to snap him out of whatever was occupying his mind.

He looked up at her vacantly and tried his best to feign interest in what she had to say. He didn't reply however, so she continued.

"Anywayyy, she's coming tomorrow, and she wants you to have lunch with us." She smiled wide, thrilled. Ree meeting her mother would only solidify his place in her life, and hers in his.
He stared straight ahead before answering a simple,
"I can't...I have lunch plans."
Trinity felt a slight lump in her throat and she wanted to protest, but she knew Ree didn't tolerate tantrums or her becoming too involved in his dealings. She chose her words carefully.
"Business?" She asked with her voice cracking. And he knew, that she knew, exactly what it was for, and that it had nothing to do with business. He was sympathetic to her disappointment, but his plans would not change.
"It's complicated."
That's all he would give her. No more, no less.
So Trinity walked away, and went to soak her frustration away, cursing Tatum the whole time.

As Trinity lay in the tub, she reflected on her fast growing and now just as fast diminishing, relationship with the man she called Sean.
About a year ago, she had taken a job at the resort, hired by Ree's father, and she had been anxious to meet his son, the sexy owner that all of the ladies had doted over.
Trinity had grown up very poor, twelve people to a shack poor. So when she realized at a very young age that she possessed attractive qualities that drew men to her, she knew from that day forward that her ticket out of a life of poverty and pain, would be a man, a powerful and wealthy man. She had been waiting on that kind of man since that day. And as she heard the stories of Ree and his family, she knew she wanted him before she even laid eyes on him. So she began her work.
She befriended his father, and learned what Ree liked, what he disliked, and purposely avoided meeting him until she was sure that she knew him like a book, front to back.
If he was coming, she was going. If he was days, she was nights. And if he was weekends, she was weekdays.

85

When she finally was introduced to him, by his father of course, she had the independent woman, not looking for a man, non-materialistic, good girl act down to a tee.

She treated him professionally and worked hard, showing him that she was of value and reliable. She worked overtime, holidays, and played him close, in a less obvious way. If he was thirsty, she would just so happen to have a bottle of water. If he was hungry, she was on her way out and could pick him up something. And if he was lonely, she was there to fill the void. Which is exactly what ended up happening one rainy night.

"Trinity, seriously, you can go home...there's nothing left to do."

Ree had come out of the back office, taking a break from his license reviews, and she was standing there, slightly leaning on the desk, and the lobby was completely empty.

"That's fine Mr. Knights, I don't mind being here... You never know when a couple with a broken down car in the rain, may want to check into a hotel in the middle of the night," she joked.

Ree chuckled.

"You've been watching too many horror movies."

She laughed, and Ree stretched, feeling the tension somewhat ease off of him. She watched his muscular tattooed arms extend and she had to look away before her lust showed on her face.

"Yeah, well you know the clerk always gets it first," she warned, assuming that she would be the first to die if this was a scary movie.

"Yeah, well they'll have to go through me first," he winked.

She knew his comment had no pretense, but it made her swoon. It made her feel protected. She went in for the kill as he checked the numbers on the computer.

"Speaking of which, what are you still doing here? I know I'm single and lonely, but you don't have a special lady at home, waiting on you?"

He looked at her and snickered, and his mind traveled back to Newark where Tatum was. She still hadn't reached out to him, and he had sent the postcard months before. Before he could respond or go any further in his thoughts, Trinity continued.

"I bet she's home now, with a nice dinner for you, a nice massage waiting, some sexy lingerie." Trinity giggled innocently but knew that she was planting the seeds in his brain that she could provide those things for him. He looked at her and realized for the first time, just how attractive she was. He also realized that she was slightly flirting with him.

"No, nobody at home...and I like it that way. You women are trouble, man," he said shaking his head.

She chuckled lightly and put her one leg slightly up on the low shelf under the desk, allowing her skirt to rise and her long legs to be on display. She then poked her average sized, but firm, ass out and arched her back.

"Trouble, huh ...well, what's wrong with trouble?"

Ree scanned his eyes over her body, but before it could go any further, he turned and made his way back into the office.

"Have a good night Trinity...go home, it's late."

She didn't give up though. A minute later, she was knocking on his office door.

"I just wanted to apologize for my behavior..." She started. "It's just being around you, and getting to know you... I've grown...attracted to you." She tried to act like it was hard to say, but really it was rehearsed. "And it's just been so long since I've...well... I thought you were attracted to me as well...I just don't want you to be upset with me."

She turned to leave and he called her back, feeling a little bad.

She was gorgeous, and he was attracted to her, that was for sure. She worked for him though, and that was a downside.

"Trinity its okay, you didn't do anything wrong... Have a good night, alright."

She walked over to him with a friendly smile to hug him goodnight, and pressed her body against his dick. The feel and smell of a woman, and her contact on him, caused Ree's semi-hard dick to grow as they embraced for a second longer than they should have.

"Goodnight, Mr. Knights," she whispered sultrily in his ear, and then used the tip of her tongue to gently trace the rim. It was the point of no return, the make or break, would he take the bait?

The greater man in Ree told him not to, but the lesser man gave into lust, and slowly palmed her ass as she kissed and licked lightly on his neck. He picked her up strongly, cupping her buttocks, and placed her onto the desk, tonguing her neck, as she pulled at his shirt and belt buckle.

"Oh Mr. Knights, I want you to fuck me…please, fuck me." She was begging for it.

Mr. Knights. That shit had him feeling like he was the president or some shit. He searched through his jeans and desk drawers for a condom, but she pulled one out of her purse.

He didn't care why she had it, he didn't care if it was planned, all he cared about at that moment, was fucking this little bitch's brains out. She wanted it, he needed it, and his tension was growing by the day.

He put the rubber on while eying her sexy body, and then he slid all of him inside of her, as she opened her eyes wide from the vast size of his dick. Her wetness engulfed him and they both closed their eyes in sheer pleasure. He began moving in and out of her, making her throw it on him.

"Oh yes, oh Sean…oh fuck me!"

He grabbed her lightly by the neck and pushed her back down onto the desk as he stood up, stroking her powerfully.

"Mr. Knights…say Mr. Knights," he ordered roughly, as he pounded into her.

"Oh, shit! Yes, Mr. Knights! Mr. Knights! Mr. Knightsss!" She screamed in pain and pleasure.

Ree fucked her long and hard that night, and since then she was at his beck and call.

She had established herself as a friend at first, and she was grateful that she had because if she hadn't, she would have been in hoe status after that night.

But instead, she was at friend status, friend with benefits. Who slowly worked her way up to manager of his hotel, and slowly worked her way up to the closest thing to a girlfriend to him, as he would ever let her be.

But was that all in jeopardy now?

She continued to soak and let the question penetrate her mind.

Ree's business meeting that night was scheduled to take place at a very fine, yet expensive restaurant called The Sugar Mill. The meeting was originally supposed to be between Ree, his father, their accountant, Bernie Meyers, and two potential partners, who owned some property in Montego Bay that Ree was interested in getting his hands on. However, as Trinity had soaked in the bathtub that night, Ree had done something that he infrequently did, he double checked his accounts.

His overseas accounts, which he kept the majority of the money that he had accumulated in the drug game, were slowly but surely dwindling. Someone was transferring small amounts to an unknown account and it was time Ree had a one on one with Bernie, being that he was the only other person with access.

He stood inside of the second level of the dark parking deck, smoking on a blunt calmly as he watched Bernie's 2010 Range Rover pull inside. Even through the slightly tinted windows, Ree could see Bernie looking skeptically at him, probably wondering why he wasn't waiting inside like everyone else.

Bernie backed into a parking spot, across from where Ree stood, and turned off his car and driving lights. As he stepped out in his brown Stacy Adams shoes, he closed the door and made his way over to Ree carrying a black briefcase, wearing an uneasy smile.

"Hey, Sean…why are you not inside? Is the meeting cancelled?"

Bernie spoke with a slight Jamaican accent attempting to be covered up by proper English. He was a middle-aged Jamaican man, with a wife, kids, nice home, solid career, numerous degrees, and apparently, no brains. He addressed Ree as Sean because he too, like many, did not know the man Respect, and he had been lucky enough not to have known him, up until now.

Ree inhaled the smoke and let it slowly maneuver throughout his system, calming his nerves, slowing his heart rate, completely relaxing him, the way he liked to be, at times like these.

"Nah Bernie, it's not canceled…everyone's inside. Just let me finish, and then we can walk together."

Ree was just as collected as he'd always been.

Bernie nodded hastily and stood in front of Ree, ready to make his way to the elevators. As Ree continued to smoke, Bernie looked down and noticed the Beretta 98 9mm down at Ree's side, in his right hand.

"Mr. Knights…," Bernie started but was frozen with fear. Should he run? He was standing so close to him, he wouldn't make it in time…besides, he'd look as guilty as he was. "What do you have the g…gun for?"

Ree calmly put out his blunt on the trunk of the car that he was leaning on and reached into his pocket for the silencer. He slowly pulled it out and began to screw it on as Bernie stuttered over his words.

"Oh this?" Ree said calmly. "Hold up, I'll tell you."

He finished screwing on the silencer as Bernie's body began to rattle with fear. His eyes were wide and focused on the gun the whole time. He now had a sudden feeling that he should have ran when he had the chance to. Would he still be able to make it?

"Don't," Ree simply stated, standing up straight in front of Bernie.

"Wha-what?" Bernie asked nervously, feeling the tears well in his eyes.

"Don't try to run yo, you'll make it worse. When I find you, when I catch you, I'll torture you…I'll make it slow, and very painful."

Bernie began to breathe heavily and shake his head no. He looked around the empty parking deck as Ree just stared at him seriously. Then, as if everything was alright, Ree put his arm around Bernie's shoulder and began guiding him back toward his car. Bernie felt as if his legs were jelly as he tried to walk and think at the same time.

"Don't worry Bernie," Ree said, comforting him while lightly patting him on the back. "I'm gonna make this quick."

Bernie figured maybe he should plead as he felt the warm piss running down his leg.

"Mr..... Mr. Knights...please...I don't know what I did. I...I have a family...a wife...please..."

They reached the back of Bernie's car which was facing the cement wall, so no one could really see them. Ree tilted his head to the side and listened to Bernie plead his case but it fell on deaf ears. Ree's heart was cold to the man who had crossed him.

"Please Mr. Knights...I am a good man...with a family..."

Ree nodded understandingly.

"That's part of it...the other part of you Bernie, is a snake."

Ree opened the trunk and motioned with the gun for Bernie to climb in.

"Get in...come on, get the fuck in... I'm hungry."

Bernie cried profusely, as the tears fell from his eyes.

"Please," he whimpered, but Ree smacked him hard with the butt of the gun, becoming frustrated.

"Stop trying to buy time mothafucka!" Ree barked.

Bernie held his head in pain and sobbed like a baby, climbing into the trunk. He looked at Ree with pleading eyes and Ree pointed the gun at his forehead.

"God no...please," he tried to beg again.

"Don't worry about the family...you got life insurance, right?"

Bernie's reply never made it from his lips as the two bullets ripped through his skull, blowing his brain matter all over the back of the SUV.

Ree looked into the wide eyes of his victim and felt a surge of vengeance. A thrill, an excitement, something he hadn't felt in a long time.

He wondered if killing was apart of his nature, because no one should feel the electricity he felt at that moment. His father, a reformed and old school gangster, would be sour about the way he handled the situation.

He objected to a man of Ree's caliber getting his hands dirty, especially with his new legit lifestyle he was supposed to be living. But Ree felt that someone stealing from him was a personal matter, and should be handled...personally.

He closed the trunk and began to make his way to the elevators and into the restaurant, with no remorse for the transgression he had just committed.

He approached the table where his father and the two business associates were already seated with their drinks.

"Good evening, gentlemen," Ree greeted with a smile, taking his seat as if nothing had just happened.

"Good evening, Mr. Knights."

"Glad you could join us, Mr. Knights."

His father looked up from his menu.

"Good evening, son. Have you heard from Bernie?"

Ree picked up a menu and the steak caught his attention, as he motioned for the waitress.

"Um, yea... He won't be able to make it."

The next day

Tatum walked nervously towards the elevator, triple checking her appearance in the hallway mirror. Although she had changed her outfit four times, trying to decide between the 'not trying too hard' shorts and tank top look, the 'I'm sophisticated' linen dress look, and the 'flirty and ready for the beach' denim skirt and sandal look, she ended up opting for the 'don't you wish you still had this' yellow miniature sundress look, that accentuated her long legs and her curves and sat her cleavage up as if on a platter. *Perfect.*

Her hair was straightened and hung long down her back, and she was wearing Ree's favorite scent for her, Escada. She rode the elevator, not believing that in a few moments she would be face to face with him, alone.

As she stepped off, she was reassured that she looked stunning by the admiring stares from the male, and some female, guests and staff. She smirked and headed to Eden, which was one of the three hotel restaurants. She was meeting Ree there for lunch.

When Tatum got to the entrance, she took a deep breath before pulling open the heavy, wooden, double doors, and heading inside of the dim and quaint establishment.

There were quite a few people in there when she looked around, but as she nervously neared the hostess, she felt someone come up behind her and rest their hand gently on the small of her back, causing her to turn around.

"You look...wow." That was all Ree could say. Tatum smiled up at him and he looked at her for a few moments, completely blinded and blown away by her beauty. "This way," he added, guiding her through the restaurant.

They walked through what seemed like the entire restaurant before coming to a stop at a small and isolated section near a bunch of large windows. He pulled out her chair and she sat, and as he took his seat across from her, Tatum's heart ached.

She watched the way he maneuvered, his debonair style, the way he sat tall, looking her in the eyes, the way he took control of things. He made her feel like a woman – desired, secure, protected.

"So, how are you enjoying your stay so far?" He asked, taking her hands into his. She felt a sensation run through her.

"Good...it's well," Tatum answered, not sure of what else to say.

He looked at her for a few seconds before continuing.

"And how long are you here for?"

Tatum studied his sexy lips as he spoke to her, almost to the point of where she barely heard what he had said.

"Oh, um...we leave tomorrow."

"Tomorrow?" Ree repeated, a bit disappointed, and she nodded, as the waitress came over and took their drink orders. When she was gone, the conversation picked up where it left off.

"So, when were you gonna come and find me...or was that not apart of the plan?" Ree asked her this with a charming smile, but Tatum avoided answering it with a question of her own.

"So, who's the chick?" It came out more direct than she had expected.

Ree chuckled, but Tatum's face had attitude written all over it.

"She's just some...chick," he said, mocking her. Tatum wanted to scream.

"And how did you meet her, when did you meet her?"

Ree sighed, not thrilled that the conversation seemed to be about Trinity, but he knew he owed her an explanation. Tatum was the only woman that could get away with questioning him like that.

"Um, she works here. I probably met her about a year ago, more or less."

The fact that Tatum and Ree's romance had only taken place over a few months and this chick had a whole year of him, infuriated Tatum.

"So what was she working first...the job, or you?" Tatum looked at him with a raised eyebrow and Ree was amused at her wit. She was so beautiful, yet so fiery. He had missed that.

"Now we gonna get some shit straight," he said firmly, but with slight humor. "She don't work me...that's not even possible, so get that out ya head."

He licked his lips and eyed Tatum.

"But that's not important,...you know what is?"

"What?" She shot back.

But he didn't say anything, he just pointed at her, causing a smile to grow on her face.

"How's the girls?" He asked sincerely. Ree had grown close to Tatum's nieces in the time that she and him had been together.

The question caused Tatum to reflect on the letter she received.

"They're doing well. They broke me for Christmas... but I got them everything they wanted, so they were happy. Chanel has a boyfriend now."

Ree shook his head, not thrilled with the news, he felt like a protective uncle or something. Tatum sighed and continued.

"Their mother gets visits with them now, she came back from the dead…and now she's *suing* me for custody." The news stunned Ree as she proceeded, wearily.

"Apart of me wants to just let them go and have a life with their mother, because I know how important that can be…but I'm so scared…Scared that she may relapse… and then in a way, I guess I'm…"

"Scared of being alone," he finished for her.

Ree knew, like she knew, that Tatum used the girls as a crutch. She loved them, but she used the obligation she had to them and to other things, to prevent her from her own happiness, like when she chose not to come with him.

She changed the subject.

"Do you speak to Chauncey?"

Ree shook his head no, not wanting to touch on anything pertaining to his old business. He prayed she didn't bring up her brother. But she didn't.

"Yeah, he's supposed to be coming home soon, that's what Sasha says. I know Aubrey will be happy… oh my god, Ree, you should see her, she's so adorable." He chuckled, imagining a little Sasha mini-diva.

Tatum smiled and took a sip of her water, she knew she was talking a lot out of her nervousness, but Ree put her at ease at how attentive and interested he was in her and what she was saying.

The waitress came and took their orders, and they talked some more about the girls, and about his father and the hotel, and Tatum and her trying to write a book, and by the time the food came, it was like two years ago, the conversation between them flowing with ease.

"So, are you happy here?" Tatum asked him, as she picked at her almost empty plate. She was feeling stuffed.

Ree put his fork down and wiped his mouth with his napkin. That was the first time anyone had asked him that, and that's what he loved about Tatum.

"It's alright...I'm content." He leaned back and stared at her seriously. "I could be better." She wondered if he meant with her being there, but apart of her already knew the answer.

"I feel you...sometimes I feel the same way."

Ree nodded, and as the waitress brought the check, a feeling of perplexity moved throughout him. A feeling of *now what?*

Even as he paid, and as they made their way out of the restaurant, neither was sure of where they stood, or where they went from here.

Ree knew she still had business in the states, things she had to handle. Tatum knew that contrary to what he said, before she had shown up, Ree had a girlfriend. However they both also knew that they didn't want this to be the last time they saw each other.

As they reached the lobby, Ree stopped and took Tatum's hands into his.

"This can't be the last time I see you, Tatum."

Tatum bit her bottom lip.

"I know...I wish I didn't have to leave tomorrow... but I do. I have a court hearing." She looked at him achingly. "I wish we had more time," she added, breathlessly.

Ree shrugged.

"Well, come back after."

Tatum sighed and chuckled. The answer shocked her, but Ree was serious. She wanted to ask him if he would still be with Trinity. She wanted to ask him what she would be coming back to.

"That's a possibility." Tatum smiled and continued to hold his hands, as the clerks at the desk and the regular guests wondered who this girl was that Mr. Knights was interacting so intimately with.

Ree still appreciated, yet scorned her stubbornness.

"At least meet me for breakfast or something before you leave tomorrow, so I can convince you," he requested, with a smile.

Tatum agreed, but didn't want to tell him that she needed no convincing. She had a lot on her plate, mixed emotions and all, but she knew she would be back, if that's what he wanted.

Ree was conflicted as well. He knew his feelings for Trinity nowhere matched the ones he had for Tatum. But Trinity knew what she wanted, and Tatum even after all of this time, seemed to still be holding back.

He figured it was since they had been apart for so long, and maybe seeing him with Trinity had made her draw back more, but he definitely wanted them to work on rebuilding at least their friendship again.

Even if they took it slow, he knew he wanted Tatum back in his life.

They shared a close-knit, lengthy hug and then Tatum made her way back to the elevator with a seductive strut, turning back once and smiling.

Ree watched her the whole time.

And Trinity, who was standing at the front desk since they had come out of the restaurant, watched him, watching her, the whole time.

"So the businesses are doing well?"

"Oh yea," Jayde responded, sipping her Pina Colada.

She and Sasha were lounging out by the pool in their bikinis, while Tatum was having lunch with Ree.

Sasha wanted to ask Jayde about the phone call, but didn't want to let on that she had been spying on her, so she chose her words carefully.

"And it's just the nightclub and the boutique, right?"

Jayde was silent for a moment, staring straight ahead with her dark shades on. She finally answered.

"And the restaurant."

Sasha nodded.

"That's right…the restaurant."

Sasha turned over on her stomach and faced Jayde. She suddenly felt solemn.

"You know, I envy you."

Jayde looked at her like she had lost her mind. The princess Sasha, Head Diva, Miss It, love my life, me, me, me, would never say such a thing. Sasha envying anyone was just absurd. But Sasha explained why.

"You're happy, you know? You've got your businesses, you're doing what you want... and you're free. Sometimes, I feel trapped. I swear if it weren't for Aubrey, I'd probably never go home."

Jayde was not too shocked by the revelation, but more shocked at who was revealing it. Sasha always appeared and wanted to appear, perfect. Even when things weren't.

"So you're not happy?" Jayde asked the obvious.

Sasha thought for a second and was glad Jayde couldn't see the tears forming behind her designer lenses.

"I hate my life," was her simple but passionate confession.

Jayde felt so bad for her, not knowing what to say. So she said what she was thinking.

"So, what are you gonna do about it?"

Sasha turned her head the other way and breathed deeply.

"Nothing."

And a tear rolled down her face.

Chapter 11 - Sex

"Mills... they want you, let's go."
Chauncey stood up and the guard opened the big steel door, as Chauncey made his way out and down the hall.
"Ay yo, good luck Chaunc," a young head from Elizabeth said as he passed.
"That's right young blood, I got a good feeling," an older Muslim cat encouraged. Chauncey sometimes would converse with the man and had gained valuable lessons from their talks.
He heard them and he nodded in response, but all he was thinking was how he needed for his lawyer to come through and get him the early release. As they neared the room for Chauncey to meet with the Head Commissioner, he reflected on his Parole hearing that had occurred two months prior, and he reflected on the reason he had never told Sasha about it.
"There's a female in there," the same officer that was now walking with him, had informed Chauncey.
"A female?" Chauncey had asked confused, wondering who it could be. His lawyer may have acted like a bitch, but he was definitely a dude. He couldn't comprehend who else would have been there, being that in most cases, outsiders were not allowed to sit in on the hearings.
He remembered feeling an intense amount of pressure as the guard had opened the door and led him into the room.
When he walked in, he remembered noticing the Parole Commission first, all seated next to each other, looking stone-faced, he remembered his lawyer seated on the opposite side of them, his Case Manager was in the back of the room, and then that's when he had seen her.

Neli was sitting there staring at him as Chauncey entered the room, and Chauncey recalled the disgust and defeat he had felt.

As he took his seat, he remembered his confident outlook on the situation diminishing. He just knew he wasn't going to make parole. Even the C.O. had shaken his own head, because he knew that when a victim showed up to the hearing, especially a female one, your chances of getting out were slim to none.

He didn't even look at Neli, and as he was sitting there waiting to begin, he couldn't believe that he had made the mistake of fucking with the broad.

"Mr. Mills, how are you today?" One of the members of the Commission staff had asked him.

"I'm well…thank you." Chauncey had tried to stay as polite as possible, but really was thinking of how they didn't give a damn about how he felt.

"Shall we begin?" She had said and Chauncey remembered his apprehension.

"Mr. Mills, you are now in your twenty-sixth month of a three and a half year sentence under the regulations of an aggravated assault charge and conviction, a felonious assault under the guidelines of section b, assault with serious bodily injury. The conviction was increased three levels, due to the severity of the bodily injury however, the victim did not sustain life threatening injuries, making a full recovery, and therefore the sentence and charge was lessened, is this all correct?"

Chauncey had looked at his lawyer and his lawyer, little bitch ass Jew boy, stood up slightly and responded a simple,

"Correct."

Chauncey couldn't stand him, but he did what he did well, being that originally they were trying to hit Chauncey with an attempted murder charge, and he had gotten it down to aggravated assault.

But that day at the parole hearing, little Jew boy had another trick up his sleeve.

After they had asked all of the basic questions of 'did he feel he was rehabilitated', 'what were his plans if released', 'did the anger

100

management counseling work', questions that Chauncey had aced with flying colors, his lawyer then added.

"Commission, I would like to call Ms. Penelope Daniels to speak. Ms. Daniels was the other party involved in Mr. Mills' case, and she would like to give her input on Mr. Mills' possible eligibility for parole." Chauncey's lawyer had avoided referring to Neli as the victim.

Chauncey remembered feeling his blood boil as he had stared at his lawyer like he had lost his fucking mind. And once she had started talking, Chauncey just knew it was over.

"Ms. Daniels, you are currently housed at the Greystone Psychiatric Hospital, when is your release date?"

"December 27th," she had said innocently, as Chauncey avoided eye contact with her.

She started her speech, and Chauncey was surprised by what had come out of her mouth.

"I just want to say… that although what Chaunc-, I mean Mr. Mills, did was wrong, I do feel…" She had paused and looked at Chauncey before continuing. "I do feel that he should be released."

Chauncey remembered being shocked as hell, and she kept it going.

"That night…at the hotel," she had reminisced. "My mind was not right…a lot of ugly things were done, on both of our parts…but I have changed. And I know that if I can change, then Chauncey most certainly can. He's a kind man…a good man…and he has a child… And I believe that he has learned his lesson."

Chauncey had remained silent but inside was conflicted. He hated Neli, but at that moment, he was thankful for her.

"That's all," she had concluded.

And it had sealed the deal, Chauncey's parole was granted and his lawyer moved right then for an early release.

Now here he was, walking back down the hall, seeing if it all had played out, and if it was really happening. His lawyer had assured him that it was good as gold, but Chauncey didn't want to get his hopes too high. Almost didn't count to him, he wanted the guarantee.

When he reached the room, he saw his lawyer shaking hands with the Head Commissioner as if the meeting was over. He stood up and made his way over to Chauncey with a grin.

"You're good," he said excitedly.

Chauncey looked at him with raised eyebrows.

"I'm good?" Chauncey asked, a little surprised. His lawyer nodded and Chauncey felt a weight instantly lifted off of his shoulders.

He was coming home.

"Congratulations Mills," the C.O. said, lightly slapping him on the back.

And as they turned to head back to Chauncey's cell, he was grateful that this would be his final days locked down. He was ready for his daughter, his life, Sasha, his money, his status, everything. He was ready for Atlanta.

But was Atlanta ready for him?

You sure you don't want to come, it's our last night," Sasha reminded Tatum, trying to convince her to come out with them. Sasha and Jayde were dressed to kill and ready to do it up their last night on the island. But ever since Tatum had come back from her lunch with Ree, she'd been zoned out and out of it.

"No," Tatum declined. "Ya'll go, have fun...I'm tired."

Sasha pouted, but then shrugged and blew her a kiss as the girls made their way out, with Tatum closing the door behind them.

About an hour after they left, Tatum was wishing that she had went with them. She couldn't get the situation with Ree out of her mind, and she found herself wondering if he was with Trinity at that moment. *I gotta get outta here.*

She grabbed a towel and her swimsuit and headed out for a late night swim hoping that it would clear her head.

The water was perfect, surprisingly not too cold for an outdoor pool. Tatum kicked her legs up and backstroked, dipping her head back into the water and attempting to completely relax.

The pool was completely empty, there were no guests and no lifeguards, and the only lighting came from the track lights inside of and around the pool. Tatum was relieved.

She closed her eyes and allowed her body to float as she tried to let all of her problems drift out into the water.

She was in a state of almost complete relaxation when she heard someone clearing their throat. She popped her eyes open and lifted up quickly.

"Swimming with no lifeguard on duty… you better not let the owner catch you."

Ree made his way to the edge of the pool and knelt down, resting his arms on his knees.

Tatum smiled lightly, slightly bashful, as she swam over to him.

"Yeah well, I'm not too worried about that…I know him."

Ree chuckled, while he gazed at her in her small white bikini, looking so tempting.

"Is that right?"

Tatum gradually swam up in front of him, and rested her elbows on the rim of the pool.

"That's right."

Ree was looking so scrumptious in his grey sweats and white tee that showed off all of those tattoos that she loved. She could tell that he had probably been relaxing at home or something. *So what was he doing here?*

"What are you doing here?" She asked.

He looked at her in the eyes and took his time as he replied.

"Well, I was home… and I uh, realized that I left something…so I came back to get it."

Tatum looked at him curiously.

"Did you get it?" She asked sincerely.

"I hope so." He looked at her seriously and repeated, "I hope so, Miss Lady."

Before any feelings could register in her, Ree slowly leaned over and kissed her softly on the lips. She found herself leaning forward for more, but Ree's strong arms gently pulled her up out of the water and to her feet.

She crossed her arms, feeling a chill and he picked up the towel and wrapped it around her.

"Thank you," she whispered.

He stared at her and then he leaned down and kissed her again, this time more passionately as he slowly wrapped his strong arms around her.

"Mmm," Tatum moaned in pleasure while kissing him back, having gone too long without his kiss. She kissed him back deeply, and their tongues were reacquainted with each other as the heat between their two bodies built.

Ree gracefully moved his hands all over her, palming her soft body and Tatum was in bliss. The way he handled Tatum so delicately, you would never guess how dangerous and malicious of a man he potentially could be.

He took a detour from her lips, and licked slowly over her neck as Tatum began to cream and her nipples poked out, begging for his lips.

Tatum could feel how hard he was as his huge dick saluted her, and she couldn't wait to feel him again. But first she had to kiss him once more. She wrapped her arms around his neck, allowing her towel to drop to the ground, and she found his lips again with hers and shoved her sweet tongue down his throat. The passion between them was crazy.

"Damn Tatum, I need you...I fucking need you."

He kissed her face repeatedly and she closed her eyes, still holding onto him for dear life, never wanting to let go.

"My room...let's go up to my room," she managed to say, breathing heavily.

He reluctantly pulled away from her and shook his head lightly, trying to break his trance. Then he bent down and picked up her towel again. This time she wrapped it around her body as she smiled at him. He looked at her with lust filled eyes.

"C'mon," he ordered sexily. And they made their way to the elevators.

First floor. Sweet tongue kisses… his hands on her back… her hands in his hair.

Second floor. His lips on her neck… her hands under his shirt…. caressing his muscular back.

Third floor. His hands on her ass… under her towel… his lips to her ear, her lips to his. *I missed you. Damn, I missed you.*

Fourth floor. Her legs wrapped around his back… His hands under her bikini top, caressing her breasts…. Intense, passionate kisses… Heat… Pure, unadulterated, fiery, sexual, heat.

Fifth floor. Her hands in his pants, stroking his largeness… His wet mouth wrapped around her soft mound of breast flesh… Tongue flicking, circling, dancing…*yes*….

By the time they made it to Tatum's room and in the door, they were at a point of yearning that they had never reached in their lives. Tongue kissing all the way to the bed, Ree undressed her slowly, removing her towel and her bathing suit with poise.
Tatum was completely nude before she even realized it, as Ree laid her gently onto the bed. He lifted her right leg, and started at her calf, licking slowly up her leg, to her thigh as he stared her in the eyes. Tatum's pussy pulsated as she squirmed from the pleasure. He repeated with the other, and then he reached her sweet center and used his thumbs to slowly part her second lips, breathing lightly on her before using the tip of his tongue to massage her clit. Before she knew it, Tatum was receiving that out of this world head that had mesmerized her the first time they had made love.

"Ooh, that feels so good."

Ree cupped her ass cheeks and danced his tongue around... steady, forceful, wet, slippery, strokes of his tongue, sending her to ecstasy.

Her body tensed and she knew it was coming as she grinded against his mouth and he grinded his mouth right back against her. Her body vibrated and shook out of control and tears escaped her eyes as she came hard into his mouth.

He continued to work her over until she couldn't stand anymore, and he kissed up her body as she pulled him up to return the favor.

Tatum wasted no time taking him into her mouth, inch by inch. He was so large, but she wanted to taste him so bad, that she relaxed her throat and tried to take as much of him in her moist, warm mouth, as she could.

Ree placed his hand lightly on the back of her head and grunted as she bobbed slowly on his dick.

"Mmm, I missed this dick so much, baby," Tatum moaned sexily, knowing that the absence of sex, and him, in her life had her extra freaky.

Ree closed his eyes and was enthralled in pure pleasure.

"Oh, shit," he whispered.

She slurped and sucked him slowly until he was about to explode, and then he lifted her up and carried her to the dresser, pushing everything off of it. He pulled out the condom he had in his sweatpants, and slid it on carefully, while looking at her beautiful face. He couldn't wait to be inside of her.

Tatum stared Ree in the eyes, feeling the intense emotion between them. So real, that she wanted to cry. She anticipated his dick, and as he kissed her face, and tenderly worked himself into her tightness, she held firm onto him and spread her legs wider, wanting all of the painful pleasure that she could take.

"Oh god yes..." She moaned, as she felt another nut building up.

She felt so damn good to him, that he almost wanted to cum right then, but he had to make it last.

"Damn, Tatum," he moaned in pleasure.

He stroked her slowly at first and it was pure lovemaking. And even when he sped up and hit her with deep, vicious strokes, it was still lovemaking. But it had the ferocity of fucking.

They indulged in each other for hours. Both raking up numerous orgasms, in numerous positions, and every time they thought they were spent, one would turn the other on in a way that they had to go again.

Tatum fell asleep in Ree's arms that night, both of them exhausted, and both of them, for the first time in a long time, completely, utterly, satisfied.

"That shit was fun...them mothafuckas really know how to get it in," Jayde exclaimed, opening the door to the suite and flipping on the lights.

"I know, but did you see that nigga with the blond dreads? He was dancing crazy as hell!" Sasha laughed hard, but she noticed Jayde had stopped laughing. She turned her attention to the kitchen where Jayde was focused, and her mouth dropped at the sight of a naked Ree and Tatum.

Sasha turned her head quick, but Jayde was frozen, taking in all of Ree, literally, before Tatum jumped in front of him. In those short seconds though, she had witnessed the Mandingo on that brother. *Damn, Tatum a lucky bitch!* She thought.

"What are ya'll doing here!" Sasha screamed, flustered and still with her head turned and eyes closed.

Tatum stood there mortified, with her hands trying to cover all of her goodies, and blocking Ree, who just chuckled in disbelief at the situation. He held his hand up to his forehead in slight embarrassment as Tatum shot back.

"What are *ya'll* doing here? I thought you guys were going out!"

"It's four o'clock in the morning," Sasha shrieked as she looked down and grabbed a couch pillow, throwing it their direction.

Tatum could only say 'oh', as the discomfort began to set in.

Jayde grinned in her drunkenness, thinking this was some treat for the night.

"Just guide me to the room," Sasha barked.

When no one said or did anything, Sasha screamed at Jayde. "Let's go, Jayde!"

Jayde grabbed Sasha's hand and led her to the bedroom giggling, as Tatum turned to Ree with her mouth wide open.

"I am sooo sorry…" She began to laugh. "Oh my god, I didn't think it was so late."

Ree shook his head at her and smirked.

"Aw man, this is all your fault… you know that right? You the one that wanted to come out here, talking 'bout, 'ooh Ree, let's do it on the balcony, let's go in the kitchen… get the ice, Ree'."

Tatum laughed hard as he made fun of her.

"Now look at you, got me standing out here, dick all out… now how you expect me to look them in the face?"

Tatum died laughing at him and the situation, doubling over and holding her stomach as Sasha screamed out of the bedroom.

"Go to bed, nasties!"

Ree pointed at Tatum seriously.

"See, you in trouble, now. That's to you right there, let her know how nasty you are."

Tatum looked at him sensuously and wrapped her arms around his neck.

"You like how nasty I am, though," she accused.

"Yeah, maybe."

They kissed long and slow and then made their way to the bedroom to get dressed.

"So, I'm gonna see you tomorrow, right? Before you leave?"

Tatum nodded solemnly, thinking of leaving Ree, and thinking of leaving him here with Trinity.

She was so conflicted, and she felt like she was getting herself wrapped up in a twisted love triangle. But at the same time she knew that what she felt with Ree was real, and regardless of who he was occupying his time with, she knew what he felt for her was the same. In all honesty though, she was terrified of getting her heart broken. *What if he really cares about this girl?*

She walked him to the door, holding in all of the things she wanted to say, as she kissed him goodnight.

Tatum went to bed that night with much on her mind.

Ree walked into his home surprised to find candles illuminating the entire living and dining room area.

"Hey baby," Trinity greeted him, dressed sexily in a red negligee. She held a bottle of champagne and two glasses in her hands.

Ree stopped at the door and ran his right hand over his face in despair. Her timing was so off.

"Hey," he greeted her nonchalantly.

He noticed the table was adorned with strawberries and rose petals and immediately felt bad, but knew it was impossible to give her what she wanted that night. He had given it all to Tatum.

Trinity noticed the void look in his face and frowned slightly.

"What's wrong, Sean …you don't like it?" She had dozed off waiting for him earlier and had rushed to relight the candles and get prepared again when she heard his car pull up. Now he seemed unfazed by her gesture.

Ree felt horrible. A part of him really did care for Trinity.

And had Tatum not sneaked back into his heart, Trinity would have eventually won it by default.

All of these emotional conflicts were new to a man who honestly had never given a fuck before.

"No, I like it…I love it," he lied, making his way over to her. "I just…I just had a long night. I'm sorry, Trini." He looked her in her pretty and disappointed eyes and kissed her softly on the forehead, before walking past her and to the bedroom.

Trinity immediately smelled the Escada perfume on him. The same perfume he had purchased for her but she never wore, because she hated it.

She closed her eyes tight and fought back the tears.

Don't you cry. Trinity, don't you cry.

But she was already crying.

"Aw shit, they done fucked up now!"

Chauncey coolly bopped out of the large metal gates with a confident smirk. He walked up and greeted his right hand man, E, with a hood handshake turned into a manly hug.

"You sure they let you out?" E joked, looking at Chauncey skeptically. "I left the car running just in case."

"Fuck you, nigga," Chauncey shot back, taking in a deep breath of new freedom.

They made their way to E's black on black Benz.

"Nah, I'm saying tho', you like two weeks early out this bitch," E noted, climbing all 300 pounds of himself in the driver's seat.

Chauncey slid in the passenger, missing the quality feel of leather against his skin, missing the quality feel of luxury. He shrugged.

"What can I say my nigga, the power of the M.O.N.E.Y," he replied, remixing Jay Z's lyrics. E nodded, knowing just what he meant. "Now get me the fuck outta here."

They took off headed for the NJ Turnpike, with their immediate future plans in the talks.

"What's these for?" Chauncey asked, as E tossed him a set of keys.

"That's the crib, it's done... I told you I'd have it ready."

Chauncey smiled, thinking of his new Atlanta home, and wondering if Sasha and Aubrey would approve. Now that he was home, he had every intention on spoiling his princess, both of them.

"It's a house right?" Chauncey asked jokingly. "Not a condo, a townhouse, a fucking loft-"

E cut him off.

"Nigga, do I look like an idiot? You said a fucking house, I know what a house is."

Chauncey had to make sure he had a home, with enough room for his family.

"Alright, good looking."

Chauncey suddenly became serious and looked over at E.

110

"What about that other thing, you got that all set up?"
E nodded, turning down the 50 cent mixtape he had playing.
"The ATL is all ready. I showed 'em what we was working with...they appreciate the quality and the price. So business is as good as done. Got about three major, major clients set up."
Chauncey nodded, thinking of how lucky he was to have Ree's connect, or connections he should say. Of course, it wouldn't be the same without his old boss, but he was planning on doing him justice, filling his shoes and making some major paper. He couldn't help but to notice the slight apprehension in E's voice with his next question.
"But Chaunc, don't you think we might be ruffling a few feathers? ...I know you wanna be down there for your seed and all, but we 'bout to have a lot of muhfuckas mad with all the shit we bringing down there...I mean I'm wit' you and all, I told you, but-"
Chauncey cut him off aggressively.
"Fuck them down south niggas. If they smart, they'll get down...and if they not, sorry for 'em. You can't make no real money without pissing muhfuckas off, E. I know you know that."
Chauncey pulled out a cigarette and lit it, inhaling the cool smoke deeply and reclining his seat. His fitted hat was pulled low over his deep waves and his face was scruffy, in need of a shape up.
"And I don't wanna be down there," he added. He looked out of the window and thought of Mike playing house with his two girls and it made his jaw clench up. "I *need* to be down there."
E nodded understandingly, and continued to drive. He said he was wit' him, and that's exactly what he meant.
A new town, a new state, a new day, a new year, and a new boss. *Let's get it!*

"Now that's what I'm talking about," Sasha said, placing her credit card back in her Gucci wallet. "Comped out, that's the way to end a vacation!"

When the girls had went to the desk to checkout, they found out that their room was comped out for the long weekend that they had been there, no charge, completely free.

"I can't believe he did that," Tatum said, starting to feel regret for not meeting Ree for breakfast that morning. But after he had left her suite the night before, she thought of him going back to Trinity, and she felt low, used, and miserable. She figured she would handle what she had to back at home with no distractions, and if he was still here, and single, then maybe it would be.

She put on her shades as they made their way out of the front doors and her heart sank.

I can't do this, I have to say goodbye.

"Wait guys, hold up." Sasha and Jayde stopped, and Tatum turned to go back inside and found Ree standing right there, in the lobby, looking at her somberly.

She made her way up to him nervously.

"Hey," she greeted him, taking off her sunglasses and trying not to look him in the eyes, as he stared at her intensely.

"So, come with no hellos… leave with no goodbyes."

He said this as if he was disappointed with her, and he was. Tatum sighed and looked up at him.

"I just…I just have so much on my mind," Tatum tried to explain. Ree looked away from her. It was always something on her mind and he was starting to wonder if it was even worth it. This was why he, up until her, had never been serious about any female. They required too much of his time and energy.

"Yea well, it's cool…you could've kept your word though."

Tatum looked down, ashamed. She should have kept her word and met him.

He felt the animosity he was giving off to her and he didn't want that. He lightened up because in a way, Tatum was like him, and they both didn't handle emotions very well. Him, because of the life he'd lived. Her, because of the things she'd been through.

Ree felt that maybe his experience had made him more upfront with expressing how he felt, and more mature.

"When's the first hearing?" He asked, changing the subject.

"In a week," she answered, finally looking at him as she shifted her weight from one leg to the next. She was dressed in jeans and sneakers, and her hair was pulled back, but she was still flawless. Ree nodded, ready to put it out there. Either this was going somewhere, or it was going nowhere.

"So when it's all over, are you coming back?"

Tatum's heart raced and she looked around the lobby anxiously. She was not prepared to answer this right now and she couldn't believe he was putting her on the spot.

"To visit?" She asked, playing clueless.

His intense stare was his response, and she figured she would put it out there as well.

"I don't know, Ree."

He looked down and nodded slowly, and then chuckled.

"We back here again?" He asked her seriously.

Tatum knew just what he meant, back in her hallway, two years ago, at a crossroads. She was instantly defensive as to how he was trying to put it all on her. He wanted to keep it real, so she would too.

"Are you going to leave Trinity?"

The questioned stunned Ree briefly before he replied.

"Are you coming back?"

Tatum's heart sunk, not happy with the response.

"That shouldn't matter. You should want to leave for you Ree, not for me. You must care about her…and a part of you must want to be wit' her."

He didn't respond and Tatum was furious, but she didn't show it. Just then, Sasha came inside.

"Sorry guys, but the car is here."

Tatum coolly put her shades back on and picked up her bag.

"I have the number here…I'll call you."

She walked away as Ree stood there and let her.

He had waited almost two years for her last time they had parted ways, and he didn't want to feel like a sucker again. It just was not becoming to him, and it made him feel weak. But he knew that if Tatum was to come back, he would be with her, no question. But did she know that?

He watched the car begin to slowly pull off from the curb.

"Wait, what the fuck am I doing?"

He made his way out of the door, lightly jogging to catch up to the car. He banged on the trunk.

"Stop!"

The car kept going and Ree ran to the front and banged on the hood with force, causing the driver to slam on his brakes.

"I said stop, muthafucka!"

He walked swiftly around to the backseat on the driver's side and tried to open the door but it was locked.

Tatum, Jayde, and Sasha watched in shock and Tatum tried to unlock the door but didn't know how. Ree banged on the driver's window.

"Unlock the door, dummy," he barked.

He heard the click a second later from the scared driver, who had instantly obeyed. He yanked the door open and knelt down to Tatum, who sat looking at him so emotional, her chest heaving in anticipation.

"I do...I do care about her." Tatum furrowed her eyebrows in confusion and anger, wondering why he had stopped the car to tell her this. He continued. "I can't lie, I care about Trinity...but not the way I care about you."

He took her hands into his and looked her in the eyes as Sasha and Jayde looked on.

"I love you, Tatum."

She gasped lightly and took a deep breath.

He kissed her lips softly and when she went to talk, he silenced her with a finger to her mouth.

"Just... just come back."

And with that, he slowly closed the door, and then he tapped twice on the trunk, letting the driver know he could pull off.

114

As the car made its way from the hotel, Tatum looked out of the back window with tears in her eyes. She watched Ree stand there and then she saw him walk back into the hotel as the car turned the corner.

"I love you, too," she whispered. "Goodbye."

Chapter 12 - Change

After dropping Tatum off, and taking the jet back to Atlanta, Sasha and Jayde were now in the back of a car service Lincoln Continental. The car was riding through the dark and quiet streets of Buckhead taking the ladies to their last destination, home.

Sasha had asked Tatum if she wanted her to come with her to the hearing, but Tatum insisted that she would be fine and for Sasha to stay home and be with her baby. After a long hug, the girls went their separate ways.

"Oh, god...I can't wait to get to my bed!" Jayde exclaimed, wondering if she would call up a little freak or hit her thousand dollar sheets alone.

I can, Sasha thought. But opted for a more appropriate,

"I know, right." She knew Mike would be there, and she felt bad for even thinking it, but she was in no rush to see him.

She thought of him in comparison to Chauncey, and although Chauncey outweighed him in almost every aspect, Mike had one huge plus.

He would never hurt me the way that Chauncey did.

Every time Sasha thought of Chauncey sleeping with her ex-friend Neli, for damn near half of their relationship, the pain went through her like it had happened yesterday. It had almost destroyed her, and unless you would've gone through it, there was no way to explain it.

"What's on your mind, mama?" Jayde asked, looking up from her blackberry. She saw Sasha just staring out of her window into the pitch black night, as light raindrops beat against the car.

"Oh, nothing...everything." Sasha paused and then turned to Jayde. "Chauncey is getting paroled soon. He may come down to Atlanta."

"Oh, I seeeee." Jayde nodded as if it all made sense. "Well, that's a good thing, right?"

Sasha shrugged and continued to look out of the window.

An instant thought ran through Jayde's mind, and she turned to Sasha abruptly.

"What is he gonna do?"

Sasha was confused.

"Huh?"

"For money...for a living. You said he used to hustle, right... well, what is he gonna do when he gets down here?"

Sasha shrugged again.

"I don't know," she answered honestly.

There was a brief silence.

"But what do you think he's going to do?" Jayde persisted.

"I don't know!" Sasha repeated, growing upset. She had not thought about it because that was another flaw of Chauncey's. He loved the streets, with a passion. "Why does it matter, anyway?" Sasha asked, a little calmer.

"Doesn't it matter to you?" Jayde sassed.

"Of course, because it matters to my daughter. But does it matter to you?" Sasha asked curiously.

"Hello no, why would it matter to me?"

They pulled in front of Sasha's house and before she got out, Sasha eyed Jayde skeptically. She sighed and then leaned over and gave her a hug, not understanding, and not really caring about the basis of Jayde's questioning.

"Alright girl, talk to you later."

They hugged tight.

"See ya," Jayde said.

Sasha climbed out of the car, and retrieved her luggage out of the trunk. She waved at Jayde as the car pulled off.

And as she made her way up the walkway to her house, she never paid any attention to the car parked on her street, or the person inside of it, watching her every move.

"10… 9… 8… 7… 6… 5… 4… 3… 2…1…Happy New Year!" The Bernstein house erupted in cheer.

Sasha, Mike, and even little Aubrey were all up watching the ball drop, blowing noisemakers, and Mike and Sasha were drinking champagne. Of course Aubrey had her matching champagne glass, filled with sparkling cider.

Sasha blew her noisemaker once more and the phone and doorbell simultaneously rang. Sasha and Mike both went for the phone.

"You…okay I'll get…okay, you get the phone, I'll get the door," Sasha said, laughing as she made her way down the hall. She wondered who it could be this late; maybe a neighbor wishing them a Happy New Year. Tipsy off of the champagne, she yanked the door open without looking to see who it was.

"Happy New Year!" She screamed, but was immediately frozen, mouth open and all.

"Happy New Year, kid."

Chauncey stood at the door, with gifts in his hand and looking oh so edible. He was dressed in all black – black jeans, black thermal, black leather jacket, his smooth black skin and black waves and goatee, Sasha took it all in.

"What are you…?" Sasha couldn't even talk. He kissed her on the cheek softly.

"Where's Bri, she sleep?" He asked, as he made his way into the house, past her. No invitation needed.

Sasha glanced at his Burgundy 2010 Bentley Mulsanne parked out front before closing the door.

His flashy ass! She thought, but they were two of a kind. And she was envious.

118

"Babe, Tatum said to call her back," Mike screamed, walking toward the hallway to meet Sasha, but was greeted by a tall and cocky Chauncey.

"Babe? Aw, I knew you liked me," Chauncey joked, making his way into the living room. Mike was taken aback.

Chauncey examined the house and nodded in slight approval, as Mike fumed.

"This is cute Sash, real *cute.*"

Sasha knew Chauncey was being an asshole. Anytime he said cute, he meant small.

Like when she used to punch him with all of her might and not do shit. That was cute. It was like they had their own secret language.

"Yeah, thanks. I'll take that. Cute fits me just fine," she shot back. She was standing there with her sexy smirk on, in her spandex tights and small v-neck tee shirt. Her hair was wild in a messy bun and she thought she looked horrendous. But Chauncey thought she looked sexy as hell.

"Where's my daughter, princess?"

"She's sleeping. I just put her to bed," Mike answered for her.

Sasha looked at Mike hesitantly; Aubrey had just been awake with them. She had taken a late nap and was not even sleepy a second ago. Chauncey turned to him.

"So, *you're* princess now, huh? I'm babe… you're princess…we really got some kinda connection going on here, huh Mike?"

Mike rolled his eyes at Chauncey's mockery while Sasha intervened.

"Let me go see if she's still up."

Sasha left the living room and made her way up the stairs, while Chauncey watched her ass, and while Mike watched Chauncey, watch her ass. Once she was upstairs, Chauncey turned to Mike, who was standing there, nostrils flaring with his arms crossed.

"What up, Mike…you remember me, right?" Chauncey used to see Mike around the hospital when Sasha used to work there, and Chauncey used to pick her up. "Damn, last time I seen you, you were pushing gurneys…you still a nurse?"

Chauncey was being condescending but Mike was prepared to get back with him.

"Nah, actually, I'm a doctor. I have a career, with benefits. Sasha doesn't have to work, or lift a finger," Mike bragged while Chauncey chuckled at his pompous attitude.

"Oh, that aint nothing new, playboy. She been living like that…See, that car you driving now, I wrote the manual on that… Put them first miles on it and everything," Chauncey boasted, referring to Sasha as if she were a car. Mike snickered.

"Yeah, you may have, but that's *my* whip now… I take care of the engine… the tune-ups… and the bodywork. And you know it need bodywork like a mothafucka," Mike quipped.

Chauncey's jaw flinched at Mike innuendos to him and Sasha's sex life.

"Yeah, a little more bodywork than you can handle," Chauncey shot back, knowing that Mike was not laying it down how he should be. "But you just remember, if you get one little scratch, I mean a dent, a nick, anything on that bitch… then we got problems, nigga."

Mike didn't take kindly to Chauncey's threats and he knew he should just leave it alone, but he wasn't going to let Chauncey get the best of him.

"Oh you aint got to worry about that, Chauncey. See, I keep that shit in the garage, aint nobody driving that but me."

"That's cool," Chauncey nodded. "But you got to know that shit's on lease anyway. Best believe it's coming back to its rightful owner."

Chauncey had a cold and promising glare in his eye and Mike was getting pissed now.

"How you figure, when I got the papers on it?" Mike pointed at his wedding band and threw their marriage in Chauncey's face, sure that he had won. Chauncey chuckled at Mike's cocky smirk as Sasha and Aubrey came downstairs.

"Daddy!" Aubrey screamed excitedly, interrupting the ego battle, and running up to Chauncey.

120

"Yeah Mike, you might got them papers, for now… But I got the insurance," Chauncey said, referring to Aubrey, as he picked her up and shot Mike a wink. "What's up, princess? Happy New Year, pretty girl."

Mike was livid as he watched them.

"What ya'll talking about?" Sasha asked, completely oblivious to what was going on.

"Cars," Chauncey casually answered, because Mike was too angry to initially respond. He finally snapped out of it.

"Yeah babe, Chauncey was just admiring my new Benz in the driveway."

Chauncey shot Mike a challenging look.

"Yeah I was," he added, still holding Aubrey. "I was just telling Mikey here that it's pretty as hell… but it's a lot of maintenance. He may wanna downgrade…or go crazy trying to keep up with it."

Chauncey smirked reading Mike's anger.

"That's what I was saying," Sasha agreed, glad that they were getting along. "You might wanna listen to Chauncey babe, he used to have one just like it."

Mike glared at Sasha hard before storming off, as Chauncey laughed quietly to himself. Sasha had no idea that she had added fuel to the fire.

"Oh my god, what did I say?" Sasha asked, confused.

Chauncey shrugged and she shook her head.

"I think he's sensitive about his car," she added.

"Yeah, maybe…Mr. Sensitivity, Ralph Tresvant ass nigga," Chauncey joked, as Sasha playfully punched him.

"Stop it."

She turned to him and watched as Aubrey nestled up close to his neck. This was supposed to be her family, but he ruined it.

"So, this is it? You're home now?"

He looked at her dotingly.

"I am, I'm home kid." He was so happy to say it too.

"And you're gonna be here…in Atlanta?" Sasha asked, but she was scared to hear the answer. How would she deal with him being so close?

"Yeah…as long as you two are in Atlanta, then I'm in Atlanta." Sasha thought of the conversation she had with Jayde earlier as she posed her next question.

"And what are you gonna do…you know, for money? I see the Bentley outside, you must not be planning on living on a budget?" Sasha was trying her best to find out if he was still going to be hustling, without sounding like she cared.

Chauncey walked over and sat down on the couch, holding Aubrey in his lap. She was getting sleepy. He knew what Sasha was trying to ask and he thought of the best way to answer.

"Well, I got a couple of things lined up." He summed it up like that. Sasha gritted her teeth, clearly upset. She wondered if he would ever give it up.

"Yeah well, just remember…you got a little girl to look out for," she drawled in her southern accent.

He nodded, loving her voice and the way her accent came out the more upset she became.

"I got two girls to look out for," he added, matter of factly. Sasha rolled her eyes, although she was flattered.

"You don't have to worry about me…if that's what you mean. I don't need looking out for."

Chauncey looked at her dismissively.

"Yeah aight, and who gonna look out for you…Mr. Softee? You think I'm gonna bank on that? C'mon ma."

Sasha could hear Mike's footsteps stomping around upstairs and she knew he was mad. She folded her arms across her chest and knew it was time for Chaunc to leave, although she knew Aubrey, nor her, really wanted to see him go.

"Okay Chaunc, I think we should 'to be continue' this reunion. It's late, and Bri-Bri had a long day." Sasha yawned herself, knowing that she had a long one too.

Chauncey looked up at her and wished he was going upstairs with her to put Aubrey to bed, and then putting Sasha to bed, in a totally different way.

"Alright, hand me those bags right there." He pointed to the large black bags that he had come with, containing individually wrapped presents.

"Yay," Aubrey screamed, waking right up as Sasha handed him the bags.

Sasha sat on the arm of the couch as Chauncey and Aubrey tore into all of her gifts from him. He had gotten Aubrey too many clothes to name, a pair of Gucci sneakers, a new baby Parka, a pair of diamond stud earrings, computerized learning games, DVDs, books, and her favorite, a huge black Princess doll. Aubrey stood up to hug the doll, which stood taller than her, and Sasha smiled.

She looked down and saw Chauncey holding a small box in his hand.

"I know you aint think I forgot you."

Sasha looked him in the eyes and cautiously took the box, which obviously contained jewelry. She tore into the paper and flipped open the box.

"Oh my god," she whispered.

She covered her mouth with her left hand as she studied the beauty of the Lorraine Schwartz diamond necklace. She had wanted it so bad, and there was a waiting list for it at Bergdorf's in New York. She couldn't even fathom how Chauncey had done it.

Sasha looked up and saw Mike standing there, grilling her. She hadn't even noticed him come back downstairs, she was so enthralled in the splendor of her present. But one look at him, and she knew she couldn't accept the $45,000 gift. At least not without a year's worth of fighting.

But oh, how hard this would be. Sasha was a material girl at heart. And diamonds were her weakness, every princess needed her diamonds. But still…

"I can't...I can't take it Chauncey." He looked in her eyes and could see how bad she wanted it and his face dropped in disappointment. Mike felt a slight twinge of satisfaction.

"Let me walk you to the door," she added, getting up.

Chauncey hugged and kissed Aubrey goodbye, and she made him hug the doll too.

"I gotta hug the doll too?" He asked her as she laughed.

"Yes Daddy," she said. "And kiss."

Chauncey gave the doll a big, long hug, and a kiss, and then he hugged and kissed Aubrey again. Sasha walked out to the hallway and Mike went back upstairs when he was sure that Chauncey was on his way out.

"Happy New Year Chauncey...welcome home," Sasha told him once they were on the front porch.

Chauncey leaned over and kissed her on the forehead softly. She shook her head, trying to break his spell.

"Chauncey, you can't be doing this...and you can't come all late like this. What if Aubrey was sleep, a normal day she would have been."

He looked at her with a smile.

"Then I would've watched her sleep...like I used to watch you."

They locked eyes for a second and Sasha's heart raced, and then Chauncey made his way down the walkway.

"Goodnight, kid."

That night as Sasha put Aubrey to bed, she couldn't get the evening with Chauncey out of her mind. She tried to think of other things as she looked at her sleeping angel.

She looked over at the huge doll that Aubrey had insisted on laying in the bed with her. *This thing is bigger than her.*

As Sasha kissed her baby goodnight, and made her way out of the room, she caught an intense glare from the doll's neck. Her heart skipped a beat as she looked closer and noticed the princess doll was wearing the Lorraine Schwartz necklace that Chauncey had bought for her.

Oh my god.

She couldn't deny how excited she was as she removed the necklace and clutched it close in her hand. It was so beautiful.

"Thank you Chauncey," she said out loud.

And then she made her way to bed, with her husband.

"Are you nervous?"

Tatum looked over at her lawyer with an uneasy smile but didn't respond.

"Don't be, this will all be over before you know it."

Johnny Carson was a New York born, well-known, high profile, shark of an attorney. He was in his mid-thirties, quite handsome, and extremely confident in his work and reputation.

He was also very good friends with Sasha's father, William Seals, and owed him more than enough favors.

As the procedures began, Tatum looked over at Nikki, who couldn't even make eye contact with her. She sat there in her cheap polyester suit, with her cheap attorney, and folded her hands across the table appearing more like a member of a choir, than an ex-coke whore. This was only the first hearing, and it was in a small court room. No jury, no witnesses, no big case, just a couple of lawyers, a judge, and two women who both wanted the best for two little girls.

As Tatum watched her lawyer present the case, making Nikki appear worse than the devil herself, she briefly considered giving up the whole thing. She loved her nieces greatly and she would always be there for them, and a part of her knew that Nikki would probably be a good mother to them, but the stubbornness in her knew nothing but how to fight.

Never mind her life and how she was barely living it.

"Nichole Samuel abandoned her children for *six years* your honor! Six long, cold, hard, years that these children spent wondering where their mother was…and six years that she spent, *high.*"

Tatum thought briefly of all of those years, and then she thought of

125

her brother. She missed him and she wondered if he would approve of this whole battle that she was going through.

The whole hearing took no longer than thirty minutes as the judge was presented with several key pieces of information, the main ones being that Nikki had abandoned her children during her stint on drugs, Tatum's brother, the girls' father, had provided for them up until his death, although the courts had attempted to track Nikki down, they did not exert all possible measures that were required to legally finalize an adoption, and last but certainly not least, Nikki had never signed any papers.

Still Tatum's lawyer was convinced that all was in their favor. The hearing was over and the next and final one was set for the following week, in which they would hear testimony from both Nikki and Tatum and the judge would make a decision.

As they made their way out of the courtroom, Johnny looked at Tatum with different eyes than he had during the hearing.

"Would you…maybe like to go and grab lunch?"

Johnny was attractive, smooth brown skin and pretty white teeth, neatly trimmed hair and goatee, expensive Brionni suit and, well, he was a lawyer.

But Tatum's interest lay elsewhere.

"No, I really should get going…but thanks for the offer."

She watched as he shrugged with a smile and then made his way down the court steps and into his waiting car. As it pulled off, she wondered if she should had gone with him, maybe had given herself an opportunity to test the waters. Her cell phone began to vibrate in her purse and she took it out, not recognizing the 876 area code.

She figured maybe it may have been a bill collector, but then she thought maybe…

"Hello," she answered, warily.

"How did it go?" A deep and smooth voice asked on the other end of the phone, causing Tatum to melt right there on the steps, never mind the cold 35 degree weather.

"It went okay." It was so cold, that just holding the phone was a challenge to Tatum, but the person on the other end was well worth it.

Tatum began to make her way to her car, so glad that Ree had called her. It had been a week since she'd last seen him and she wondered how she had gotten through those two years. She was in agony.

"You know you're timing is impeccable," she added. "I just walked out of the courthouse."

Ree laughed effortlessly and Tatum could hear the smoke exhale out of his lungs as he spoke.

"Yea well, I try to be as precise as possible...especially with you." Tatum grinned.

"Or maybe it's just luck." She imagined him, his arms, his tongue, his eyes, his hands, his lips and she couldn't help herself from saying, "I miss you."

Ree was a little surprised by the admission, but it felt good to hear those words from her sweet mouth. The same words spoken by any other would have meant nothing at all to him.

"I miss you, too...that's why I had to call. I had to at least hear your voice, you know?"

Tatum smiled hard and they continued the conversation for about twenty minutes or so. He asked her if she had given any thought to coming back, for good. And she said that she had, but didn't go too much further than that. She told him that she just wanted to see what happened with the whole situation with the girls, but really she just needed to think about it altogether. As he was about to end the call, and they said their goodbyes, Tatum knew there was one more thing that she needed to tell him.

"Ree, I have to tell you something."

There was a silence as he waited for what she would say.

"I'm all ears," he encouraged.

Tatum took a deep breath and closed her eyes before she proceeded.

"Ree...I love you. I'm in love with you. But I'm scared...I'm so scared. I don't want you to hurt me."

Ree's heart felt heavy hearing her speak this way. He knew at that moment that he had to end it with Trinity. He couldn't lose Tatum, again.

"I won't...," he assured her with sincerity. Just then, Trinity entered his office and shot him a flaccid smile. He looked up at her unreceptively.

"I won't," he repeated to Tatum, and then he disconnected the call.

"Trini, come here...we have to talk."

Chapter 13 - Envy

The rain beat down hard against the window of the old burger joint, as Chauncey sat serenely, sipping on his soda and occasional picking at his French fries and burger. He was only halfway entertaining his food, which was pretty tasty, but it wasn't the reason he had come to the west end side of Atlanta, known as the rough Bankhead hood.

He had come to meet with a pretty major player in the game, a player who was interested in purchasing the goods that Chauncey could supply for him, a Georgia native hustler by the name of Capo. Capo had started out as a low level corner hustler but was working his way up slowly but surely. He had gone from his own corner, to his own blocks, to now his whole section of the town. Between him and another rival squad known as the J-crew, they had the city of Atlanta padlocked down. Capo and Chauncey's right hand man E were cool, so E had set up the exchange.

Chauncey could see a light-skinned cat with long braids make his way inside, and judging from the description that E had given, this was the man he had come to see. Chauncey could see the look of deliberation enter the young man's mind, and Chauncey gave a half nod to assure him, as the guy made his way to Chauncey's booth.

"New York?" Capo drawled in his southern talk, double checking before sitting down.

"My man, Capo right?" Chauncey shot back, never mind that the southern niggas referred to them as New York niggas, even though they were Jersey all the way.

Capo breathed a sigh of relief and took his seat across from Chauncey.

"That's right…" Capo looked around at the mostly empty joint before continuing. 'So, what's up? We expecting snow down here, or what?" Capo was speaking in code for the keys of cocaine that he was anticipating from Chauncey.

"Yeah," Chauncey answered. "But with the shit I been hearing, I'm thinking more like a blizzard, you feel me?"

Capo smiled wide, appreciating what he was hearing.

"Something like, 17, 18 inches right?" Capo asked hopefully, as Chauncey furrowed his eyebrows like 'get the fuck outta here'.

"Nigga, I don't know where you getting them stats from, but it's more like 20, and you know it."

Capo scratched behind his ear and Chauncey stared at him, his blood starting to rise and feeling like he was being tested.

"20? Damn…I thought since it was another one on the way, it wouldn't be that much." Capo figured that since he would be purchasing frequently, he could get them for less than 20G's. Chauncey was no herb though; he knew what Capo was accustomed to.

"Nah, 20 it is. Y'all aint getting no less than 20. And it's still better than that 30 y'all got before…but I aint got time for the bullshit, so what's up?"

Capo could see Chauncey becoming frustrated and wanted to put the ease back in the situation. He was used to paying 30 from Father, and the quality was half of Chauncey's.

"Nah, nah 20 it is…20 is good, it's better than good. I was just fucking wit' you New York."

"Don't make a habit of it," Chauncey warned, wiping his mouth with the napkin. He peeled off a twenty and threw it onto the table as the two men prepared to make their way out of the restaurant.

"E let me know the drill, follow me to the body shop around the corner…take it all apart." Capo told him, making his way to his car.

Chauncey hopped into the old Lincoln town car and followed Capo out of the parking lot, as E tailed him.

Chauncey looked around at the town as they drove. This was the real hood, nothing like the Buckhead area that Sasha lived in.

Once the guys reached the auto shop, Capo had a few men there waiting.

They brought the car in, broke the car down, and removed the product from the compartments, tested it, and approved of it, thoroughly. Chauncey and E counted the money and once it was concurred that both parties were satisfied, they proceeded to make their way out.

"Pleasure doing business with you," Capo stated, shaking both Chauncey and E's hand. He knew that he was about to come up in a major way with Chauncey and E.

"Pleasure's all minc," Chauncey replied, feeling good. Feeling real good.

Atlanta was a reckoning, a renaissance, a rebirth. And it may have been one of the most colorful places in the country, but Chauncey was about to paint the town white.

We bout to make it snow in the south, we bout to make it snow.

"Ikaw Na Nga! Ikaw Na Nga! Ikaw Na Nga!"

"What the fuck is going on with Capo?" Father barked, in the middle of his hot-stone, deep-tissue massage. The Filipino woman went to place another stone onto his ridiculously fat back, while singing a song in her native tongue, but he swatted her away in frustration.

"Get! Go! Get the fuck outta here...no more stones!"

She obediently walked away to give him and his partner, some privacy, while still singing.

"Ikaw Na Nga...Ikaw Na Nga..."

Father breathed deep, his obesity causing his breaths to squeal when exhaled.

"I know his business aint slowed, that mothafucka just recruited new workers. Got the J-Crew retreating every time he take a new block, so why my money slow?"

His partner shrugged.

"He only copped half of what he usually do last time we saw him. And that was a minute ago. I'm not sure if it's much to it, but streets is saying he fucking wit' some New York boys."

Father fumed inside and his face read one of confusion.

"New York boys?" He questioned audibly.

His partner had a thought.

"You remember that Jamaican cat, that fucked with them Dominicans? That crazy mothafucka from up north, didn't Capo mention before that he knew him?"

Father was silent as if he was deep in thought but he knew exactly who he was talking about.

"Respect?" Father asked as his partner nodded profusely. He had heard stories of him and knew that was one situation he didn't want to see come their way. Father shook his head.

"Nah, Respect is out the game...besides, he would never do no shit like that. You don't play the game like that. Everybody that come down here know, the south, we got a way of doing things. We gangsters, but we gentlemen. That's why it's called southern hospitality. You come down to a man's city, you start going on his blocks... taking his clients, taking food out of his mouth and you don't even stop by to say hello? Nah, this got to be some young mothafuckas...that think they got that I don't give a fuck in them. Find these niggas, I wanna meet them. I wanna have a *discussion* with them."

His partner nodded and made his way out and the Filipino woman made her way back in.

Father rolled over onto his back and pulled away his towel, revealing his erect, no more than three inch penis.

"Now, I done got all tensed up. Grab those stones Noki, come work it out of me."

She bowed slightly and grabbed her stones, and made her way over to him and began to massage Father's small dick, obediently.

"Ikaw Na Nga... Ikaw Na Nga... Ikaw Na Nga..."

"The court calls Tatum Mosley."

Tatum made her way up to the stand thinking of the testimony from Nikki that she had just heard. She wondered if they would be asking her the same type of questions, which were basically what made her a better provider, how the kids behaved around her, what their grades were like, things like that.

Tatum did have to admit that Nikki did a pretty convincing job on her commitment to stay clean, and her commitment to being a good mother. She even had a sworn statement from her mother who vouched for her and assured that she would be there every step of the way helping Nikki. Tatum had to fight the urge to tear up when Nikki began to cry. Back when her brother and Nikki were set to get married, Tatum had loved her, but when she fell off the wagon, Tatum had found it hard to forgive her. Hearing her testimony today though, she actually started to look at drug use as a habit, a sickness, a disease, and not a conscious selfish decision.

As she began to answer the simple questions, she was sure she was doing just as well of a job as Nikki had done, but was also sounding a little more competent, being that she had no demons, like Nikki. Her lawyer had asked her repeatedly if she had ever done drugs, been arrested, anything like that, and she had secured to him that the answer was no. He smiled at her as she seemed to ace the cross questioning from Nikki's attorney.

"And do you have steady employment to where you can provide for the children?"

"I do…I am a beautician and I make a pretty good living doing so."

The judge seemed pleased to hear that.

"Are there any aspects of your lifestyle that may situate the children in any danger?"

Tatum looked at her like she was crazy.

"No, not at all."

Nikki's lawyer nodded and then asked.

"Have you ever placed the children in any direct danger, knowingly?"

Tatum shook her head no and the judge informed her,

"Please answer the question aloud Ms. Mosley."

"Oh, no. No I haven't."

Her lawyer looked at her pleased as the questioning was wrapping up, and then…

"Who is Sean Knights?"

Tatum's heart stopped.

Nikki's lawyer noticed the look of surprise on Tatum's face and used it to her advantage.

"You seemed surprised Ms. Mosley. Do you not know who Sean Knights is?"

Tatum's lawyer looked at her suspiciously and Tatum's face grew hot.

"Um, n-n-"

"Please remember you are under oath Ms. Mosley," the lawyer reminded with a smirk, and the judge turned to Tatum. Tatum dropped her shoulders in defeat.

"Yes."

"Excuse me?" The lawyer probed.

"Yes…yes, I know who Sean Knights is."

Tatum's lawyer looked on with disbelief, knowing that this was not good.

"Well, maybe your honor, you are not sure who Sean Knights is. Ms. Mosley, let us include everyone on who Sean Knights is. Sean Knights, was Ms. Mosley's boyfriend. He was…is…also a major drug dealer, murderer, and gangster-"

Her lawyer jumped in.

"I'm sorry, but was he ever convicted? I believe you should use the words alleged." Although he had no idea that Tatum was connected to Respect, he, like every judicial person in the tri-state area, was aware of who he was and how bad the state was trying to get him two years ago. They were also aware that it was undo-able.

"Oh, I'm sorry *alleged*...but still...do you take eight and ten year old little girls across state lines with a possible criminal? You did go to Florida with him, correct?" She didn't even give Tatum a chance to answer as she continued to tear into her. "A possible criminal who your brother allegedly worked for, selling drugs? A possible criminal, that if your brother would have lived to tell it, his testimony would have put Mr. Knights away, for running one of the largest drug and criminal rings of this decade...*allegedly*."

Tatum felt faint and felt ashamed. In a way, she was no better than Nikki. She was just on the other, more glamorous side of the game. Dealers, users, still all in all, the same kind of people.

"Did you, or did you not do this Ms. Mosley?"

Tatum sighed and let out a barely audible, 'yes'.

"No more questions, your honor."

And the court rested.

"Please, close my door...can I get you gentlemen anything?"

Father was seated at his ivory desk in his humongous office, and Chauncey and E were seated across from him. There were deer heads and stuffed birds all around, and rifles and various other weaponry lined the walls in glass cases.

Chauncey wore a blank expression, one that was hard for Father to read, however E's mean mug, ice grill, expressed all of his animosity. He knew why Father wanted to see them, and he was prepared for anything.

The bright sunlight pierced through the wall length windows and two of Father's henchmen stood posted next to the door, both with black suits, black shades, and black Mac-11's in their hands.

Chauncey and E declined his offer for refreshments, so Father proceeded to get right down to business.

"You know, when I heard of some New York niggas making their way down here... pumping some shit through my streets..."

"Your streets?" Chauncey questioned, cutting him off.

"That's right," he agreed.

"I'm sure the J-crew would have something to say about that," Chauncey quipped, knowing that they had just as much of a lock on Atlanta's drug trade as Father did.

Father's jaw tightened in aggravation.

"J-crew knows their place."

He leaned forward and folded his hands, breathing heavily.

"Like I was saying… when I heard of this, *situation*, I had no idea that it was you. Now that I know, I am sure we can come to some…resolution."

Chauncey rubbed his chin, slightly interested in what Father had to say.

"What do you suggest?" He asked, taking the bait.

Father, relieved that it was up for negotiation, took out a piece of paper and scribbled a number on it. He handed it to Chauncey and waited for a response.

Chauncey looked at it and then back to Father.

"For what?"

"To get the fuck out of Atlanta…you and your product."

Chauncey chuckled and crumpled up the paper, a clear sign of disrespect.

"Get the fuck outta here."

Chauncey felt as if Father was trying to play him like a sucker, meanwhile, Father's anger was growing by the minute.

"Either that, or we talk about you working for me. You can't just come and take my customers, man. That's not how we do things. Capo is under me."

"Capo is his own entity, as far as I'm concerned," E butted in.

"Capo is money. He has what I want, I got what he needs. Anything personal needs to be handled between y'all," Chauncey added blase-like.

Father cracked his neck slowly.

"You know, you New York niggas been doing this shit for years…thinking we some bamma mothafuckas that you can just come around, set up shop, take shit from our plates, and we just

136

supposed to fall in line. Is that how you think shit supposed to work?"

Chauncey could see his point and that what he was doing was fucked up, for them anyway, but the way he looked at it, he had the ill connect. Best product, best price, that's business.

"How about you do business with us…we supply you, everybody eats," Chauncey suggested, feeling generous. He felt like he was doing him a favor, get down, or lay down.

That's when Father became agitated.

"Nigga, I don't work for nobody! And I'm loyal to my people. How dare you insult me, in my own office?"

Father was foaming at the mouth and Chauncey was cool as a breeze. He could see the meeting going nowhere.

"Let's just cut the shit," Father said angrily. "You continue to supply mothafuckas, my mothafuckas, down here, and we got ourselves a problem, youngin'."

Chauncey laughed hysterically.

"Really? Is that really what you wanna do?" Chauncey leaned forward. "You know, I thought we could do business together…but I guess you must've forgotten the company I keep."

Father matched Chauncey's intense stare, knowing exactly what he meant.

"And you my young friend, must've forgotten that your boss…your *former* boss…is out. No Respect… equals… no respect."

The men eye boxed for a few seconds before Chauncey stood up, followed by E, and began to make his way to the door.

The goons at the door remained stone faced, and as Chauncey and E made their way out, Father shouted behind them.

"You have three days to reconsider…And that's only a pass for the company you *used* to keep."

Father had much respect for Ree, but he'd put his young, knuckle-headed protege in the dirt if he had to.

Chauncey paid him no mind as he continued to walk confidently out of the office. If he was preparing to takeover, then a war was expected. He just needed to make sure that he was prepared, because one thing he didn't have, was home field advantage.

"What are you saying, Sean?"
Ree exhaled deeply before responding.
"Trinity, we went through this already. I don't...I don't understand, why you're not getting it."
"You said space Sean, space. It's been days, you haven't called me. You see me at the desk, and you tell me to get the reports, like...like I'm a worker." Trinity was trying to keep her emotions in check but she felt like she was losing him, and she didn't like it. She knew she would never find another man like Ree.
"You are a worker," he affirmed.
"Is that all I am?" She questioned, hurt.
"Trinity, I apologize. But I can't give you what you want. Not now...not ever. I'm sorry, sweetheart."
Her body shook as she began to sob, and Ree's heart went out to the girl. He had genuinely cared about her. He tried to be easy on her before, but it seemed as if it didn't get through the first time. Now he tried a more direct approach, and he felt bad knowing that direct was also painful.
"This is about that girl, right? I know it is, it's about that damn girl."
"What girl?" Ree feigned ignorance.
"You know what fucking girl! That *bitch* that came down here, and fucked your head all up...now you treat me like this. For what? For *her?* Where is she Sean? She left!" Trinity cried harder and got on her knees in front of him, while he sat in his office chair. Ree looked into her wet and heartrending face.
"She left you Sean. But I'm here, I'm right here."
She leaned in and tried to kiss him, but he pushed her away lightly.
"Trini, please."
She cried harder at his rejection and in the moment of desperation, she tried to throw herself onto him. She pulled at his clothes, tried

to grab his face, his dreads, his arms, his legs, anything. She needed to touch him, to have him, to keep him.

"Please, please just hold me, Sean. Please, hug me like you used to, make love to me, please. Please, I'll do anything for you. Please, don't leave me." She was on her knees, begging. Touching him, grabbing him and Ree firmly grabbed her arms and pushed her back, causing her to fall back on her ass, and then he stood up.

"Trinity! Stop it!"

She looked up at him as he walked over to his bar. He was so tense, so angry, so intimidating, so powerful, and it was so captivating.

She knew she could do one of two things. She could stand up, and walk out with the little dignity she had, or she could keep trying. She looked at him as he focused on pouring his drink and she knew she couldn't give up on him.

She began to unbutton her crisp white blouse as she stood up and made her way over to him, while undressing.

"Sean...please..."

He looked up and saw her walking over to him in her small black skirt and black bra, her shirt now in her hand. She was sexy, she was beautiful, and he knew that he was hurting her. As she reached him, he felt a little submissive, especially by his guilt. She wrapped her arms around him and began to kiss on his neck as Ree contemplated hitting it one last time. As she made a bee-line for his lips, a thought of Tatum popped in his mind.

He backed up from her.

"Nah, Trinity..."

She grabbed his dick and squeezed it lightly, feeling it come to life faintly.

"Ssh, Sean. Let me help you forget about her," she whispered.

Ree snapped back into reality and pushed her away, forcefully.

"You gotta get the fuck out."

He grabbed her arm roughly and pulled her to his door as she fought him, once again trying to grab for him.

"No! I'm not leaving!"

He snatched her shirt out of her hand and wrapped it around her, trying to get her to put it on, but she pushed it away.

"Put your shirt on!" He demanded.

"No! How could you do this? I loved you!" Before she knew what she was doing she slapped him hard across the face.

There was a brief pause as he put his hand to his cheek and felt the sting, and she looked on in apprehension. And then Ree's natural instinct caused him to grab her roughly by the shoulders and push her hard against the wall, gripping her frail neck with one hand. His adrenaline was pumping while he tried to tide his rising temper.

Trinity looked at him, eyes wide with fear and her mascara running, making her appear crazed. He stared at her long and hard, with an intensity that frightened her.

"Get. Out."

He opened his door and strongly shoved her out and tossed her shirt into her hands as Elsa and another desk clerk looked on.

"It's over Trinity."

And then he slammed the door on her loud, causing her body to jump, and her heart to break.

Chapter 14 - Greed

Chauncey and E were riding along the Highway 78 when a drop top SLR pulled along the left side of them. The driver of the car, a young looking dude, motioned with his right finger calmly for them to pull over. Chauncey, who was in the passenger seat, cocked his nine, but told E to oblige. Chauncey had read the vanity plates through the rear-view and had an idea of who the person was.

"Fuck this nigga want?" E questioned, cocking his also, always prepared for whatever.

They turned off of the highway, and pulled over, as the Benz pulled up behind them and the driver got out. He approached E and Chauncey in a nonthreatening fashion, his hands were empty, his walk was easy, so Chauncey and E stepped out of the vehicle.

The young nigga smiled casually and extended his hand out to Chauncey.

"What up yo... Bleek," he introduced himself. Chauncey nodded and returned the handshake.

"C," he stated, but Bleek already knew who Chauncey was. His name rang all types of bells.

Bleek turned to shake E's hand and Chauncey caught the tattoo on his neck. *J-crew.*

He had been waiting to run into one of them, and was even considering going to look for them. But it seemed like they had found him instead.

"So what up? Why the urgency?" Chauncey asked, leaning against the car. His dark Versace shades, button up, and Mauri sneakers masked the ruthless hustler that Bleek had heard of. Bleek was dressed more for the part in his hoodie, baggy jeans, and boots get-

141

up. His smooth youthful face was filled with confidence and experience, yet with a sense of eagerness and hunger. He was like Chauncey five years ago.

Bleek nodded, knowing that they were curious as to why he had pulled them over.

"I got somebody that wants to uh, get better acquainted wit' you," Bleek informed Chauncey.

"Yeah well, pardon my lack of concern, but if it aint bout no money, then…"

Bleek interjected.

"Oh, it's always about money, shawty. And lots of it…I don't play around when it comes to money."

Chauncey nodded and E smirked, he definitely was a reincarnation of a young and cocky Chauncey.

"Well, lead the way," Chauncey said, and the men all retreated to their vehicles and re-entered the highway.

When they arrived at the location, which seemed to be a nightclub of some kind, Bleek led them to the back door.

Even in the daylight with no flashy lights and crowds of people, Chauncey could see that it was still a pretty upscale establishment.

Bleek knocked three times, quickly and hard.

"Judas!" He yelled, and Chauncey wondered if that was what the J stood for in J-crew.

The door opened slowly and Bleek, followed by Chauncey and E entered the dark and empty club. When the door closed behind them, a large man approached.

"I need to pat ya'll down."

Chauncey took off his shades and looked at him aggressively.

"Nah, that's not an option."

The big man became agitated.

"Well, it's a requirement…especially if you going to see the boss."

The two men stared each other down although the other man had height and mass over Chauncey. He was even bigger than E, who also held an irate gaze.

"It's alright," a voice based from up the stairs. "Let them up."

Chauncey and E made their way past the Biggie impersonator and followed Bleek up the stairs, as the man looked at them with distaste.

"Big man 'bout to get his shit pushed back," E barked.

"Fuck all that," Bleek said, walking ahead of them and dismissing the petty altercation. "Boss right in here…Big J, J-Murder some say."

Chauncey had definitely heard the name. Bleek knocked twice and then opened the door, and instantly Chauncey and E took in the richness of the room.

Gold draping, gold floors, gold couches, everything was lavished in gold, giving off a rich and wealthy vibe.

A tall, dark man stood at the other end of the room with a beautiful woman on his arm. Chauncey and E tried not to look too hard at her, but she was bad as hell. The couple walked towards E and Chauncey, and faced them, while Bleek stood on the side.

Chauncey extended his hand to the mysterious man, ready to meet the infamous J-Murder, the well respected hustler and gangster, face to face. But it was the woman who returned the handshake, completely throwing Chauncey off guard.

"Pleased to finally meet you Chauncey, I've heard a lot about you."

Chauncey furrowed his eyebrows at her and Bleek wore a smirk.

"I'm sorry, do I know…"

"Big J…or maybe you know me as J-Murder," the sexy, green-eyed beauty announced.

Bleek looked from the sidelines at Chauncey and E's shock, and he thought of the episode at her condo they had shared. They'd be surprised by a lot of things about Jayde.

She turned to the man at her side.

"Can you excuse us for a minute baby?"

He nodded and then made his way out of her office, closing the door behind him.

Jayde turned ferociously on her heels and strutted back to her desk, her cream Chanel suit hugging her curves.

"Please! Have a seat," she boomed loudly. "Make yourself as comfortable in my office, as you are in my streets!"

Chauncey chuckled at her wit and at the sheer fact that he was thrown for a loop. It took him a minute before he and E walked over and sat down at the chairs facing her desk. Her back was still to them as she searched her bookshelf for something. Finally she turned around and threw the book onto the desk with a sharp look in her eyes.

"Open it," she demanded.

Chauncey looked at her and then grabbed the book and opened it to the first page.

It was a photo album, and the first picture was of a little girl and a man. A man, that Chauncey had seen before…

'Mickel…Mickel DuPree?"

Mickel DuPree was a street legend from the Islands. Chauncey saw that the little girl in the picture had striking emerald eyes. It started to make somewhat of sense to him.

"Mickel DuPree was your father."

She finally took her seat.

"Let me tell you a story," she said, taking a sip of her Nuvo drink. Bleek sat on the side wanting to hear the story as well, Jayde was the J-crew's leader, and he still didn't know too much more than that.

"My father…Mickel…as you probably know… ran arguably one of the tightest, longest, and best drug empires for almost three decades straight. His reign started in '79, that's when he hooked up with the Columbians and supplied almost every single city, in some way, shape, or form, in much of the bottom East Coast. He supplied them all with the most quality, delicious, fucking coke, ever. Shit, when I was a little girl, I spent so much time around Columbians, I thought I was one of them... We were family with them, close, so they treated us well." Jayde paused and took another sip before continuing.

"When my father was murdered five years ago, his um, business partner... who really was like his fucking flunky... Ernie Hobbs, called himself taking over things. He was so incompetent, so disgusting..." Jayde's face twisted in repulsion as she spoke. "He was so fat and greedy! And the Columbians did not want to do business with him, they preferred to work, with me...yours truly. So, Ernie's thinking, I deal with the connect, for him, he runs things. You see, he wanted me from the beginning, even when Daddy was still here. But with Daddy gone, he figured we could run the city together. But more like, he run the city you know? I sit on my ass, look pretty and deal with the connect... He wanted to be Mickel. He wanted the love and respect Mickel had and he wanted me to be devoted to him, like I was for my Daddy. He even wanted me to call him a nickname, Father. When I refused, that fat mothafucka changed his name to Father so that everyone would call him that, and I wouldn't have a choice... But he didn't know me. He didn't know little J, had grown up. I started mingling, mixing, meeting so many people, big people, and found that people...clients...preferred me. They liked me. So I took myself, and my sweet connect, and I parted ways with...*him.*"

She looked at Chauncey and E and leaned back in her chair.

"Me and Father keep a mutual understanding, and so far we seemed to magically coexist in this town. He has people that respect him, and he's got goons so people fear him, but he's garbage. I could never afford to war with him physically, by myself, and since this fucked up recession shit, I can't even compete with product." She looked at Chauncey with much sass. "But now, I guess that doesn't matter... 'cause you, my friend Chauncey, seem to be the man to see....You've got the goods, the price, and you will eventually leave me and Father squabbling for crumbs."

Chauncey tilted his head to the side, somewhat seeing her point of view.

145

"Well, not exactly. No matter what... you're J-Murder. You have your clientele, this is your hood.... I'm just a freelancer. You're the store."

She smiled, glad that he had walked into her vision.

"Exactly. But... what if I could combine... in a perfect world... my army, my soldiers, my government officials, my judges, my lawyers, my police, everyone that looks out for me, looking out for you... combined with your product, your prices, my clientele...and Father's clientele."

"How would we get Father's clientele?" Chauncey questioned, but was already well aware of the answer.

With Father out of the picture, Jayde and Chauncey could take over the city, shit the state and maybe even the lower east side. Her connections and his connect, would be a beautiful marriage. Sure Father's goons may want justice, but with Jayde's home team squad and Chauncey's out of state pull, they'd be no match.

Chauncey rubbed his chin at her cleverness, she was smart and deadly. He thought of all of the ruthless tales he had heard of J-Murder and couldn't believe that they were committed by this feminine woman. She smirked as she let him take it all in.

E looked over at Chauncey knowing that he was deeply considering her offer. He would play it cool, but he was sure he would agree to kill Father and run things with Big J.

Chauncey nodded deep in thought as Jayde's eyes became even greener with greed. Blcok and E both were excited thinking of the possibilities as well.

They were about to have the city on lock, The J-Crew, Chauncey, E... and Jayde.

Tatum's stomach did somersaults as the plane began to descend.

"Ladies and gentlemen, we are now approaching our destination. Please keep all safety belts buckled and make sure your seats are upright. Approximate arrival time, eight minutes..."

Eight minutes. Eight minutes. Am I doing the right thing? Of course…

She reflected on her last conversation that she had with her nieces.

"Auntie Tatum, I don't wanna leave…can't you come with us?"

Tatum had felt the tears building up in her throat, but she tried to remain strong as she walked the girls to the car.

"I can't come baby girl," Tatum said, looking into Tangee's sad eyes. "But I can come visit you, and you can call me everyday if you want."

Tangee half smiled knowing that it wouldn't be the same, as Chanel rolled her eyes.

"But I don't wanna go to Virginia. I wanna stay here with you, and my friends…and Dashun." Chanel didn't want to leave her little boyfriend.

Tatum gave them a big bear hug and kissed them both.

"I know this is hard for you girls…it's hard for me too. But you'll be fine. You guys have to go to Virginia, because that's where your mommy's mother lives, and they're gonna take such good care of you. You'll have your own rooms." Tatum tried to sound excited for them. "And most and best of all, you get to spend the summers with me, so we'll have something to look forward to."

She could see their faces brighten a little and a thought went through her head. *What would I be staying here for?* Then she added.

"What do you guys think about summers in a really warm place…like an island?"

They both gasped, excited, and Chanel being the oldest and knowing way more than she should said,

"With you, and…you know who?"

Tatum had told them a long time ago never to say Ree's name, being cautious of his situation. And they never did. She assumed Chanel had been picking up on her and Sasha's many discussions over Ree, so she was not too surprised at her comment.

Tatum smiled and shook her head with tears in her eyes. She was going to miss Chanel's sass.

"Yeah…me, and you know who."

They cheered, thrilled with the proposition, they adored Ree. And as they were getting situated in the car, Tangee pulled Tatum's coat sleeve, something she did when she wanted to tell her a secret. Tatum leaned her ear down to her and Tangee whispered softly.

"I'm happy for you Auntie Tatum. Go live happily ever after."

Tatum looked at her purely shocked and at a loss for words, and then she kissed her on her precious forehead.

As the car took off and a piece of Tatum left with it, she figured she just may take Tangee's advice.

Now here she was, doing so, and she was so nervous. Deep down inside though, she knew this was the way it should be. She had heard that people that have an easy start on life, usually have their rough times later. Well, Tatum had her dose of rough times, so maybe now was her time, to be easy.

As the plane landed, and people began to de-board, she picked up her cell phone, and made a call.

"I'm here," she said, sounding happier than she had in a long time.

"That's great! Oh my god, I can't believe you're doing it," Sasha admitted, starting to cry like a softie. She was going to miss Tatum. Knowing that she was in Newark felt a whole lot better than knowing she was in Jamaica. But it was time for her to live her life and Sasha couldn't be happier for her.

"I guess at least one of us gets the happy ending, huh?" Sasha asked, reflecting on their conversation a few years ago about choices.

Tatum wasn't sure what to say to that, so she said what was in her heart.

"I love you."

"I love you too, girl," Sasha said, tears of joy lining her face. "Now go get you some!"

The girls laughed and Tatum ended the conversation, promising to call again later. As she made her way outside, she found a taxi waiting and approached him.

"Where to pretty gal?"

"Botanical Bay, Botanical Bay Resort," she said without doubt.

"Sure thing...and welcome to Jamaica!" He exclaimed, as Tatum smiled wide.

Welcome home, she thought to herself.

The ride was brief, and when Tatum stepped out of the cab, a flutter of butterflies went through her. She grabbed her two roll away luggage bags and her duffle, the only things that she had brought with her. All of her furniture and other miscellaneous items, Sasha promised she would take care of.

Tatum walked through the pretty glass doors and approached the main desk. There were not even half as many people in the lobby as there had been when she was there previously.

A new clerk was at the desk, and was all smiles as Tatum made her way to her.

"Gud aftanoon, can I help yu?" The woman asked in her Jamaican accent.

"Um, yes. Is Re-Mr. Knights available please?"

The woman looked at Tatum skeptically but then retreated to the back office.

She gently knocked on his office door and he told her to enter.

Ree was sitting at his desk, elbows deep in paperwork, even wearing his reading glasses. He asked what she needed without even looking up.

"Eh Mistah Knights, there is sum lady here, she wud like to see yu."

"What does she need?"

The clerk shrugged.

"I dunno."

Ree shook his head.

"Tell her Trinity can help her. I'm busy."

She nodded and closed his door back. She approached Tatum with an uneasy smile.

"Sorry, Mistah Knights is terribly busy. Wud yu like ta talk wit Miss Trinity, she da hotel managa, she cud help yu."

149

Tatum chuckled at the irony before responding.

"No, no, I don't want to talk to Trinity...at all. Can you please tell Mr. Knights that it's terribly important and that it will only be a minute...please," Tatum asked, extra nicely.

"One moment." The clerk retreated again.

She knocked once more, timidly and a little nervous. This time Ree came to the door.

"What is it?"

"She insists on speaking wit' yu Mistah Knights. I try ta tell ha, but she don't want Miss Trinity."

Ree sighed, annoyed, and made his way out of the office and toward the front desk while removing his glasses. He looked around and then his vision began to focus.

The sight of Tatum standing there, looking radiant, could've stolen his breath from him.

"Wow," he said, thrown off as he approached the desk. His face couldn't reveal how happy he was if it wanted to. Tatum beamed wide.

"I was just wondering...if I can possibly...get a room," she teased.

He smiled at her before answering.

"Well, let me see what I can do. If you're uhm, planning on staying short term, we can maybe get you a suite," he said, playing along. Tatum scrunched up her nose and shook her head. He nodded and continued.

"No, okay. Or if maybe you want to try one of our extended stay rooms?"

She smiled and shook her head again as she leaned over the counter.

"Nah...you know what? I was thinking something, a little more...domestic. A little more, intimate." She was thinking of with him, at his home.

He smiled wide and bit his bottom lip.

"Well how long you plan on staying Miss Lady?"

She breathed deep and looked in his eyes.

"A while," she confessed. Ree opened the small wooden door that led behind the desk.

"Get in here…"

She practically ran to him and into his arms, as he grabbed her and held her tight.

"Look at you…" he said sexily. He kissed her slowly, deeply, and passionately on the mouth, and Tatum felt like she was floating.

"Mmm…" he moaned and she creamed. And in a sexy low whisper, he asked, "A while?"

"A while," she repeated. She looked into his eyes and felt overwhelmed with emotion.

"A lifetime," she corrected, in an expressive soft voice. And he kissed her again.

Trinity froze in her tracks as she watched Ree and Tatum embracing so affectionately. She blinked away her tears as she continued to lead the new maid crew through the tour of the hotel.

"Um, right this way ladies," she instructed them, but still keeping her eyes on the lurid couple.

It was like a bad car wreck, horrible to look at but impossible to look away from.

Ree had broken her heart in the worse way, and hadn't even given her time to heal.

"Fuck 'em," she thought to herself.

But even as she turned to lead the crew through the halls, and forced her eyes away from them, she knew it wouldn't be that easy. She was scorned. She was scorned something serious.

"Put the giraffe over there," Sasha ordered, while pointing across the room.

"You sure?"

"Yes…trust me. It'll look nice."

Chauncey looked at her skeptically but then carried the gold and ivory giraffe statue to the other side of his spacious living room.

He looked around at the paintings, statues, and drapings all scattered around the floor and wondered if asking Sasha to help him decorate was wise. Just spending this time alone with her was worth it though.

"What's up with the giraffes, though? I don't know if I'm a giraffe kinda nigga."

Sasha rolled her eyes and giggled.

"I have taste...the giraffes, perfect touch." She shot him a wink and plopped down on his brand new eggshell European sofa, which was still sitting in the middle of the room because they hadn't decided where to place it yet. She thought of how this could have been her home, their home, but this punk nigga had to go thinking with his dick.

"Maybe I should check on Aubrey," Sasha figured, proceeding to get up. Chauncey sat down beside her and grabbed her arm lightly, pulling her back down.

"C'mon, I just put her down for a nap. She good."

Sasha nodded and then looked over at him. He was so *fine.*

The phrase tall, dark, and handsome should've just been renamed *Chauncey.*

He looked at her with such a cool yearning that she wasn't sure what would come next. She briefly thought of Mike and how she had told him that she was dropping Aubrey off at Chauncey's, and then going to have lunch with her parents before they went back to Jersey. A little white lie that her mother not only justified, but had commended. Now, here she was.

"I think I need something to drink...I'm thirsty from all of this moving around." Sasha got up quickly and headed toward the kitchen, trying her best not to be wooed by him.

"You aint do shit but point, I moved everything," Chauncey cracked, getting up behind her and watching her ass and hips in her skin tight jeans, as he followed her to the kitchen. He knew from her reactions to him that he was breaking her down slowly.

"Shut up," she shot back, finally reaching the fridge and bending over to get a bottled water. When she stood back up, Chauncey was right behind her, all in her space, and her heartbeat quickened. She turned and faced him, with only inches between them, and held his magnetic gaze.

"What?" She asked nervously, her breath in short spurts.

"What you mean what…I'm thirsty too," he said, nonchalantly. She stood there looking at him as if she were under a spell. Their lips were so close, and just like in her dream, she could almost taste him. She felt herself becoming moist.

"Well?" He asked.

"Well," she answered, still looking up at him dreamily. Chauncey smiled his killer smile that brought out his dimples.

"Well, you wanna grab me one…or move your pretty ass to the side so I can get my own."

Sasha was thrown. He didn't try to make a move on her. She was almost positive, halfway prepared, for him to try to kiss her. *What the fuck?*

"Oh," she stated simply. "Here."

She handed him her water and bent back down to get another, this time poking her ass out even further. Chauncey walked away and leaned back on the counter, watching her, with a sly smirk.

Oh, he laughed to himself, knowing Sasha like the back of his hand.

Sasha closed the refrigerator and walked over to the other side of the kitchen. She hopped up on the counter facing him, and opened her water, taking a long swig. She looked around at the huge steel designed area and realized how much she loved his home. It was almost three times the size of hers; it was like her dream house.

"You did good. Your house if fly," she complimented.

"You like it?" He asked, taking a sip of his own.

"I do," she assured him. She put her water down next to her and released her hair from her ponytail holder, running her fingers slowly through her long tresses. She closed her eyes and enjoyed the sensation, knowing that she was bringing Chauncey to his knees gradually.

153

This was a weakness of his, a turn on. This, and when she used her forefinger to pull her hair behind her ear subtly. It drove him crazy, she didn't know why, but it just did. It was his *thing*.

Chauncey watched her closely, his mouth slightly agape. He could feel his lust building. He sighed and looked down, and Sasha fumed silently. She didn't want to fuck Chauncey. Well, she did, but she knew that she couldn't. But either way, she wanted him to want her. In fact she couldn't even deal with him not *needing* to fuck her. She wondered if he was dealing with any females down in Atlanta yet.

"So, I have a question," she posed, hopping off the counter and walking over to his side.

"Shoot," he said coolly.

"How is it? You know, not...being, uhm...intimate with anyone, for *years*?"

He raised his eyebrows, slightly shocked by her question. Sasha bringing up the topic of sex told him many things at once. He played with her.

"What you mean?"

She sucked her teeth, and then she delicately licked her lips.

"I mean...you know...sex. Does it like bring you to a whole new mental level, or something? Or is it like, not even that important anymore... when you go so long without it?"

She really wanted to know why he wasn't pressing her. Chauncey chuckled and shrugged.

"You tell me."

This time it was Sasha's turn to be shocked.

"What you mean by that?" She shot back defensively.

"You know exactly what I mean," he boasted arrogantly and then smiled. Sasha squinted at him and crossed her arms. She hated how he could do that, read her like a book and then turn the tables.

"How you figure?" Was all she could reply.

Chauncey leaned in close to her ear and whispered.

"You're good looking...you got a beautiful body, beautiful legs, beautiful face...all these guys in love with you...only you got a look in your eye like you haven't been fucked in a year..."

He smiled and she laughed lightly at his impersonation of Scarface, reciting the infamous Tony Montana quote to her.

"Whatever!" She giggled, and leaned over on the counter, using her finger to pull her hair behind her ear. She realized what she had done and looked back at Chauncey and bit her lip, as he stepped behind her with a sexy yet serious stare.

He pressed his dick firmly against her ass and she went to stand up. They were so close that if it weren't for their jeans, they'd be fucking.

"Stay like that," he demanded in a sexy baritone, as he pressed down on her back and bent her gently back down onto the counter.

"Chauncey, no," she whined, trying, but not really trying to stand straight up and get away.

"Ssh," he whispered, pressing her down again. "Keep yo' ass right there."

Sasha gave up and closed her eyes, her face pressed against the cool counter and Chauncey slid his hands under her shirt and grinded seductively on her from behind.

His fingertips were slightly cold and foreign to her as he slowly moved up her back and sides, to her perky breasts. He cupped them with his strong hands and then gently pulled her bra down, rolling her nipples between his fingers.

"Oh," she moaned quietly as her pussy quivered. He moved away from her breasts and lifted her shirt up little by little and then pulled it over her head and threw it on the floor. He delicately licked and kissed her back and Sasha breathed heavily, completely in ecstasy. She was at the point of no return but she didn't care.

"Ooh, Chauncey, I need you to fuck me...please, fuck me," Sasha panted.

Chauncey unbuckled her pants from behind and peeled them down to her ankles as she stepped out of them. He ripped off her pink lace panties and bit her ass cheek gently and then sucked on each one of them.

Sasha rubbed her titties, completely turned on. She had never been this horny in her life.

She could feel him behind her standing back up, but she kept her eyes closed. She heard his jeans unbuckling and she anticipated his dick. Finally, she could feel the hardness, the largeness, pressed against her bare pussy from behind. Chauncey ran his dick from her ass to her wetness, lubricating her entire womanhood.

"Stop teasing me boy," she gasped sexily. "Put that shit in me."

"You want it," he based, his veins poking out as his dick reached its full capacity.

"I need it," she confessed, arching her back and preparing for something she hadn't felt in so long.

He grabbed her juicy ass cheeks and spread them wide, opening up her second lips and sliding into her pink prettiness, inch by inch.

"Oh god, yes!" Sasha declared as she creamed instantly on his dick. Once he was almost all the way in, he slid the last five or so inches in at once, causing her to cry out in pain and pleasure simultaneously.

"Chauncey!"

He smirked and closed his eyes. She felt too damn good.

He sat there, mid motion for a second and then began to steadily stroke her, gripping her hips as Sasha held the counter for dear life.

"Damn," he grunted, realizing how much he missed fucking her.

"Chauncey, this dick is so good. Oh, it's so fucking gooddd," she moaned, as a tear escaped her eye and rolled down onto the counter.

He began to move faster and faster, pounding her as her head danced around like a bobblehead.

"Gimme that pussy," he ordered as she threw it back at him.

"Take it!" She shouted back, getting so into it. It had been too long since she had felt this.

She grabbed the dish rack on the counter, knocking over forks and knives, and cooking utensils everywhere. She was trying to grip something, anything.

Chauncey used his left hand to pick up the spatula that had fallen, and smacked her swiftly on the ass with it, still gripping her with his right hand and pumping in and out of her.

That was why she loved fucking him. He was so in control, and so spontaneous.

"Oh yes! Do it again," Sasha begged, loving it. He slapped her ass again with the spatula, causing Sasha to cream all over him again. He felt her body shake as she came and he felt his nut building up.

"Oh! Again!" She yelled, in the midst of her orgasm.

He slapped her again and then threw the spatula down, strongly grabbing her titties with both hands and going deep inside of her. She felt his dick twitch and it gave her a rapturous feeling.

Chauncey bit his bottom lip and his body tensed.

"Oh...Sasha...," he groaned, releasing deep inside of her.

"Chauncey, I love you," she cried out.

"I love you too, girl," he replied, and then he covered her back with loving kisses.

Interlude

The black hoodie concealed their face, as swift movements guided them across the street, and back into the car.

Once comfortably nestled inside, and sure to be undetected, they anxiously proceeded to play back the video they had just recorded, not believing how juicy it was.

"Oh, Sasha."

An instant feeling of nausea developed as they watched Sasha and Chauncey go at it in his kitchen on the camcorder.

The shadow fast forwarded through all of the details, unable to stomach them. There was one part that was crucial, the most evident. *Here it is.*

"Chauncey, I love you," Sasha cried out on the tape, a look of bliss on her wicked, yet gorgeous face.

"I love you too, girl," Chauncey had answered, sounding like he had really meant it.

The culprit stopped the tape and started up the small hooptie, slowly driving off.

Gotcha bitch!

Chapter 15 - Malice

"You know, I can't believe you asked me to come here...I haven't seen you in so long. And I've never seen you like this."

Father lay back on the black silk sheets of Jayde's king sized bed as she placed soft, wet kisses, all over his oversized, blubbery stomach. She wore a sheer black thong and sheer black bra with black six inch stilettos. And Father was in total awe of her.

"Well, like I said at dinner...we have to work together now. Outsiders are thinking that they can come into my...our city," she corrected. "That's no good."

She sat up on her knees over him and slowly unlatched her bra, as his bug eyes were glued to her always forbidden, now suddenly within his reach, perfect C-cup breasts. Jayde reveled at her control over him. Getting him there, with no bodyguards was almost too easy. He actually had believed her sob story of being terrified of Chauncey's possible competition and war. Now, he was at her mercy.

"Now what do I have to do, to get you to join forces with me?" She probed.

Father studied her as if he were in an anatomy class and rubbed his chin as if in deliberation, knowing that he was delighted to have Jayde on his team. He was secretly not so confident in the potential conflict with Chauncey, and was glad to have an ally.

"I don't know," he mused. "Why don't you show me what you can do?"

He licked his lips greedily; he wanted to lick every inch of her. He was nasty like that.

"Better yet," he said excitedly. "Why don't you come and have a seat up here, and I'll show you what I can do... I'm giving moustache rides, baby."

Jayde had to force herself not to frown. She loved getting head, but doubted she would enjoy getting it from her arch nemesis. She would see though.

She made her way up and turned around to sit on his fat face, her ass pressed against his nose.

I wish I could smother this mothafucka with my pussy, she thought as she felt his slimy tongue probe her sugar walls.

She daydreamed about all of the money she would soon be making as he licked and sucked her, and she was surprisingly delighted when a sensual feeling shot through her like a bolt of electricity.

"Ooh," she quivered. *Damn, I must really love head, 'cause this shit is starting to feel good.*

"Mmm, mmm, mmm...thith ith tho good," Father tried to mumble through Jayde pressing against his mouth. She chuckled.

"Ssh baby, don't talk with your mouth full."

Jayde leaned over and jerked his small penis as she lifted off of him and turned to face him. She didn't want an orgasm to throw her off. *Kinda like a fighter, no sex before the big brawl.*

"I wanna know more about you...Father." It was hard for her to call him that. "I want us to build with one another."

She gave her best impression of a regular girl who had genuine interest in a guy. She continued to jerk him slowly while she looked at him innocently.

"What's your favorite food?" She asked. He looked at her incredulously.

"What?"

She shot him an award winning smile.

"C'mon. What's your favorite thing to eat?"

He leaned his head back in disbelief but continued to enjoy the dick massage, although she was not as good as Noki.

"You," he answered with a sinister laugh, that reluctantly made Jayde chuckle. She licked her lips, ready for the main attraction.

"Okay, last question. What's your favorite movie?"

"Come on, climb up on this dick," he urged.

Jayde stopped rubbing him and leaned over to unbuckle her sandals.

"That's not a movie...I'm serious, favorite flick?"

He sighed and closed his eyes, ready to make a flick of their own.

"I don't know...Casino, I guess."

You're no Sam Rothstein, Jayde pondered.

"You wanna know mine?" she asked, slipping out of one of her sandals. Father shrugged as she continued. "It's Single White Female."

"Never sccn it," he said dismissively, anticipating her.

Jayde's eyes turned cold as she unbuckled the other shoe.

"I like the part...when she sleeps with the guy...and he's lying back in the bed."

Father sighed loud.

"I said I never seen it," Father repeated. But Jayde kept talking, blocking him out.

"And then she takes her shoe...and he's so helpless...he doesn't suspect anything..."

Father was becoming irritated.

"Baby, is we gon' fuck or what?" He shouted.

Jayde looked at him, her Christian Dior spiked heel in her hand, and she finished, laughing hysterically.

"And then...she stabbed the mothafucka right in the fucking eye, with her fucking shoe! Can you believe that shit?"

Father sat up slightly, hearing the last part and before he could get his "what the fuck" out, Jayde brought the heel of her shoe straight down into his right eye socket.

"Aaaarrggghhhhh!" He hollered, in complete pain and terror.

"Fat...fucking... bastard!" She screamed, demented.

Father felt himself blacking out and continued to scream, reaching for the shoe as blood and pus oozed from his face. Jayde quickly grabbed the .32 that was taped under the bed and fired four shots into his fat chest.

"Shut!" Pop!
"The!" Pop!
"Fuck!" Pop!
"Up!" Pop!
His body jolted and then relaxed, blood pouring from him onto her bed. She breathed heavy and eyed him closely, checking his pulse and heartbeat.
"Done!" She screamed, as Chauncey, E, and Bleek came from out of her walk-in closet. They were there in case anything would have gone wrong.
"Damn!" E exclaimed, looking at the naked and dead Father with a shoe in his right eye.
Bleek shook his head from side to side and stretched.
"You aint worried about the neighbors?" Chauncey asked calmly, referring to the gunshots.
"Soundproof walls," Jayde shot back, walking over to Father's body in her nakedness. Chauncey, E, and Bleek watched her as she stood over him, and leaned down.
"Fuck you doing?" Chauncey asked, bewildered.
Jayde grabbed the Dior sandal and twisted and turned it until she was finally able to pry it out of Father's eye socket.
"My fucking shoe!" She said, examining it and then wiping off the blood on the sheets. "I paid a grip for these shits."
She walked away and Chauncey followed her, so that they could discuss the next step.
And E and Bleek stayed behind and did what any real gentlemen would do; they cleaned up the mess, and took out her trash for her. The city was now theirs.

"So like I said, if you can't get a hold of me, Tatum can make any on the spot decisions that need to be made…I want you all to respect her. And I just wanted to formally introduce you all to her."
"Ree," Tatum protested, feeling self conscious of her portrayal to all of his staff. He was putting her on some type of pedestal.

He had been chauffeuring her around the island, introducing her to everyone and in return, she was treated like a Queen. In fact, that's exactly what she felt like, and unbeknownst to her, that's exactly what she now was considered in Jamaica. Royalty.

Tatum didn't understand how the people of the island held so much respect for a man whose family represented crime, murder, and drugs, but she realized that the way these people lived, Ree and his family seemed to care more for them than their own government. They were loyal to him, and now, her as well.

"I'm not answering to her," Trinity mumbled, feeling like a spectacle.

Even though she and Ree had kept their relationship under wraps, many of the staff workers knew that they were dating, mostly due to her. This was embarrassing.

"Is there a problem Trinity?" Ree asked boldly.

He knew she was going to be upset with him being with Tatum, but hey, life goes on. He wasn't going to hide his relationship or put it on hold for her. And he definitely wasn't going to jeopardize Tatum's feelings for hers. If she wanted to continue working there, then she would have to find a way to deal with it.

"No," she answered meekly, as Tatum glared at her with an arched eyebrow.

"Good," he responded.

The crew dispersed after showering Tatum with warm smiles and kind words. They all were either trying to get or stay on Ree's good side. When the area was cleared, Tatum turned and wrapped her arms around his waist.

"So, this is us…this is my life," she said, still not believing it.

"Yup, this is us. I have one more thing I want to show you a little later." He held her hips and stared at her. Now he was at ease.

"Okay," Tatum said, curious as to what it could be. Then she added. "And I have one more thing I want to ask you."

"Ask it," he urged.

Tatum looked down and then back at him.

"This is it, right?" He looked at her not really following what she meant, as she continued. "You know what I mean…no more street stuff?"

Ree sighed and stared her right in the eyes. How could he tell her that no matter what kind of business he was in, he would always be a gangster? It was in his DNA.

"All money is legal, now," he said, hoping that it would be enough. She smiled and kissed him on the lips, and he figured that it was.

"So what else do you have to show me?"

The car crept up a hill as Tatum took in the breath-taking scenery. All of the buildings were classic, almost historic looking, and beautiful fields of trees and flowers surrounded them.

"Ooh Ree, look at that building over there, I wonder if that's someone's home?"

"It is," he confirmed, looking out of the window on her side at the old mansion he had admired since he was younger. He wrapped his arm around her waist as they sat in the back of the Maybach, gradually approaching their destination.

"Oh my god, and look at that! I know that can't be someone's house too." She pointed at a white colonial style estate that resembled a castle. Tatum was in complete awe of the beauty that surrounded them and Ree loved it.

"It is," he stated.

"What? Oh my god…must be someone really important, huh?" Tatum was like a child staring at the huge property.

The car slowed down gradually and then finally came to a complete stop in front of the building Tatum had been admiring. Ree got out of the car and walked around to the other side to open the door for Tatum

"It is…a very important person."

Tatum stepped out slowly, looking up at him in confusion. She wondered who he was going to introduce her to now. Her head was spinning from all of the new acquaintances she had made.

He grabbed her hand, helping her out of the car and then he smirked.

"It belongs...to you."

Tatum dropped her jaw.

"Nah-unh," she laughed in amazement.

"Ya-huh," Ree said back, making fun of her juvenile, yet incredibly cute choice of words.

She smiled and shook her head in disbelief as Ree closed the door to the car.

"Would you like for me to wait Mr. Knights, or will you be staying?"

"Wait...please," he instructed the driver.

He let go of Tatum's hand and walked ahead swiftly.

"Come on, let's go," he said, as Tatum looked around at the front of the estate.

The horse ranch, the pond, the garden, the stone walkways, large metal gates with two huge reflecting K's encrypted in them.

K is for Knights, she figured.

"Come on Miss Lady, I got somewhere to be soon," Ree hurried Tatum, with a slight smile. She double stepped to catch up to him, and they finally reached the huge front door.

"What do you mean, it's mine?" She asked intriguingly, as he opened the door and led her inside.

"Just what I said. This is my home...and now it's yours."

"Her heels clicked against the marble floors as she watchfully made her way inside, taking in the spaciousness of her vicinity. It was breathtaking.

"But Ree, I've been to your house...I've been staying at your house." She looked at him as if he had amnesia as he leaned coolly against a mahogany table in the living area.

"My beach house."

"What?"

"We've been staying at my beach house. But this is my...and your...real home."

She stared at him a second longer and then slowly grinned wide, making her way over to him. She wrapped her arms around his neck and pressed against him.

"I love you, Mr. Knights."

"Yea…yea…yea…," he joked, looking up at the ceiling blasé like, with a smirk. She punched him playfully and he smiled and grabbed her hips. He looked deep in her eyes, his stare, so tantalizing.

"I love you more," he answered, kissing her in a way that made Tatum weak. His kiss was so in control, so firm, yet gentle. His kiss was like liquid sex.

Tatum felt his hands making their way to her ample ass, palming her behind through her silk wrap dress.

"Mmmm," she moaned, as his strong hands caressed her body. She could have him right then and there if he had wanted to be had. But she remembered him saying he had somewhere to be.

With the heat he was inducing, she knew they were heading in the direction of a sex down.

"Wait…wait. Don't you have somewhere to be?" She reminded him, as his tongue traced her neckline. His hands sliding under her dress and up her thigh was his response.

"But what about the driver? Didn't you ask him to wait?" She questioned almost inaudibly, closing her eyes and biting her lip.

"And that's exactly what he'll do," Ree responded seriously, kissing her again.

Mmmm definitely, liquid sex. And then they had each other right there, in the living room, on the floor, of their home.

"Just one more block to go," Sasha murmured to herself, as she jogged down Lindbergh Drive. The sun had recently set, catching her in the middle of her workout, and as she started to make her way home, a sense of eeriness came over her.

She tried to fill her thoughts of her latest dilemma with Chauncey and her husband to not become too creeped out, but even that wouldn't do it.

As she turned onto her street and saw her house, she got that same feeling that she had gotten two years ago when those thugs had broken into her apartment and tried to kill her. The same thugs that she later found out were sent by Neli.

Sasha looked around at the now dark and empty street and didn't see anything out of the norm.

Maybe I am tripping. This whole thing with Chauncey has really got me bugging anyway. I'm probably just being paranoid.

She reached into her small Coach pouch and fished for her keys, and that's when she heard heavy footsteps fast approaching from behind.

Oh no.

Thump, thump. Thump, thump. Thump, thump.

Sasha turned around quickly to face whoever it was, but found no one. She hastily looked around, in front, behind, side to side.

I'm on some white girl, scary movie shit now, she thought.

But to be on the safe side, she sped up her jog to her front door.

As she neared the door, her feeling of apprehension heightened to the point where her heart pounded and her palms were sweaty.

She didn't feel alone, she felt someone there, and she felt scared. She struggled to get the key into the lock, feeling the presence of someone else become stronger, and closer, and nearer.

She dropped her keys in a haste to open the door.

Shit!

Sasha bent down and picked them up quickly, not wanting to waste time turning around. She just wanted to get into the house.

Mike's car was gone, he was at the hospital, and Aubrey was with Chauncey. She knew the house was empty.

She finally found her key again and slid it into the lock and she could literally sense someone behind her. As she pushed the door open forcefully, the wind brushed against her hair... or maybe it wasn't the wind?

Either way, she was finally in. She slammed the door behind her and locked all three locks, breathing heavily.

Sasha quickly flicked on the hallway light and stared at the front door. After thirty seconds of waiting, she sighed deeply, trying to calm herself down.

What just happened?

She went to look out of the peephole hoping to see nothing, and that would maybe confirm that she was just tripping because she had too much on the brain.

As she leaned into the door, she slowly put her left eye to the peephole.

Nothing. Just an empty porch.

See, nothing.

She turned to head into the kitchen deciding to give Tatum a call. The dead silence of the house had her feeling lonely. Sasha began heading down the hallway, feeling relieved, and then…

Boom! Boom! Boom!

Three loud knocks on the door caused her to jump almost out of her skin. She turned slowly toward the door, but stood still in her tracks, and her eyes widened in fear.

Boom! Boom! Boom!

Her heartbeat could've won the New York City marathon, it was going so fast.

"Who is it?" She yelled, trying to sound confident, but her voice was shaking.

There was no answer and Sasha's hands began to shake.

Maybe I should call the police...

And tell them what, someone's knocking on my door?

She shook her head at her own foolishness.

Maybe I'll just ignore them and they'll go away. She turned to head back to the kitchen.

Boom! Boom! Boom! ... Boom! Boom! Boom! ... Boom! Boom! Boom!

Each pounding on the door made Sasha's body jump.

"Who is it?" She screamed, angrily.

168

Boom! Boom! Boom!
Sasha looked over and saw a fire poker leaning against the wall. She grabbed it and headed slowly toward the front door. She figured she would check who it was through the peephole.
A million thoughts raced through Sasha's mind as she reached the door. She closed her eyes briefly, and then re-opened them, leaning in to look out of the peephole.
Here goes nothing.
Her blood instantly was on boil from the sight before her and she was no longer scared, but she decided to hold onto the fire poker…maybe for other reasons.
Sasha snatched the door open, fire poker in one hand, other hand on her right hip.
"What the fuck are you doing at my house?" Sasha hissed, through clenched teeth.
Her nostrils flared and her eyes were lowered to slits of anger.
"Hi Sasha."
Neli was standing there with an uneasy smile on her face.
"You look…great," Neli complimented out of nervousness.
"What…in the fuck…are you doing…at my god damn house, bitch?" Sasha's words were so full of venom, her face was scowled and if she wasn't so scared of prison, she would've stabbed Neli right through her evil, hateful heart with the fire poker.
"Sasha…I didn't say who it was… because I was scared you wouldn't answer. I know, you weren't expecting me-"
"*Expecting* you?" Sasha asked, bewildered. "Bitch, you really are fucking looney…you lucky I don't kill yo' stupid ass!"
Neli sighed audibly, nodding her head.
"I know…trust me I know, Sasha. I…I did a lot of bad things, but I need you to hear me out…"
"I'm not hearing shit, hoe! Fuck off my doorstep before I call the cops and have you arrested for trespassing," Sasha barked, waving the fire poker like a weapon. "And were you just following me, you psycho hoe?"
Neli didn't budge, and kept her same innocent and serene look.

169

"No! Sasha…" Neli protested. It was not easy for her to humble herself to her arch nemesis and put up with the name-calling, but if it was one thing Greystone had taught her, it was to be responsible for her actions. And Neli had caused Sasha a lot of pain, so she had a right to be upset. "Sasha, I have to let you know something. I know…I know you're upset with me about Chauncey…and about Kim…but…"

Hearing Neli utter Kim's name sent Sasha over the edge. This bitch was the reason her friend was dead and she wanted to bring her up. Sasha grimaced and charged at Neli.

"You! Fucking! Bitch!"

She dropped the poker and grabbed Neli by the collar, pushing her to the edge of the steps. Then she pulled her fist back and connected powerfully against Neli's right jawbone.

Crack!

Neli went tumbling down the stairs.

She lay crumpled at the bottom of the steps in horror and shock. Her blood dripped from her mouth and she looked up at Sasha.

Neli had never expected Sasha to hit her, but she had underestimated Sasha's hate for her.

"Now you got ten seconds to get yo' ass away from my house before we have a replay of your little bathtub episode. And this time, won't be no fuck ups 'cause I'll be the one doing the slitting!"

Sasha was referring to Neli's suicide attempt and Neli fought back the tears in her eyes. It was a low blow.

Neli got up off the ground, still holding her face. As she walked away, she turned back toward the house in one more feeble attempt.

"Sasha…"

"Fuck you!" Sasha screamed in a rage, and slammed the door so hard it rattled the house. Neli stood there and stared at the closed door. She sighed.

"Don't say I didn't try to tell you," Neli whispered. And then she made her way to her little hooptie ride.

When Sasha reached the kitchen her insides were on fire, she was full of rage and she was seeing red. Tears of anger and pain fell from her eyes. Anger because she wanted to do so much more to Neli. Pain, because she knew no matter what she did, it would never bring Kim back.

She searched for the cordless but couldn't find it so she grabbed her cell phone out of her pouch.

She dialed Tatum in Jamaica, but there was no answer. She tried her house and then cell, still no luck. She left an urgent message for her to return her call on the machine and at the front desk of the hotel.

Next she tried Mike, but they said that he was in a surgery.

She thought of the third person she had to call, and was surprised that he wasn't her first thought.

"Chauncey!" She screamed when he answered.

"Where are you? Everything okay?"

Chauncey always asked where you were first. He figured he'd get the most critical information first and then at least he could get to her, and find out what happened later. He hated when people asked what happened first, it was like okay, you know what happened, but if you cant find out where they are, you cant do shit about it.

"I'm home...and I'm fine, now."

Chauncey sighed, relieved.

"Okay, what happened?"

Sasha told him all about the running episode, the scariness, the banging, and then who it ended up being.

"What! Get the fuck outta here." Chauncey was thrown. He hadn't seen Neli since his hearing and was sure, based on what she had done for him, that she was at least halfway stable. But coming to Atlanta?

"Yeah!" Sasha yelled. "I told her she come near me again, I'm a slit her wrists my damn self, and I won't do it halfway...I'm a follow through."

171

Chauncey ran his tongue along his jaw in anger before responding calmly.

"Don't worry 'bout that. She come near you again, I'll finish what I started… and *I'm a* follow through."

Sasha was quiet remembering that Chauncey had damn near killed Neli before. She didn't want him to go back to jail. If something happened to Neli, Chauncey would be public enemy number one.

"She won't…I think she got the message. Especially when I snuffed her," Sasha cracked.

Chauncey chuckled at Sasha getting gangsta on her ass.

"That's my girl. So what's up…you alone?"

Sasha sat down on a stool, feeling more at ease. Chauncey always calmed her. Big shit just didn't seem big when Chauncey was around.

"Yeah," she responded. "He's at the hospital."

"So why don't you come over here? Me and Aubrey just ordered pizza…and I don't want you to be alone."

A night with her family, her real one, sounded like the perfect remedy. And some more of what Chauncey had broke her off with on the kitchen counter sounded like a fucking cure. She caught chills just thinking about it.

But then she heard the keys dangling in the door…

"I can't," she said in a low whisper.

"Why not?"

Before she could answer, Chauncey heard Mike's voice through the phone.

"Babe, are you okay? The receptionist said you called…said it was an emergency-" That was all Chauncey got and then the line went dead. He held the phone to his ear for a few seconds in anger. But in reality, his anger was masking what he was really feeling, heartbroken.

"Who you talking to?" Mike asked Sasha, seeing that she had her phone in her hand.

"Uh…no one. I was just trying to call Tatum."

Mike remained silent and just stared at the phone in her hand, but then he walked over to her and wrapped his arms around her, kissing her forehead.

"Are you alright?"

She brightened a little.

"I am...now."

He beamed, just knowing that she meant now that he was home. But what she meant, was now that she had spoken to Chauncey.

Mike cupped her face with his hands and looked at her lovingly.

"I love you so much...you know that right?"

Sasha continued smiling but wanted to cry. *He's such a good man.*

"I know...I love you, too."

I can't hurt him. I can't do what Chauncey did to me...I can't break his heart.

Chapter 16 - Power

"The fucking city…is ours!" Jayde screamed, raising her Margarita, sitting poolside of E's new lavish home.

When Jayde's customers had gotten a hold of Chauncey's product, at Chauncey's prices, they all went bonkers. They bought it so quickly, copped twice as much, sold twice as much, and the money was coming in. It was pandemonium in the streets.

The icing on the cake was that besides Father's main goons, who E and Bleek had taken care of, all of his other workers got down with the program. It was the easiest transition that Jayde had ever seen.

"Fucking recession…and niggas still wanna get high," E quipped.

Jayde tilted down her D&G frames.

"Fucking recession and niggas will get twice as high…that's what depression does to you. We're feeding off the weak. Cashing in their unemployment checks and shit. Shit, we should tell our workers that they need to accept those shits! Bring your fucking unemployment check straight to us!"

Jayde laughed obnoxiously and E chuckled. He thought Jayde was alright, but something about her rubbed him the wrong way, well, except the way she looked.

"Yeah, that'll be some shit."

Jayde took another sip of her drink and turned to E.

"Did you handle that nigga from the bottom like I told you?"

E had to look around to make sure no one else was present.

"Told who?"

"Told *you,* fat mothafucka!" Jayde cracked. "You were sitting right in my office, and I told you to handle that nigga."

"Yeah well, I must've misunderstood, 'cause I woulda gracefully declined... I don't think we should do that anyway," E stated.

Jayde snatched off her sunglasses and looked at him.

"It wasn't a *suggestion*…it was an order."

E turned and looked at her incredulously.

"Oh, well I *suggest*…you find out who I take orders from."

Jayde sucked her teeth.

"So you will take orders from Chauncey…but not me?"

E chuckled as Chauncey made his way through the sliding doors and out to the back area.

"I take orders from nobody….but my dick!" E boasted, with arrogance.

Jayde eyed him bitterly and Chauncey approached them.

"Play nice children," he soothed, taking the lounge chair between them.

Jayde swung her long legs over the chair and got up, strutting away in her leopard print bikini. She was fuming and they knew it. When she was more than an earshot away, Chauncey turned to E.

"What's up yo, you got a problem working hand and hand wit' a female?"

E shook his head.

"Nah, I got a problem working hand and hand wit' a bitch!" E sat up and leaned into Chauncey. "Yo, it's one thing, for her to handle certain things, because you know, this her hometown. But she aint gonna be running me around like a fucking flunky. The bitch aint working wit' a full deck…Bleek said she just wanna dead that nigga from the bottom 'cause he wouldn't hit her off wit' some head!"

Chauncey threw his head back in laughter at the notion.

"C'mon son, I doubt that's the case. And what's the difference, you drop niggas all the time…I know you always got my back when some shit go down."

E shook his head.

"She aint you, C. I aint dropping nobody for her personal shit."

Chauncey nodded and sipped his Heineken.

"Don't worry about it…I'll holla at her."

175

Chauncey wondered how he was going to get them to see eye to eye. E would have to understand that between Chauncey and Jayde, many of the decisions would be made. But Jayde would have to understand that E was not like Bleek, he was no one's soldier. He was a warrior. She would have to respect him.

"The fucking toilet paper is rough as sand paper!" Jayde barked from inside the house.

"That's 'cause this a man's shit," E mumbled. "And she could get out, and go find some Charmin."

Chauncey laughed.

"Maybe you should go in there and hit her off wit' some head, then ya'll can be friends."

E looked at him and gave him the middle finger.

"Fuck you, muhfucka."

Chauncey laughed harder because he knew E well.

"Aw man, yeah. You got a problem working with a female," he concluded.

E twisted his mouth up and took a sip from his beer.

"A bitch…," he reiterated. "A bitch."

"See, that's what you get, going jogging and shit like some white woman in Central Park," Tatum joked, as Sasha cracked up laughing.

"Shut up, Tay! I told you, I wanna lose like ten pounds. Shit, my ass is getting too big…it looks like yours," Sasha cracked. Tatum sucked her teeth and laughed sarcastically.

"Ha...Ha... Ha…whatever!"

Sasha sighed and smiled, glad that she was talking to her best friend. Tatum had returned her call and couldn't believe the chain of events that Sasha had filled her in on.

"But seriously Tay, can you believe that bitch had the nerve to show up at my house? Talking about she had something to tell me."

There was a pause as Tatum pondered on what the reason could have been for Neli's surprise visit.

"Yeah, that's crazy. I would have at least found out what she wanted though." Tatum was beyond curious.

"Please Tatum, she wanted to stir up more drama. Probably try to get inside my head or something. Or offer some punk ass apology. But she could save it!"

Tatum nodded, knowing Sasha was probably right, she had other bones to pick with Sasha though.

"So, what are you gonna do about Chauncey? And I'd hate to say it, but I knew this was gonna happen." Tatum was not shocked at all to learn that they were fucking.

Sasha bit the skin off of her lip in nervousness and laid down on her couch. She was so conflicted.

"I don't know, girl. Why did he have to come and fuck shit up?" Sasha thought aloud.

"Sasha, it's not Chauncey's fault. You should've never married Mike, knowing that he wasn't what you wanted."

Sasha became defensive.

"Well, I *thought* he was what I wanted."

"No, you thought he was what you *needed*."

Sasha remained quiet, knowing Tatum was right. She wanted to change the subject.

"So, how's paradise?" She sang happily. Tatum smiled and shook her head. *Same old Sasha.*

"Listen Sash, you don't have to tell me what you're gonna do, but you *are* gonna have to make a decision, mama. You can't keep stringing them both along. Chauncey loves you, but he aint the type of dude that'll take the backseat to Mike for long." Tatum knew by Sasha's silence that she was not in the mood for her lectures so she eased up. "And paradise…is amazing. This man…damn." That's all Tatum could say.

Sasha smiled, truly happy for her.

"Aw, Tay. I'm so happy for you. Have you spoken to the girls?"

Tatum broke out of her reflection on her Ree fantasy and thought of her nieces. She missed them dearly.

"Yeah, they're actually doing good. Tangee's crazy about her mother now, and Chanel...she's crazy about boys. She said she has two male friends now. She goes no, auntie, they're not my boyfriends. They're boys, who are friends."

They both laughed and Sasha snickered.

"See, I knew that was my secret child right there."

The girls chit chatted for a few more minutes before Sasha had to leave. She was going to start applying to medical schools, against Mike's wishes.

He kept reiterating to her that she could just be a housewife. But even in Sasha's spoiled nature, independence was always a quality she loved to possess. He would just have to deal with it.

"Knock 'em dead girl, good luck," Tatum encouraged.

"Thanks girl, love you."

"Love you, too." And then they hung up.

"Miss Trinity, please...why are you doing this?"

"Shut up, Rodney," she whispered, pushing him against the wall, and locking the janitorial closet from the inside.

Trinity had Rodney the bell boy under hostage, and he was terrified. She had approached him on the elevator and told him that she needed to speak with him, and when she directed him to the closet and he questioned her in confusion, she pushed him inside. And now, here they were.

"Please Miss Trinity, I do not want any trouble."

"For the last time Rodney, shut the hell up," she hissed.

Trinity began unbuckling his pants as Rodney breathed hard in bewilderment. All he could think about was his job, his family, and not jeopardizing either.

When she pushed his pants down to his ankles, she could see that he was not erect. Probably from the surprise and fear that he was experiencing.

Shit!

She tried a different approach.

"Okay Rodney, don't worry," she whispered sultrily. "I'm gonna make you feel good, okay? And I won't tell anyone, it will be our secret."

She was stroking his dick and whispering in his ear.

Rodney looked around the dark closet anxiously. He was so baffled.

"Please...I do not want to feel good...I just want to do my job. Please."

His self righteousness was really pissing her off.

"Rodney!" She yelled. She realized how aggressive she was coming off and went softer.

"Rodney, I will pay you... Five hundred dollars, Rodney."

A million things ran through Rodney's mind. His wife. His job. How bad he needed that money. But all he really could manage was...

"Wh...wh...why?"

Trinity licked his ear seductively.

"Because I want you," She lied.

She dropped to her knees before he could protest further and took his ashy dick into her moist mouth fully.

"Oh my," Rodney gasped, surprised and still rigid and tense.

As she continued, he couldn't help himself from enjoying it, and he really couldn't stop his growing erection. Here Trinity was, his manager, his beautiful manager, sucking him off in the closet.

She could feel his dick jump, ready to ejaculate.

Damn, already, she mused.

She stood up and hiked up her skirt and then leaned against the wall, pulling him in front of her and pushing all five inches of Rodney into her.

"That's right Rodney, fuck me. Fuck me baby," she encouraged. Trinity was moaning sexily, trying to really put him into it. It didn't take much, and before long Rodney was shouting.

"Oh my gudness Miss Trinity, it's cumin, it's cumin...oh yes."

179

He went to pull out of her but she grabbed him tight and held him close.

"No!" She screamed. "Keep it in."

"Huh?" Rodney asked, still lost in pleasure and in his pre-ejaculatory phase. He pumped in and out of her, feeling himself on the verge.

"I said keep it in," she repeated still holding him tight. "Cum in me, Rodney...Cum in me."

Sasha finger combed her hair as she approached the front door. She stopped at the wall mirror in the entrance hallway and admired her appearance. Her red, knit, HOD sweater dress really hugged her curves and made her caramel complexion and shiny jet black hair sparkle. She smiled in satisfaction and then pulled the door open.

"Hey," she greeted Chauncey, casually. She reached into him to take a sleeping Aubrey out of his arms. "How was she?"

"She was fine...she was, Bri. She's my daughter Sasha, I wasn't babysitting," Chauncey reminded her.

Sasha rolled her eyes.

"I know that...I was just saying..."

Chauncey looked her up and down as she stood there. He couldn't get her off of his mind, and he didn't know how long he would be able to handle this situation with Mike.

"You look good," he complimented. She raised her eyebrows as if she wasn't expecting it, although she was anticipating it.

"Really... thanks."

Chauncey nodded and placed his hands in his jeans.

"Can I come in?"

"For what?" Sasha shot back, defensively. She wanted to look good to him, she wanted him to want her, but she didn't want to become weak and sleep with him.

Chauncey chuckled at her suspicion.

"To use the bathroom."

Sasha stood there and bit her lip in deliberation. Mike would be home at anytime.

"I don't know…Mike will be home soon…."

Chauncey looked at her like she was crazy.

"So? The fuck Sash, you act like this nigga be beating you or something. Let me find out yo… I'll kill his soft ass."

Chauncey made his way inside, moving past her with no invitation, clearly upset. "My fucking daughter live here, and you telling me I can't come in?"

He kept walking through the house, toward the guest bathroom. Sasha sighed and closed the door, and then went upstairs to put Aubrey in her bed.

She laid Aubrey softly down and shook her head from side to side.

"This nigga really think he run shit," she mumbled, pulling the covers over Aubrey.

"Oh, and I don't?"

She turned around startled, and found Chauncey standing there, leaning against the doorway with a smile.

"What are you doing up here?"

He didn't answer. Instead he just stood there, undressing Sasha with his eyes. She shook her head, knowing what he was thinking.

"Unh-unh…no. Not gonna happen."

She went to walk past him but he grabbed her firmly by the arm and pulled her into him.

"No," she murmured softly.

He pulled her into the hallway and held both of her arms, bringing his face to hers.

"Get off of me, Chauncey."

She struggled with him, truly not wanting to take such a major risk.

"Come here," he whispered deeply, pinning her against the wall.

"No…" But he silenced her with a zealous kiss.

She couldn't help but to kiss him back.

Damn.

Then, his hands slid under her dress.

"Please Chauncey…"

She could feel his fingers begin to play her like a guitar. "What…what if Mike comes?"

Chauncey kissed her deeply again and picked her up, holding her ass with his hands. He carried her into their bedroom; he wanted to leave cum stains on Mike's side of the bed.

Sasha knew what she was doing was wrong, horrible. But Chauncey was her drug; he was like the purest dope.

He threw her onto the bed and stood up and unbuckled his pants, as she breathed heavily in lust.

"We have to be quick, okay?"

He didn't answer; he just stared at her hungrily.

As he laid her down and proceeded to enter her, Sasha's mind traveled to a fucked up land where pleasure meets deceit. Her heart felt heavy as she thought of what she was doing to Mike and how no matter what, she didn't want to stop.

"God…I wish I knew how to say no to you," she moaned to Chauncey as he began to stroke her.

"No you don't," he whispered, hitting a spot that made her yelp in satisfaction. "No, you don't."

After the episode, Chauncey stood buckling his pants as Sasha combed her hair down.

"We can't keep doing this," she confessed.

"I agree," Chauncey concurred nonchalantly, ready for her to kick Mike to the curb.

She turned to look at him, truly not knowing what she wanted. She loved Chauncey, but Mike was what she needed. She still wanted to be a doctor, and she still wanted to lead a straight life, with a straight family, no worries. She shook her head in confusion but the footsteps that she heard coming from downstairs snapped her out of it.

"Oh shit!" She whispered.

Chauncey remained calm but looked at her like, 'well, what you want me to do?'

"Go in Aubrey's room...go!" She ordered silently. "I'll say you came up to put her to bed."

Before Chauncey could say anything, Sasha heard her name being called.

"Sasha...Sasha, you here?"

She put her hand on her chest and breathed a sigh of relief.

"Oh my god, it's just Jayde...Come on."

"Who?" Chauncey asked, confused and making his way down the stairs after her.

Jayde saw Sasha coming down and met her at the stairs.

"Girl, your door was wide open! What the hell is wrong with you?"

When she saw Chauncey coming down behind her, she knew what was up, and judging by Chauncey's wide eyes and slightly open mouth, she knew he was shocked to see her.

"Wide open?" Sasha asked, knowing that she had closed the door. The revelation gave her a creepy feeling. She tried to shake it off and turned to Chauncey.

"Jayde, this is my...Aubrey's father, Chauncey. Chauncey, this is Jayde."

Chauncey grilled Jayde, or J-Murder as he knew her, with disbelief and extended his hand.

"Jayde...as in J...like with a J, right?"

Jayde was cool as a cucumber.

"That's right...pleased to meet you."

"Uh-huh...yeah, okay." Chauncey couldn't believe this shit.

Sasha looked at Chauncey, feeling like he was being a tad rude to her friend. She heard a noise upstairs and figured Aubrey was up.

"Excuse me for a minute," she said, nudging Chauncey on her way up the stairs. She gave him a face like a mother gives a child who's in trouble. Once Sasha was up the stairs, Chauncey turned to Jayde with cold eyes.

"What the fuck is going on?"

"Nothing...I can explain."

"Fuck is you making friends wit' my people for?"

183

"Chauncey...me and Sasha have been friends, for a very long time."
Chauncey furrowed his eyebrows.
"So you knew about me?"
"Of course," she stated calmly.
"So why the fuck you aint say you was Sasha's friend?" Chauncey asked, animated. Jayde shrugged.
"What difference would it have made?"
"Maybe that would have affected if I chose to do business with you or not."
Jayde laughed at his erratic suggestion.
"I think not...you know how sweet that deal was. Besides, Sasha doesn't know what I do, and I didn't want it to come from someone else's mouth when it hasn't even come from mine."
Chauncey folded his arms across his chest.
"Yeah, well it's about to come from one of our mouths, so you choose."
Jayde was taken aback by Chauncey's anger in the situation.
"Why are you so upset?"
Chauncey could hear Sasha's footsteps upstairs, so he leaned into Jayde to answer quickly, knowing she would be back.
"Because...Sasha had enough fucked up people and shady ass friends in her life... and she don't need no more. I gave my word that I would never keep no more shit from her, and I'm not fucking that up. So you tell her...*Fucking tell her*," he hissed.
Jayde nodded slowly and leaned against the wall. She really preferred to keep her position unknown, except to people in the business. But she figured Chauncey was right, she didn't want to be another person to hold a killer secret from Sasha. She stared Chauncey in the eye.
"So I guess you done had your share of fuck ups, huh...you aint fucking up no more? I'm glad... at least I know you won't be breaking her heart again."
Chauncey's answer was a cold gaze and Sasha began making her way back down the stairs, with a smile.

"I'll tell her," Jayde consented aloud.

Sasha reached them and breathed a sigh, hearing Jayde, but not thinking too much of it due to the calmness of her voice.

"Tell me what?"

Chauncey put his hands behind his back and stared at Jayde sternly as she turned and faced Sasha stone-faced.

"I'm a queen pin, Sasha. I sell drugs…and I sell a lot of them."

Chapter 17 – Trust

"Now, why it gotta be all of that?"

"I'm just saying…hurry up. 'Cause I'm starving."

Ree turned and looked at Tatum and shook his head playfully as she laughed.

"That's a damn shame…you willing to leave me, just to make the reservation? For real?" Ree asked with a smile, unlocking his office door.

The lights were out and there was no one around, so the back area was dead quiet.

"It aint my fault you left your wallet, man," Tatum quipped, ready to head to this new hot restaurant that they had reservations for.

"Yeah, well I don't think you would really leave me. Nah."

Ree hit the light switch and did a double take. Both he and Tatum's eyes fell onto the sight on top of his desk.

"What the fuck?" Tatum mumbled.

"Oh my god! I thought you would be alone."

"What?" Ree asked, not knowing what else to say at the moment. The situation had him off guard.

Trinity stood up, covering her breasts and her private areas with her hands. She had been lying naked on Ree's office desk awaiting his return. She was now disappointed and humiliated that Tatum was with him.

"Elsa said you forgot your wallet…she said you were coming back for it…"

Ree furrowed his eyebrows wondering what kind of psycho broad he had gotten involved with, as Trinity rambled on as if her lying there naked had been no big deal. But it was a big deal, and Tatum was about to show her.

"Are you fucking crazy, bitch?"

Tatum didn't know what to think. Was Ree still fucking this broad, is that why she felt like she could do this? Either way, she would deal with him next. Trinity was disrespecting and she needed to be reprimanded.

"You fucking hoe bitch!" Tatum screamed, lunging at Trinity. She grabbed her hair and punched her hard against the side of her head before Ree grabbed her by the waist and pulled her back.

"Tatum!"

Trinity held her head in pain and screamed distraughtly.

"Get your ghetto ass away from me!" She scrambled from Tatum, who was trying her best to get to her.

"Let me go, Ree! You protecting this bitch?"

Ree pushed Tatum over to the wall and held her against it, trying to calm her down.

"Fuck her Tatum, calm down!"

"Fuck me, Sean?" Trinity cried. "Fuck me?"

Elsa made her way to the back and dropped her jaw in amazement. The boss... the boss' new lady... Miss Trinity naked... juicy, juicy, juicy.

"I hate you Sean! How could you do this to me?" Trinity continued to yell as Ree held his weight against Tatum, who was breathing heavy with slit angry eyes. She was trying hard to still break free.

"Calm down, okay?" He whispered in her ear composedly. "I'm gonna handle this."

Tatum matched his stare, not responding.

Security made their way in the room but quickly paused when they saw that the situation involved Ree.

"Is there anything you need for us to do, Mr. Knights?"

They looked at a naked Trinity who was too hysterical to put her clothes on. She was bawling crying.

Ree could feel Tatum's body become less rigid and he knew she was calming. He ran his hand over his head.

"Yeah, uh, step outside... and keep an eye on her," he said pointing.

187

"Me?" Tatum asked, bewildered. "You want *me* to step outside?" Her face was twisted in anger and hurt.

"Nigga, you must be crazy."

She was fuming and Ree looked at her sternly.

"Tatum. I told you I will handle it. Trust me to do that."

Tatum stared at him blankly, wanting to yank him by the dreads. He could see her fury.

"Please Tatum, step outside and wait for me."

The security guard reached for her arm but she snatched it away and stormed out the room, her Christian Louboutins leaving smoke in her tracks.

Once everyone was gone and the door was closed, Ree turned to Trinity. He picked up her clothes and handed them to her, slightly embarrassed for her.

Then he sighed and tried to choose his words wisely, knowing that she wasn't working with a full deck.

"Look, Trini...I'm sorry. I know...I know, this may be hard for you to deal with. And truthfully, I didn't know your feelings were that involved..."

Trinity chuckled at that statement, while she dressed, and he continued.

"You're a good girl...you really are. But Tatum, she's the one. We have something that...I don't know."

He looked at her and could see her heart break, but he didn't care. She had to hear it.

"I will not tolerate this behavior...this blatant disrespect for her, or for our relationship. You know the type of person that I am, so don't try me."

The last statement frightened her. There was a frigidness and threatening tone in the way he said it, and Trinity did not want any parts of it.

"I'm...I'm sorry," she muttered halfway meaning it. She was fully dressed now.

"It won't happen again," she added sincerely.

Ree nodded promisingly.

"I know."

He turned and headed for the door as she stood wondering what he meant, until he faced her, halfway out of the room.

"You're fired, Trinity. You gotta go."

A sharp pain went through her heart and she was speechless, but Ree just walked out and walked over to security, informing them to escort her out.

He felt like he owed her enough to tell her in private and to allow her to get dressed, but that was all he owed her. She was done.

Tatum sat in a chair on the side, away from everyone, shooting Ree venomous rocks with her livid eyes. He looked at her, knowing that she was upset, but he felt Tatum had something to learn as well. When he told her that he would handle it, she would have to learn not to question him and trust that he would do so.

But Ree failed to realize that Tatum had trust issues, her heart was fragile. And little did Ree know, he had for the first time, given her reason to doubt her trust in him. Their estate was about to be the War of the Roses that night. *Round one!*

"So now you don't wanna eat?"

No answer.

"Tatum."

Silence.

"Tatum."

Silence.

"Tatum!"

"What!"

"I asked you a question...you don't-"

"No!" She screamed, as the car stopped in front of their house.

She stormed out and slammed the door and Ree took a deep breath, trying to maintain his composure before he would follow her inside.

"So, will that be all for the evening Mr. Knights?" The driver asked nervously, breaking the silence.

Ree sighed and opened up his door.

"Yeah, that'll be all. Have a good night."

He strolled unhurriedly up the walkway, toward the front door, and Tatum, who was already inside, watched him from the second floor window. She saw him reach the porch and then disappear, so she knew he was now inside.

"Tatum," his deep voice based.

She didn't respond. She was so livid with him.

"Tatum, get down here," he demanded.

Fuck it.

She approached the steps and made her way down, looking at him standing at the bottom.

"What?" She asked, with much attitude, standing on the third step up, with her hand finessing her hip.

Ree stared at her, already knowing what the predicament was. He knew women, so he could understand her anger. But the issue to him went much deeper than the surface.

"What's the problem?"

Tatum laughed before answering.

"Nothing."

"Nothing," Ree repeated, tilting his head to the side. Tatum shrugged and shook her head.

"Nope, nothing. Everything is fine."

"No it's not," he stated the obvious. "But we're gonna stand here and talk about it, until it is."

Tatum rolled her eyes.

"Well, you must plan on standing here an awfully long time then."

He didn't answer her; he just stared at her, encouraging her with his eyes to tell him what she was feeling. She became frustrated and turned to go back upstairs, she didn't want him to see her emotional.

Why he had to talk to her in private, though?

"Stay right there, Tatum," he commanded firmly. She halted and he then spoke a little softer. "Stay right there, and tell me exactly what the problem is."

She chuckled, turning to face him.

190

"The problem? Oh, I think you *know* the problem, Ree. The problem is you...playing me in front of your little *girlfriend*... making me look stupid by kicking me out of the room to talk to her. What did you have to say to her that was so private, huh Ree?"

"So is the problem how you think I made you look, or is it you not knowing what I said to her?"

"Whatever, Ree! You know what the fuck I'm talking about...why are you trying to analyze shit, huh? Why can't you just tell me the damn reason for your shady ass actions? 'Cause you hiding shit, that's why!"

Ree could feel his temper building but remained composed. He had to keep reminding himself that she was upset, but he was not used to this at all. No one, absolutely no one, had, and would ever...

"Maybe..." He spoke slowly. "What I had to tell her...was embarrassing enough, that I didn't need to do it, in front of an audience...while she was naked."

Tatum sucked her teeth.

Ree actually wanting to spare Trinity further embarrassment upset Tatum and made her face turn sour. She leaned into him.

"And maybe..." She waved her finger in his face. "You've been fucking her this whole time...and that's why the bitch felt comfortable enough to be naked...in your office! Maybe that!"

She poked him hard in the forehead and Ree grabbed her finger strongly with the quickness of catching a cobra before it strikes. So quick, and so forceful, that it scared Tatum.

He took a deep breath and squeezed her finger tighter, leaning close to her in all seriousness as her eyes grew wider. He spoke in a calm weightiness.

"Enough. I don't play these games Tatum, and I refuse to go back and forth about this. Trinity is the past. I handled that shit like I said I would. You're who I want and everyone on this island is well aware of that, including her. The fact that you are challenging that or second guessing yourself is preposterous to me. If we are going to be in a relationship, share a home, share a life, then we need to have a level of trust. I understand you may have to get used

191

to that and I'm willing to work on that with you, because I love
you." Tatum swallowed hard, feeling a little bad for her behavior
and slightly frightened, because of his. He still had a firm grip on
her finger as he spoke and there was no smile in his eyes. He was
dead serious. But she knew he would never hurt her, however she
had pressed his buttons.
"Don't ever doubt me Tatum, and don't ever question me. And
don't ever, ever put your hands on me, okay?"
She nodded slowly and felt so juvenile in her actions. She now
could see how love could have you acting completely out of
character.
"I'm sorry," she admitted, hating to apologize but knowing that she
was wrong. She should have never touched him.
He loosened his grip and the warmth slowly returned to his face.
He kissed her finger as a sentiment of affection, and stared her in
the eyes.
"How did that sorry taste coming out of your mouth?"
She snickered and shook her head from side to side.
"Um, like shit."
He laughed and then he pulled her close by her hips.
"Come here, crazy girl." He kissed her tenderly on her lips. "What
am I gonna do with you?" He asked smoothly.
Tatum raised an eyebrow and smiled.
"I can think of some things."
The two kissed again and the discussion was officially dropped.
The War of the Roses, was officially over.

"What do you want for your birthday?"
"Nothing," Sasha answered, focusing on the Sex and the City rerun
that was playing on her bedroom plasma. Aubrey lay asleep beside
her.
"Come on…I know you want something," Jayde probed, standing
next to the bed.

Mike had told Jayde that Sasha was upstairs and she had found her lying in her sweats, eating Doritos and watching television.

"I can get you anything you wanttt," she sang, trying to tempt her.

"I bet you can," Sasha quipped without looking up. She was referring to the fact that Jayde had revealed her drug cartel status to her.

Jayde rolled her eyes and folded her arms across her double breasted Dolce & Gabbana suit jacket.

"How long are you going to give me the cold shoulder for this?" Jayde finally asked.

"How long were you planning on keeping the secret?" Sasha shot back, finally looking at her seriously, letting her know that she wanted an answer. Jayde shrugged.

"I don't know…not long."

Sasha pursed her lips and turned back to the screen.

"Well, in that case. *I* don't know…not long," she added sarcastically, answering Jayde's question.

"I've apologized a million times, Sasha. Come on. That's not the kind of thing that's easy to tell someone…I mean, I didn't completely lie, I told you that I took over my father's business, and I did."

Sasha had never met Jayde's father when they were younger. She had only known Jayde's mother who had remarried when Jayde was a baby, so she had then known Jayde's stepfather as well. She had no idea that this whole time, Jayde had gotten into this life.

"Is that why you kept asking me what Chauncey was going to do when he came down here?"

Jayde nodded.

"I had a feeling that he would try to set up shop down here, yes."

Sasha chuckled mockingly.

"*Set up shop*, that's how you talk? Ms. Socialite my ass."

Jayde giggled at Sasha's snaps and Sasha had to fight back her own growing laughter. She still wanted to be mad at Jayde but found herself becoming less and less angry with each day that passed. She already had a feeling from the hotel conversation that

193

she had overheard that Jayde was into some other stuff. But Sasha loved having the ball in her court, people always spoiled her extra when she was mad at them.

"How about a party?" Jayde suggested. "I can get some big names to come through, lots of people, red carpet event."

Sasha sucked her teeth.

"Who, you and your drug lord friends, Jayde? No thanks Nino Brown. I'll pass."

Jayde pressed her lips together and let her have her fun.

"Okay, well what about a dinner? Twenty, thirty people tops. Dim lighting, linen tablecloths, your favorite cuisines-lobster, sushi, pasta, nice music, champagne, Hawaiian and Hummingbird cakes from Lulu's…"

Sasha knew Jayde had her there. She lived for Lulu's, who had the most scrumptious specialty cakes in Atlanta.

Sasha shrugged nonchalantly.

"Whatever…dinner's fine."

Jayde smirked and turned to head out.

"Very well then…I'll put it together boo." She started out but Sasha called her back.

"Jayde!"

She turned and waited, and Sasha added.

"And the Coca Cola cake."

Jayde snickered and waved as she walked away.

One woman, one party, one night, one birthday… three birthday cakes. *Gotta love Sasha.*

"Are you sure that you told her 7pm? Where is she?"

Sasha was rushing around the kitchen, putting the back on her earring, making sure all of the emergency numbers were on the fridge, and making sure that everything Aubrey may need was on hand.

"I told you…she'll be here. She is driving from campus, Sasha. And it's only 6:50," Mike reminded her. He grabbed her by the waist and pulled her close.

"Hey, relax. It's going to be fine, babe. Happy Birthday." He pecked her on the lips and she smiled lightly.

"Maybe I should just take her to my aunt's," Sasha reconsidered. "Or maybe I should just stay home."

"Sasha!" Mike exclaimed, laughing. "Amanda is a good kid, she'll take good care of Aubrey."

Mike's cousin Amanda attended Georgia Tech and had offered to watch Aubrey for them while Mike and Sasha attended her birthday dinner. She loved kids and could really use the extra money being that most college kids, were broke. Sasha had met her before, and could tell that she was a responsible and sweet girl.

"Here, have a drink with me."

Mike took out a bottle of white wine and poured them each a glass. He handed Sasha hers and smiled lovingly.

"To you…Happy Birthday."

"To me," she said raising her glass in a toast, but her elbow accidentally knocked the bottle over.

"Shit!" She cursed, as it spilled all over the counter and floor.

"It's alright, get the kitchen cleaner," Mike said calmly, grabbing some paper towels. Sasha went to the bottom counter and took out the pine cleaner.

Knock. Knock. Knock.

"That must be Amanda," he added.

Sasha wiped up the wine with the cleaner and water as Mike went to answer the door.

"Mommy, you did a boo-boo?" Aubrey asked cutely, walking into the kitchen.

"Yeah Bri-Bri, now go in the living room. Mommy doesn't want you around these chemicals."

"Hi Sasha," Amanda greeted warmly. "Whew! That pine is strong," she said covering her nose playfully.

"Yeah, I know. I'm clumsy. You can open up a window if you want," Sasha said, throwing the wet paper towels into the trash. Amanda walked into the living room and Sasha could hear her playing with Aubrey.

"Hey Aubrey! Hey girl! We gonna have fun, tonight."

"Sasha, come on, we have to go," Mike rushed her.

The dinner started at 7:30 and he knew it was no less than a half hour away.

"Okay," she agreed, knowing the floor was clean enough. She went to Aubrey and hugged and kissed her.

"Bye baby girl, mommy will be back soon, okay?"

"Okay Mommy," she murmured.

"I love you. Listen to Amanda, okay?"

Aubrey shook her head yes and Sasha kissed her again.

"Okay Amanda, my number and the number to the restaurant, as well as her father's and my aunt's number are all on the fridge. No beverages for her after 8 pm and she's bathed already. No scary movies, and no milk, okay?"

Amanda nodded.

"Okay Sasha."

Sasha turned and headed for the door where Mike was already standing and Amanda called after her.

"Oh, Sasha!"

"Yes," she said, turning around anxiously.

"Happy Birthday."

Le Cove was a brand new, fine Italian restaurant in which Jayde had rented out and shut down for Sasha's dinner. It was not hard for her to do at all, being that she was a partial owner in it.

"Happy Birthday!" She yelled, as Sasha and Mike made it through the door. Sasha looked truly gorgeous in a chocolate satin A cut dress that lay against her skin perfectly and showed off her toned legs. Her hair was pulled back in an elegant ponytail, displaying her dangling diamond earrings. Her long eyelashes curled and almost appeared false and her lips were succulent in a beige iridescent lipstick. She looked breathtaking.

"Thanks mama! Oh my god, it's gorgeous in here!" Sasha exclaimed, making her way into the dim restaurant. Jayde had it set up so nice, with floating candles in glass bowls of water. A long table with a row of roses in vases going down the center was in the middle of the room, and servers walked around serving champagne and hor'duerves to the select group who were standing around, conversing. Sasha wished that Tatum could've seen it.

She spotted a few familiar faces, like girls from the salon where she got her hair done, people from Mike's hospital, Jayde's mother, and finally, Jayde's new business associate, Chauncey. Sasha acknowledged him with her eyes, but made her rounds, saying her hellos with Mike by her side, as Chauncey's eyes stayed glued to her beauty.

"Oh, Sasha, this is Dr. Winslow," Mike introduced eagerly, as they had almost made their way around the entire room. She shook his hand and smiled, but focused on Chauncey who was now talking with some average faced, big butt female that she recognized from the salon. She noticed Mike becoming enthralled in the conversation with the fellow doctor, and used the opportunity for her escape.

Grabbing a flute of champagne, she stepped in the direction of Chauncey.

"Hello," she said to Chauncey, interrupting the girl's sentence. Her greeting dripped with a territorial sass and the girl turned and faced her.

"Oh, hey Sasha. Happy Birthday," the girl said, as if she knew her well.

"Happy Birthday, baby girl," Chauncey added with a yearning smile.

"Thanks." Sasha kept her eyes on Chauncey and waited for the girl to catch a hint. When she didn't, Chauncey broke the silence.

"Can you excuse us for a minute?"

The girl, obviously disappointed, half smiled and then walked away.

"Who was she?" Sasha asked, not masking her jealousy.

"Damn, you look good as hell." Chauncey said that like he had a hunger for her.

"Chauncey, I'm serious. Who was that chick?"

"I don't know, she just came up and started talking. But for real ma, you look *good*. I think I might need you tonight," he added in a deep whisper.

"Chauncey," she whined, starting to blush.

He took a sip of his champagne, stepping closer to her, and eyed her sincerely.

"I'm serious. You might as well tell homie that you coming home with me, you and my little princess... and that, you know...it's a wrap."

Sasha didn't answer because she felt an immense amount of pressure. She noticed Mike stealing glances in their direction.

Just then, a familiar face made their way up to them and Sasha smiled wide.

"E! How are you... how you been?"

"I'm good...how you?" He greeted with a smile.

E hugged Sasha and wished her a happy birthday and Sasha reflected on how long it had been since she'd seen him. Back in Newark, E was the one she would talk to about all of her and Chauncey's bullshit.

"Where is Bri, anyway?" Chauncey inquired matter of factly, breaking up the reunion.

"Oh, she's at home with the babysitter," Sasha said, taking a sip of her champagne.

"Babysitter?"

"Yeah, Mike's cousin Amanda...Excuse me guys, I gotta work the room," she said glancing around, noticing all eyes on them.

She strutted away, leaving them standing there and finished her rounds. E started talking to some female and Chauncey watched

Sasha, and then as if he could sense it, he looked up and noticed Mike was watching him, watch her.

They locked eyes with each other.

Both held a stare of challenge and defiance.

"Ladies and Gentlemen, I'm going to ask that we all be seated at this time," Jayde interrupted loudly.

Everyone made their way to the table and began to take their seats, with quiet chatting. Sasha and Mike sat side by side and Chauncey sat almost directly opposite of them.

Jayde, who was seated towards the end of the table, stood up, drink in her hand and tapped the glass with her fork lightly. When she had everyone's attention, she proceeded.

"I'm gonna make this quick, 'cause 1 know everyone's hungry." Everyone giggled. "I just want to make a toast... to a beautiful woman... a fantastic mother... a wonderful wife..." Sasha swallowed hard at that part as Mike wrapped his arms around her. "And an amazing friend...Sasha Seals. Oops, I mean Sasha Bernstein!" Jayde corrected, laughing, while Mike smirked. "To Sasha!" Jayde toasted and everyone followed suit.

"To Sasha!"

Sasha smiled wide, loving the attention. She noticed the waitress coming over and she was ready to eat, until...

Ding...Ding...Ding...

Chauncey tapped his glass with his fork and rose.

"If I could...just have a moment."

Everyone's eyes fell on him and Sasha noticed how almost every woman stared with lust. It was infuriating.

Mike's friends from the hospital wondered exactly who Chauncey was.

Chauncey looked at Sasha with his deep brown eyes and she tried to remain composed sitting there in Mike's arms.

"I just want to say...you and me, we been through a lot kid. A lot good...a little bad," he chuckled. "But you always held me down."

Sasha breathed hard and Jayde smiled, as Mike's friends wondered what Chauncey's thug vocabulary meant.

"You gave me a beautiful daughter…you've been a great mother to her…and I love you with all my heart for it."
Sasha felt her eyes become misty and she contemplated jumping up and kissing him right then and there, but she was scared. Chauncey stared her right in the eyes, not caring about Mike's scowl.
"I hope your day is everything you want it to be, you deserve it…you deserve the best." Chauncey said the last part with some sadness, as if he knew that he wasn't the best for her.
As he took his seat and everyone drank to the toast, Sasha eyed him speechless. She couldn't move. Mike stood up abruptly, ready to top it.
"Excuse me, I just want to make one more toast," Mike boomed, sounding flustered. Sasha noticed the waitress coming over to her.
"Excuse me, are you Sasha Bernstein?"
Sasha smiled.
"Yes, I'm sorry. You guys can start serving," she whispered as Mike stood ready to talk. She was ready to get to the good food.
The woman had an uneasy, almost worrisome look on her face and it caused Sasha's smile to slowly fade.
"I'm sorry, there's a phone call for you. They say it's urgent."
Sasha's heart beat stopped and she stood up quickly, walking hurriedly across the room.
My baby, my baby. Please let everything be okay at home.
Sasha finally reached the front of the restaurant and spotted the phone sitting on the hostess stand. She lightly pushed the hostess out of her way and frantically reached for the phone.
"Hello! Hello!"
"Mrs. Bernstein," a woman said in a comforting tone when Sasha picked up the phone. Sasha was relieved that it wasn't Amanda calling and she breathed a sigh of relief.
"Yes, this is Mrs. Bernstein," she said, warily.
"Mrs. Bernstein, this is Kathleen Philips…I'm calling from St. Joseph's hospital…in regards to your daughter, Aubrey Mills…"

The air left Sasha's body and she could only hear key words as her body began to tremble uncontrollably.

"Come here immediately…unconscious…critical condition…"

She closed her eyes and her head began to spin. Tears formed at her heart. It was like a bad dream, a worst possible nightmare.

Somebody wake me up. Please, somebody wake me up.

Her body shook violently and she dropped the phone. She had to get to the hospital, but she couldn't move.

Oh my god, my baby…My baby…My baby…My baby…

"Miss, are you okay?" The hostess asked as she noticed how pale Sasha had become and how bad she was shaking. Sasha broke down crying and grabbed onto the woman for dear life.

"Oh my godddddd! Noooooo!!!!" She wailed in dire agony and terror.

Chauncey, Mike, E, and Jayde all heard the screams and made their way quickly to the front, all fearing the worst.

Oh no, not Aubrey, Jayde prayed. *Please don't let it be Aubrey.*

Chauncey and Mike reached her first, with Jayde and E right behind them. She was holding onto the poor frightened woman who had no idea what was going on.

Chauncey grabbed her by the arms.

"What happened?" He asked, scared to his bones from her crying. His heart broke at the thought of it being something with Aubrey.

"Babe, are you okay?" Mike asked, concerned and trying to grab her from Chauncey.

"Get away from me!" Sasha screamed at Mike. "It's your fault! Your stupid ass cousin! My baby!"

She was frantic and Jayde teared up and shook her head no as E just dropped his head in worry.

Chauncey's face filled with pain as he gripped her hard. He needed answers.

"Sasha! What the fuck happened?"

She snapped into reality and realized they had to go. They had to get to their baby girl.

"We gotta go Chauncey. She's at the hospital…Bri-Bri's there," she cried hard, her words coming out in mumbles and getting caught in her throat. "And she…she won't wake up."

She broke down in his arms and tears poured from her eyes. Chauncey closed his eyes tight and squeezed his fists in pain - pure, heart wrenching pain. And something else he'd never felt before, complete fear.

"Let's go. We gotta go."

They raced to St. Joseph's in Chauncey's car, terrified and praying. When they reached the entrance, they double parked and jumped out, busting through the doors, and all sprinting to the emergency area.

Sasha, Chauncey, and Mike ran up to the receptionist.

"Please, Aubrey Mills," Chauncey said with pleading eyes.

Please tell me a room. Please, if it's a room number, then she's fine.

The young girl entered the name into the computer and gave them a solemn look.

"The doctor will be out to talk with you shortly."

Chauncey's face went blank as he cradled Sasha strongly in his arms who cried hard, hoarse moans of pain coming from her throat which sounded like a dying animal.

"Oh god, Chauncey," she cried. "Why…why can't we see her? Oh god, it's all my fault…I'm a bad mother…I left her! I left her, Chauncey!"

Chauncey could feel himself breaking down but had to remain strong, Aubrey had to be okay. She just had to.

"Can you at least tell me what happened?" He asked the girl, in almost a begging whisper. He had been unable to get anything out of Sasha.

The girl looked on, not knowing what to do. Chauncey was about to get irate, but the doctor approached.

"Mrs. Bernstein…Mr. Bernstein…" He greeted Sasha and Chauncey hastily.

"Actually, I'm Mr. Bernstein," Mike chimed, who had been playing the background the whole time, truly not knowing what to say up until this point. Anytime he tried to comfort Sasha, she would pull away and lean on Chauncey. Chauncey shot him an ice cold look and Mike retreated back to the sidelines.

The doctor ignored the unimportant comment.

"Your daughter is in ICU. She's ingested a vast amount of poison and her nervous system and vital organs are in terrible danger. We've tried a gastric lavage, in other words, the stomach pump but it seems like we may need to attempt a second option."

"A nasogastric aspiration," Sasha mumbled, knowing the procedures from medical classes.

"Yes," the doctor agreed. "She was unconscious when she arrived but we were able to revive her, although she is not stable…"

"Will she be alright?" Chauncey needed to know, not following too much of what the doctor was saying. Sasha looked up with hope, needing to hear that answer as well, but the doctor frowned slightly and dipped his eyebrows low.

"I…I'm not sure. But we're doing our best."

Chauncey's strength was gone. He wobbled slowly over to the wall and ran his hands over his face, collapsing down and sitting on the floor, with his knees to his chest.

He couldn't lose Aubrey, he couldn't lose his life.

Sasha opened her mouth in pain, like she had been stabbed in the heart, but nothing would come out. Tears clouded her vision as she gradually moved her feet, and made her way in front of Chauncey. She squatted down in front of him and laid her head on his knees, but he kept his hands over his face. Nothing short of Jesus Christ himself promising her that Aubrey would be okay would heal her agony.

She cried hard onto him, her tears and snot covering his jeans, and Chauncey felt his own tears falling, wetting his face.

Mike walked over and crouched down, rubbing Sasha on the back soothingly.

"I'm so sorry babe…it's gonna be okay. It's gonna be fine."

E sat in the chair with his head hung low, praying for little Aubrey, and Jayde covered her mouth in shock and sadness. The scene was all too unreal.

Jayde walked over to them and leaned down.

"I'm gonna call your parents, okay baby?" Sasha didn't answer, and Jayde felt her own cry coming on, seeing Sasha in so much pain. The pain of the room was so strong. "I'm gonna call Tatum too." Jayde knew how close they were, they were like sisters.

Jayde turned around and her heels clicked down the corridor as she made her way out of the exit to make the calls. She hurried faster when she felt herself breaking down. She wanted to remain strong, because that was all that she knew. But as she reached the night air, her tears ran like they were pouring from a faucet.

It didn't matter if you were the strongest of the strong, the bravest of the brave, everyone's heart went out to baby Aubrey that night. *Bri-Bri, pull through. Pull through, little Bri-Bri.*

Chapter 18 - Sin

"I can see it in your face, son…don't lie to your father, it's not wise. I'm the one person you can not fool."

"What are you talking about?" Ree asked, feigning ignorance to his father's accusations. They were seated in his living room, both with their choice of poison. Ree's being a blunt and his father's, a drink.

"You know exactly what I'm talking about Sean. And let me just add, your discontentment will always lead you in search of new things. And new things, won't always mean better." His father's warning came accompanied with a worried smirk.

Ree massaged his temples with his forefinger and thumb. His father's logic was giving him a headache.

"Pop, I don't know what you think you know…but I'm content. I have what I want…I have *who* I want…I'm satisfied." Even as the words came out of Ree's mouth, he knew they were not totally true.

"Really?"

"Really," Ree assured confidently.

"Okay, so even the smallest part of you has no desire to dabble into anymore of your past lifestyle? No drugs, no fast money… no murder?"

Ree let the question penetrate and then he shrugged and shook his head no.

"Nah. Why would I?"

His father laughed like he knew something Ree did not.

"So, if that's the case, why didn't you quit long ago? You've had enough money for years, correct? So it wasn't the money."

Ree and his father shared an intense stare as his father continued.

"No son, I would say…I would say it was the thrill that kept you. The allure of the game. You were a gangster, like myself, and like your grandfather, because you were good at it. And now that you aren't anymore…you don't know what else to be. Of course, Tatum being here has made it better. You know, getting the girl always makes it better…" His father chuckled. "But all in all…you're miserable. You're bored."

Ree inhaled his weed smoke and looked on blankly. He could only produce one response.

"Once you get away, it's idiotic to go back." His statement came out more as a question and Ree's father nodded, knowing that he knew his son well. Before he could reply, Tatum came storming into the room. She was distraught in tears.

"I…I have to go."

Ree stood up and went to her, concern on his face. His father looked on, also concerned.

"What's wrong?"

She covered her mouth and her voice cracked as she spoke.

"It's Aubrey…she's in the hospital. Jayde says she's in critical condition…I have to get to Sasha."

Ree sighed, devastated to hear the news. He knew this was crushing for Sasha, and Chauncey.

"Okay, I'll call the jet."

He grabbed Tatum up and held her close, and she wept. He placed his hand behind her head as she cried into his chest.

"Oh my god, Ree. What if she doesn't make it?"

"It's gonna be alright Tatum. She's going to be fine." And then he pulled back, holding her shoulders, and looked in her eyes, seeing how scared and worried she was. It caused him to decide. "I'm coming with you."

"Are you sure, that this is…you know, smart?" Tatum asked, as her and Ree boarded his jet. She was devastated and her mind was on Aubrey, but she also knew that the last time she had checked,

Ree was a fugitive on the run. Now he was flying with her back into the states.

"It's fine," he replied, taking his seat next to her.

"But, what if someone recognizes you?"

Ree looked out of the small jet window into the black night and answered.

"No one's gonna recognize me."

Tatum stared at him and couldn't believe how calm he was.

"But what if-"

"Ssshhh," he said, cutting her question off, and caressing her face with his hand. "It's okay. No more what ifs, okay?"

Tatum nodded and softly kissed the inside of his palm and he pulled her face close and kissed her forehead. As they began to ascend, the fleeting thought of coming clean to her briefly entered his mind.

Tatum had asked him before if he had been back to the states since he'd left, and he had told her no. She had also asked if he had spoken to Chauncey, and he had denied that as well. As the small plane made its way into the air, Ree reflected on when he had made this same trip back to the states about two years ago.

"You got five minutes," the correctional officer had whispered to Ree.

"Five minutes? Is that what fifteen g's is worth these days?" Ree had humored. "That's almost half your salary, nigga."

The guard snickered.

"Yeah, well if I get caught, then that's my job."

Ree chuckled at the rip off, and sat in the darkness in the middle of the quad, on a bench.

It was almost 1 am. and he was inside of the Prison in Rahway, waiting for Chauncey to be brought down out of his cell.

After a few minutes, he could see the dark figure make its way to him, dressed in his prison uniform and accompanied by another sideways C.O.

"Damn, nigga. You everywhere, huh?" Chauncey whispered with a smile, amused at Ree's power and pull. Respect was the only man in Chauncey's life that he had ever...well, respected. Meeting him when he was so young, Ree was almost like an uncle, or a big brother to him.

Ree stood and the two went from a hood handshake to a half way hug as Ree patted him on the back.

"How they treating you in here?"

"Cant complain. Bricks and bars, aint nothing."

Ree nodded and looked up to make sure the officers were a distance away.

"Alright. Well look, I don't have too much time, but I wanted to let you know...everything is all set up for you. I know we didn't talk about it to this extent...but a few things came up. Everything is on you now, I'm out."

Chauncey looked on with a million emotions in his face - honor, eagerness, disappointment, and surprise just to name a few. Ree continued.

"I know you got a lot to learn, but at the same time, you're a natural born leader, so you'll learn on your own. The only thing I can tell you is...you gotta tone it the fuck down. No more shine, no more floss, and no more temper. Everything is calculated from now on. You're a boss, so move accordingly."

Chauncey took it all in and then lightly smiled.

"Man I don't know why you telling me all this shit for...you gonna lay low 'til shit cool down, and then you gonna come back." Chauncey laughed, in a way wanting his words to be true. I mean, of course he wanted to be boss, who doesn't. But at the same time, he and Ree were a balance. And with that Ree status, comes a lot of problems and headaches. *Could he handle it?* Chauncey added.

"Man, plus you got too many sweet things lined up, boss. That new connect. Not to mention your master plan you been working on, that's all you."

Ree sighed and nodded.

"Well, that's your master plan now. And that connect, he gonna be waiting on your call when you get out. You make sure you get E to set up your shit for you while you in here. He's your next in command, and he's a good choice. He's loyal to you. Don't say shit on these phones... and remember don't let none of these niggas catch no breaks. Make them respect you, just be smart."

Chauncey soaked it up like a sponge but felt like he should be holding a pen and a pad. *Would this be his last conversation with his boss? ...Former boss?*

They stood, knowing that the five minutes was long up, and as they shared another manly embrace, Chauncey could literally feel the passing of the torch in the air, and Ree could feel a part of himself being left behind.

He left the jail, never looking back, and had one more stop to make before heading back to Jamaica.

It was the next night and Ree had been sitting in front of Tatum's house for hours.

The dark blue van was almost invisible against the night, and he relaxed in the passenger seat, blowing on his signature premium blend of herbs.

His monotony was broken when her Escalade pulled up on the street and parked right in front of her house. He glanced at his Audemars Piguet watch and saw that it was past 9pm.

She must be coming from her night class.

He watched as she stepped out of her truck, dressed in jeans, boots, and a leather jacket for the January weather. Her long hair blew in the night briskness. It had been about six months since he had left her standing in her hallway and she still stopped his heart. Unfortunately he couldn't say anything to her, because this trip was not in her favor.

"Yo boss, I don't know if this nigga coming back here tonight? You sure you don't want me to just handle it?" Deets, one of Ree's soldiers, had asked.

"We wait," Ree ordered, not taking his eyes off of Tatum.

209

She picked up her book bag out of the backseat and looked around with apprehension at the empty and dark block. Ree could see the slight nervousness in her eyes and body language, from it being so late.

Don't you worry sweetheart, I'm here. Nobody would dare do anything to you.

She closed the door and put the alarm on her truck, hurrying to her house and up her steps. As she unlocked the door and pushed it open, Ree's face dropped in regret.

Goodnight, baby girl.

She closed the door behind her, without looking up, and then she was gone.

About another four hours had passed before they saw what they had been waiting for, and Tatum's brother Chris pulled up onto the block in his Beamer. Just to their luck, Tatum had taken the last spot on the opposite side of the street, so Chris had to park two spaces behind the van. Ree smirked as he heard the Mobb Deep beats vibrating the quiet of the night from Chris' system, even through his closed windows.

Son they shook, cause aint so such thing as halfway crooks
Scared to death, scared to look. They shook!

He figured the scene ironic being that Chris was the most shook, halfway crook that he had ever encountered.

You aint a crook son...
You just a shook one...

As the beats came to a sudden halt, Deets discreetly exited the van and crouched down behind it, nestled in between another car. Ree slid gradually over into the driver's seat.

He could see through his rearview as Chris exited the car and stumbled drunkenly down the sidewalk. Chris approached closer to the van and Ree's veins turned cold as if they were pumping ice. Cold, for revenge.

Just as Chris neared the van, Deets swiftly jumped out and yoked him up, pressing the burner to his neck.

"Surprise mothafucka!"

He opened up the back door and threw Chris into the van, jumping in behind him, and Ree slickly pulled off into the night.

As Deets held the gun pressed against Chris' cheek, Ree looked through the rearview mirror with a smile.

"You missed me, sugarfoot?"

Chris looked up at the cold murderous glare and threw up instantly. He just knew that his sister had spared his life before, but he was wrong.

"Aw shit, this mothafucka threw up!" Deets screamed, smelling the Hennessey mixed with Kennedy fried chicken. "I think some of that shit got on me!"

Deets smacked him with the gun out of frustration, and Ree laughed smoothly.

"That's enough Deets, don't worry...we have time for all of that."

Chris lay on the floor of the van with a pounding, bleeding head but he heard Ree's words.

"Where...where are you taking me?" He mumbled, incoherently. *Why weren't they just shooting him and calling it a day?*

Ree looked through the mirror again with a serious expression.

"Oh, we're taking you somewhere fun...you like fun right?" When Chris didn't answer, out of pure fear and defeat. Ree just nodded.

"Yeah Chris, we're gonna have some fun."

Ree walked through the long, dark, and narrow tunnel, the ankle high water splashing every time he took a step. He had waited in the van for about twenty minutes as his boys warmed Chris up, aka, beat the shit out of him. And now, he was ready to wrap it up. He reached a circular metal door at the end of the tunnel and pushed it open.

When he entered, he saw Deets and Fats, along with a few other soldiers, out of breath and doubled over, saturated in blood.

Fats, obviously named for his obesity, was the most out of breath, sounding as if he were having an asthma attack as he held a metal baseball bat in his hand, covered in blood.

Chris hung from the ceiling in chains, in the middle of the room, butt naked and only semi conscious from the agonizing pain. The place was damp and dark, and rodents scurried sporadically around.

"Yall niggas need to get ya stamina up," Ree mused at his soon to be former crew.

He walked up to Chris and tilted his head to the side, placing his hands in his pockets.

"Damn Chris, you don't look so comfortable, man."

Chris cried, although no tears were coming out. He now realized that snitching on Ree was the worst mistake of his life. He should have ate whatever numbers those cops hit him with. At least he would still be alive when he was done serving them.

"I'm sor…" he whispered weakly.

Ree nodded understandingly.

"I'm sorry too, Chris…You know, I'm sorry that you're not having as much fun as I thought you would. I thought you would feel at home in the sewer. All rats, should feel at home…in the sewer."

Chris tried to talk, but Ree just pulled out his Glock and pressed it to his own lips.

"Ssshhh, don't talk Chris. It's pointless."

Chris whimpered as the rest of Ree's crew stood up, ready to leave the pungent sewer.

As Ree neared Chris, he managed to make out some of what he was mumbling.

"My sister…my daughters…"

Ree shook his head affirmatively.

"Oh yeah, don't worry about them. They'll be fine," Ree assured him. "They're better off without you. You would've brought them more harm than good anyway."

Chris dropped his head in defeat and Ree aimed his gun.

With his finger on the trigger, he lowered it to Chris' manhood and pulled.

"Aarghhhh!" Chris shouted in agony, from the feel of his dick being blasted in pieces.

"Shit," Deets, grunted.

Ree thought he would enjoy seeing Chris suffer but in all actuality, he just wanted the snake dead. Off the earth.

He had a fleeting thought of Tatum and it fucked him up. Seeing her had taken some of the joy out of this. He shook his head at how she had crept into his thoughts at a time like this. She was a true weakness.

He lifted the gun, aiming at Chris' head and as he squinted, ready to fire, he heard Tatum's voice, back in her hallway when he was ready to kill Chris the first time.

If you do this, I will never forgive you.

Ree closed his eyes trying to block the images of Tatum out, and then he re-opened them, looking Chris in his sad and pathetic face. And then, without a second thought, he pulled the trigger.

Boom!

"What are we doing back here, boss?"

Ree paused for a second before answering.

"Just give me a minute."

He toyed with Chris' keys in his hand, and then swiftly hopped out of the van, took a look around, and then headed for Tatum's house. As he walked up the steps and entered, the smell of lavender and vanilla penetrated his nostrils.

The house was dark, but he could hear the television from upstairs on. It was after 3 am. so Ree knew that Tatum had fallen asleep with the television on, as she normally did.

He crept up the stairs, and made his way past the room that Chanel and Tangee were asleep in, and then he approached Tatum's bedroom at the end of the hall.

He could hear her lightly snoring, so he made his way quietly inside and could see the imprint of her gorgeous body through the blanket. Her long black hair was fanned out against her pillow, and her serene face peeked from under the covers. She appeared angelic.

Ree watched her sleep for a few moments, and then he leaned over and placed his nose to her hair, inhaling deeply. He used to love to fall asleep with her head on his chest, adoring the smell of her hair. He used his finger to softly trace the bridge of her nose and she stirred gently. He froze and after a few seconds, she was back in her sleep. He didn't want to risk her waking, so he knew that he had to leave.

Ree leaned down for one final moment with her, and kissed her so soft, it was as light as a feather on her cheek. And then he whispered in her ear.

"I'm sorry...I had to."

When Tatum awoke a few minutes later, he was well gone and she was sure that it was just another one of her dreams. This time, she could smell him, so it was a good one. She found the large roll of money on her nightstand and figured it was a gift from her brother.

"Thanks Chris," she whispered.

And that would be the last gift that her brother had ever given her.

"Where are you right now?"

"Huh?" Ree asked, snapping back into the present.

Tatum used her forefinger to tap his temple.

"Here...where are you in here?" She wanted to know where his mind was, and she hoped it wasn't on second guessing this trip. She appreciated his support but she didn't want him to take any huge risks, and she didn't want to risk losing him either.

He grabbed her hand and brought it to his lips, kissing it.

"I'm here."

He couldn't believe it either. He was there, and more importantly, she was there.

Tatum rested her head back on the custom leather seats in the leer jet and sighed.

"I can't believe this is happening. I really hope Bri-Bri will be okay..." Tatum couldn't fathom anything happening to little sweet and innocent Aubrey.

Ree held her hand tighter, and knew as her man, his job was to rest any worries that she may have, regardless of his own.

"She will be…," Ree affirmed, hoping that his words were true. "She will be."

"Mrs. Bernstein," the receptionist called lightly to get her attention. Sasha lifted her head and turned, her face swollen and red from crying.

The receptionist approached her, accompanied by a tall, thin white woman who stared at Sasha blankly. Sasha stood up, sensing the enmity, and Chauncey stood next to her.

"Yes."

"Mrs. Bernstein, this is Ms. Cross from…"

"Child Protective Services," the woman interrupted, looking at Sasha confrontationally. Sasha furrowed her eyebrows in anger.

"Okay?" she responded, defensive, as Chauncey sucked his teeth dismissively. Their daughter was in critical condition, and here these mothafuckas wanted to come with this bullshit.

"Okay?" The woman spoke sarcastically. "Okay…so you left your daughter alone. Okay, so you're one year old daughter ingested hazardous materials. Okay, yeah. That's okay."

Sasha flinched, ready to knock this lady's teeth in, but Chauncey gripped her by the hips.

"I didn't leave my daughter *alone*. Are you crazy, lady? I would never do that! I left her with a babysitter. I left her with my husband's cousin."

At that time Mike had made his way back from the vending machine and stood on the other side of Sasha.

"What's going on?" He asked, but no one answered.

"Where is she, anyway?" Chauncey asked, wondering where this little bitch of a babysitter was.

"*She* is nowhere to be found, if there is a *she* at all. When the police arrived, there was no one in the home and it appeared there hadn't been in a while."

What? Sasha thought not believing that Amanda had left her baby. Sasha was also sickened by this woman's condescending tone and she rolled her neck and squinted her eyes.

"And how did the police get called? If there was no one home, how did anyone know to call the police?" Sasha asked as if saying 'duh'.

"I don't have time for this. My baby is fighting for her life, and you want to come over here with this bullshit!"

"Yo lady, I think you need to go 'head with all this. It's not the time." Chauncey waved his hand at her.

"And you are… the husband? Was it your cousin who was the alleged babysitter?"

"Alleged?" Sasha shot angrily, as Chauncey chuckled at the woman's ignorance.

"Nah, I'm the father."

"I'm the husband," Mike added.

"Nigga, is that your signature line for the night? We know you the mothafuckin' husband!" Chauncey barked, getting angry and walking up on Mike, who stood with his shoulders squared ready to fight.

Sasha jumped in between them.

"Chauncey! Stop it!"

The woman scribbled in her pad.

"So let me get this straight? Your daughter is only one year old, yet you are married… to someone who is not the father?"

This time Sasha was the one ready to fight.

"Fuck you, lady!"

"Okay, lets all calm down," the receptionist intervened, placing her hand on Sasha's chest.

Mike took a deep breath after scowling at Chauncey, and then he turned to the woman.

"Miss, Sasha's daughter will actually be two in March, not that it means anything…and my cousin, Amanda Bernstein, was the babysitter. She's a student at Georgia Tech, you can look it up."

The woman nodded.

"And do you have any idea why she wasn't present when police arrived on the premises?"
Mike shook his head as Sasha stood with her arms folded. Chauncey turned his back, not giving this woman any more of his time.
"I…I don't know why she wasn't there. But I hope that she is okay."
Sasha hadn't even considered that maybe something had happened to Amanda, she was just so upset with her for not being around.
The woman looked at the group and then nodded again.
"One more question…do you always leave chemicals accessible to your daughter?"
"My house is baby-proofed, lady. All of my cabinets have safety locks," Sasha sassed.
"Really?" The woman asked challenging.
"Really."
"Well, the police found a half bottle of pine cleaner on the kitchen floor…but I guess that's a safe place for it, huh?"
The woman could tell by the pain and shame in Sasha's face that she had touched a nerve. Mike shut his eyes, remembering them rushing out of the house and Sasha sat down slowly in one of the chairs, as if the wind had been knocked out of her. Tears began to fall from her eyes.
"I…I made a mistake," she whimpered.
Chauncey didn't know the full story but he knew that he didn't like seeing Sasha so upset, especially with what was already weighing on her brain. He knew Sasha was a damn good mother, so all of this extra stuff was irrelevant.
"Okay, I think that's a wrap," Chauncey instructed, guiding the woman with his hand on her back.
"Please don't touch me," she warned.
"Well, then get the fuck outta here," he ordered.
She took one final look at them and made her way towards the doors.

"You'll be hearing from me soon," she threatened over her shoulder and Sasha closed her eyes.
Please wake me up...somebody wake me up.

Chapter 19 - Strength

The all black, tinted out Yukon truck pulled up to the back of the Wingate Hotel, with the back passenger door only feet from the fire exit and employees only entrance. This was the same Yukon that had greeted Tatum and Ree at the steps of their jet, as if they were President Obama and First Lady Michelle.

A middle aged white man, dressed in a blue suit and red tie, stood at the door, holding it slightly ajar with a welcoming smile.

"Good evening sir, welcome to the Wingate by Wyndham of Georgia," he greeted in good spirits, as Ree stepped out and escorted Tatum inside of the small entrance.

"Good evening," was Ree's casual response as he took the plastic keys from the manager.

"Good evening ma'am," he addressed Tatum. Tatum smiled through her thoughts of baby Aubrey and Sasha.

"Good evening."

As the man directed them to a back stairwell, he spoke quickly.

"Hopefully sir I have accommodated you to your liking in the short notice that I was given. Please feel free to let me know of anything, and I mean anything, you may need during your stay here."

Ree nodded and Tatum followed them up the narrow staircase that she was sure was not the one for general access.

She noticed the oversized black man who had driven the Yukon, was also following them up the steps, and was walking close behind her. He hadn't spoken more than two words since they had gotten into the car. And those two words were a 'what's good' directed to Ree. She wondered who he was.

When they reached their floor, and approached the first door in view, both the hotel manager and the big man went their separate ways and Tatum and Ree entered the room.

"Who was that?" Tatum asked once they were inside. The room had a slight chill but did have a fireplace going, and she noticed a jacuzzi off to the side which had a bottle of Ace of Spades on ice. But she doubted it would be of use, being that this was not a pleasure trip. She could see however, that the manager had done his best to have the room to Ree's standards.

"You mean the big dude... that drove us here?" Ree finally responded.

"Mmmhmm," she nodded as he tossed his duffel bag onto the bed.

"That's my man, Crush. He's a friend of mine that stays here in Atlanta." Ree walked over to the opened wall-length curtains and closed them quickly with the remote. "I've known him for a very long time. And he will be accompanying you to the hospital."

Tatum furrowed her eyebrows.

"You're not coming, too?"

He looked up at her and started to make his way over.

"I wish I could sweetheart... but I don't think that's wise. I'll be right here though. And trust me, Crush will look out for you."

Tatum shook her head nonchalantly and waved her hand, feeling silly.

"No...I'm not worried. And that was a dumb question anyway."

He held her by the shoulders.

"No question of yours is dumb, cut it out."

He kissed her forehead.

"Give Sasha and Aubrey... and Chauncey, my love. Call me as soon as you find out what's going on, okay?"

There was a light tap on the door and Tatum nodded.

"Okay," she agreed.

Ree walked over to the door, his swagger more dominant in every step, and when he opened it, Tatum saw that it was the same big man.

"Ready?" big man asked, in his deep husky voice.

Okay, three words, Tatum thought as she made her way to the door, hospital bound.

"Oh my god, I'm so happy you're here," Sasha confessed, holding Tatum tight in the middle of the lobby.
"Are you crazy? This is my god baby we're talking about…how is she?" Tatum asked, concerned and nervous.
Sasha sighed.
"Well, she's conscious. They're still working on her, making sure her nervous system is okay. But the doctor says it's looking good."
Tatum exhaled in relief.
"Oh thank god! Did your parents make it?"
"We still can't get in touch with them," Sasha revealed.
Tatum saw Mike seated at a small chair next to the water cooler and she waved at him with a friendly smile.
As he nodded and waved back, Tatum noticed Chauncey and E making their way down the hallway from outside. She walked over and met them halfway.
"Hey E," she greeted. "Come here, big bro," she added, embracing Chauncey in a big hug. She hadn't seen him in so long. "How you holding up?"
She could smell the smoke on him and could tell that he was probably out having a cigarette; she could imagine how shot his nerves were. Chauncey shrugged and ran his hand over his head.
"Best I could I guess…that's my baby girl in there, you know?"
Tatum nodded and half smiled in an attempt to comfort.
"But she's gonna be okay, Chaunc. I know she will."
"Yeah, I know…anyway, I hear you an island girl now. How's that?"
Tatum smiled, seeing the multiple dimensions in Chauncey's question.
"It's good. He sends his love," she added. Just then Jayde made her way up to them and Tatum gave a generic smile. Ever since Sasha

had told her about the whole queen pin, drug pusher scenario, Tatum didn't know what to make of her.

"Hey Tatum," she greeted. "How are you?"

Jayde engulfed Tatum in a warm hug and Tatum could smell her prestigious perfume. She tried her hardest to maintain her same demeanor as the last time she'd seen her, pre-drug lord revelation.

"I'm okay...under the circumstances."

Jayde shook her head.

"I know. I'd say it's nice to see you, but that doesn't even feel right."

"Yeah," Tatum agreed, reflecting on what she had just said.

"Are you alone?" Jayde asked, looking past Tatum and around the room.

Tatum squinted her eyes at Jayde.

"I am. Well, me and...him," Tatum informed her, pointing at Ree's friend/driver/bodyguard who stood posted by the door.

Jayde looked over at Crush and pursed her lips.

"Oh, I see," she giggled. *This bitch really came up, personal escorts and all,* Jayde mused. *Lucky girl.*

She took in Tatum fully. She could tell Ree had her living like a queen. Her wardrobe and maintenance seemed to be just as well kept as before, there was no drastic change there. But there was an aura of prestige and of stature that only a fellow boss bitch could recognize in another. Jayde had to give her the props; Tatum carried her new queen bee title well and effortlessly.

The doctor emerged from the double doors at the end of the hall, breaking up the small talk, and everyone approached him in anticipation.

'She's gonna be okay," he declared with a smile, and you could literally hear everyone's sigh of relief. He continued.

"We're going to keep her for a few days for observation, but other than that, she will be good to go. She's a trooper."

Sasha clasped her hands together and thanked god and Chauncey smiled wide and wrapped his arms around her, causing Mike to frown lightly.

"You could go see her shortly. Parents first," he instructed, shooting Mike a look, and then walking off.

Everyone took turns hugging Sasha, truly thrilled that Aubrey had pulled through and Tatum took out her cell phone, ready to fill Ree in on the good news.

"I'm sorry Miss, no phone calls in here," the receptionist informed her.

Tatum rolled her eyes lightly.

"Okay y'all, excuse me for a minute. I'm going to call…," She paused and looked at all of the watching eyes. "I'm going to make a phone call." And then she headed down the corridor. She couldn't wait to tell him.

Ree saw Tatum calling, but didn't answer. He couldn't. He was stunned into silence as he held the phone to his ear. For the first time since he could remember, he couldn't think straight or rationally.

"This is not even possible," he finally managed to utter.

"How do you figure that, Sean?" Trinity sniffed through the phone, and he could tell she was crying. "You've slept with me more than once. At one time, you even shared your bed with me."

Ree sat on the hotel bed and stared blankly at the flickering fireplace. He couldn't believe it. And to think, he wasn't going to answer Trinity's call, but after the tenth time, he decided against his better judgment.

He ran his left hand over his face in frustration as he held the phone with his right.

"Trinity…I've always used protection with you. Always," he reiterated. Ree was not stupid, he knew Trinity was the type of woman that would love to luck up and have his child. He never slipped with her.

"Well, that's why it's not one hundred percent Sean!" She screamed. "When you decide to sleep with someone, there is always a possibility!"

Ree closed his eyes for a few seconds and then opened them again. He knew she was right. But something about her voice, the venom in it. He just didn't believe her. He contemplated on whether if it was the fact that he didn't want to believe her.

"Trinity, listen to me. If I find out you're lying to me…if I find out this is a scheme or something…I'm going to…," he paused, and changed the course of his words, not wanting to threaten the potential mother of his child, if she was in fact telling the truth. "It just…it just wouldn't be a good idea for you to play around like that."

There was a silence and he could tell she was taking in what he was saying, another sign that gave Ree a red flag. But she insisted.

"Sean! I am pregnant…with your child! I'm sorry if this doesn't fall into your little *fairytale* with your American project princess…but you are going to have to deal with it. And before you even ask it, suggest it, offer it, whatever. I will not terminate my pregnancy!"

It wasn't a thought in Ree's mind yet, to suggest that. But he already knew by her temperament that it was not happening. He wondered how Tatum would take the news. *Could she handle it?*

"Alright," he finally simplified.

Trinity was taken aback by his cool demeanor.

"Alright?" She asked, not able to mask her surprise.

"Yup, alright… Let me know what you need."

"Really?" She asked, feeling like maybe she had a chance to come back into his life, and his heart.

"Yeah," he agreed. "And when the baby comes, we will do a blood test."

Trinity's heart sank. Well, first it shattered, and then sunk.

"How…," her voice cracked. "How could you even say that to me? There's been no one else, Sean."

"Trinity," he spoke softly. "It's nothing personal. I just know… It's for my own sanity."

She cried.

"Sean, I'm having your baby…how is that not personal?"

Ree sighed. He knew that if it was the small possibility that she was telling the truth, then he was handling the situation all wrong. He would have to be a man, and face up to his responsibilities. But in the end, there would be a blood test, and Trinity would not be able to escape it.

"Don't worry," he assured her. "I'll…I'll be here. Just call me if you need anything."

He disconnected the call and dropped his head into his hands and wondered how this had happened. Things like this didn't happen to men like him. Careful, well-calculated, men like him.

He sat in that position for an hour and a half, deep in thought, until he heard Tatum unlocking the hotel door, breaking him out of his contemplation.

She walked in, looking radiant. Her skin glowing and her face lit up with happiness. He dreaded the fact that he was about to cut that happiness short.

"Guess what, Ree?" She walked hurriedly over to the bed. "She's fine! Aubrey's fine…I seen her!" She beamed. He smiled through his deliberation.

"That's great baby."

"I tried to call you, did you see?" He didn't answer.

"Did you see me calling you, Ree?" She asked again.

He looked up at her, feeling a million emotions at once, a million emotions that he had never felt.

"Tatum," he spoke seriously. "We have to talk."

She faced him with curiosity and he proceeded.

"There's something I have to tell you."

"I don't know about you, but I'm starving," Jayde admitted, making her way to the parking lot with E in tow. She had asked Bleek to get her Range Rover from the restaurant and meet them up at the hospital so that he could give them a ride home, being that Chauncey, Sasha, and Mike were staying at the hospital.

She was relieved that Aubrey would be okay, but was more than curious as to what had actually occurred.

Jayde had called Sasha' parents for her and left a message that everything was okay, a follow up to the message that she had left before saying that they needed to be on the first flight to Atlanta. Now that all seemed to be calm, her hunger was kicking in.

"Yeah," E said blandly. He was trying his best to give Jayde a chance, thinking that maybe working with a female was something that he just had to get used to. Lately he had been being really hard on her, especially since the pool incident. Anything that she had asked of him, he ignored. And he knew that was no way to treat someone on his team. He lightened up. "That food at the party was looking type good too," he humored.

Jayde chuckled.

"Yeah, I know. I should go back to *that* bitch and eat."

They approached the truck and Bleek hopped out of the driver's seat and threw his head into a nod at them.

"What up Bleek?" E said in response as Jayde just smiled and watched Bleek climb into the backseat. Her mind traveled back to when she had mounted his face in her living room after he had protested, preaching about his girl and his baby. She wondered if they could have an encore tonight, he definitely had a killer tongue game.

E climbed into the passenger seat and Jayde changed the CD from the Tupac that Bleek was blasting, to her Mozart classical music.

"Bleek, next time, don't touch my shit."

E raised an eyebrow to the classical symphony that serenaded them and turned and looked back at Bleek, who just shrugged. Bleek knew that eventually, E would realize how strange she really was.

"Y'all wanna hit the waffle house?" She asked over the piercing violins.

It was close to 4 am, and with the exception of Bleek, neither of them had eaten anything.

"That's cool," E said, looking out of the window as they cruised down Peachtree Dunwoody. It was dead, like a ghost town.

"I can definitely eat," Bleek agreed from the back, checking his phone messages.

Oh you definitely can, Jayde thought and smirked through the rearview. Bleek matched her eyes and knew what she was thinking. He was down, but only if he could go all the way. E was lost in his thoughts, oblivious to their secret signals.

As they approached a red light, a black tinted out Escalade pulled up beside them. E glanced at the vehicle but then faced forward.

He contemplated if maybe they should bring some food to the hospital for Sasha and Chauncey.

"Yo J, you think we should-"

"E duck!" Bleek shouted from the back, as bullets began to rip through Jayde's Range Rover, turning the passenger side instantly into Swiss cheese.

"What the fuck!" Jayde shouted, trying to drive off but noticing a car in front and one on her left side had them boxed in. *A set up.*

E tried to crouch his large frame down, reaching in his waist for his nine as Bleek blazed shots back at the firing Escalade with his .45. The way the bullets were raining on them though, Bleek could tell they were working with Mac-11 machine guns, and he couldn't match it.

"Drive J, drive!" Bleek shouted, arm out and firing like a true soldier.

She dropped her seat all the way down and threw the car into reverse quickly, backing up and escaping the parade of shots. Bleek looked through the back window and guided her as she continued to floor the gas.

"Alright, bust a U-turn! Bust a U-turn!" He yelled.

She sat up, when she knew she was a distance away from the other cars, quickly spun a U-turn, and raced down the opposite end of the street.

E stayed crouched down in the seat.

They looked back and didn't see anyone following so they breathed a sigh of relief, and Jayde let up lightly off of the gas.

"What the fuck was that!" Bleek screamed, adrenaline pumpkin. His baby face was full of rage and animation. "You think that was some of Father's peoples that we didn't lay down?"

Jayde shrugged and shook her head in disbelief, looking around, as Bleek contemplated. He thought him and E had laid everyone on Father's side down, or got them to get down.

"I don't know what the fuck is going on...you alright?"

Bleek leaned back and nodded.

"Yeah I'm cool."

Jayde turned to E.

"You alright, E?

She saw the light turning red, but quickly ran it; she would not be stopping at anymore lights.

"E?" She repeated, but already knew what it was when she saw that he was still slouched in his seat.

He wasn't crouched down, he was slumped. And now Jayde could see the blood pouring from his white button up.

"Damn," she whispered, dropping her head.

Bleek sat up in worry.

"What...what you mean damn? Yo, E."

Bleek leaned up to the front passenger seat.

"E!"

But then he saw the same sight, and he closed his eyes in distress, his jaw tightened in anger.

In the short time that he had known him, Bleek had grown close to E.

"Yo, we gotta take him to the hospital!"

Jayde continued to drive at her regular pace, her face filled with sadness.

"J! We gotta get him to the fucking hospital! Floor it, yo!"

"He's gone, Bleek!" When she realized that she was shouting, she lowered her voice. "He's...he's gone."

She could see E was as lifeless as a doorknob, so she reached over and placed her right hand over his face, closing his eyelids. Bleek buried his head in his hands as they drove through the Atlanta streets in the shot up Range Rover.

"Rest in peace, E," Jayde whispered.

"I don't know how to tell you this."
"Just say it baby," Tatum urged. Ree was beginning to scare her. She was hoping that they weren't in any kind of trouble. "Is everything okay?" Her voice dripped with alarm.
He took her hands into his and looked into her eyes. Then he took a deep breath, and...
"Trinity says she's pregnant."
That was it. He could've punched her square in the nose and it would've felt better.
"H-huh?" Tatum couldn't find any air for anything. *Where did all of the air go? I can't breathe.*
"I said...Trinity called me, she said-"
"I *heard* you, Ree!"
Tatum jumped up off of the bed and Ree did too. He watched as her body trembled and as she placed her hands to her ears, as if that would prevent her from hearing anymore of what he had just told her.
"Tatum...I am so sorry that this is happening. But I need to know..."
"You had unprotected sex with her, Ree? I thought you said it wasn't that serious?" Tatum couldn't help the tears that began to fall from her eyes. "I guess it's just not meant for us, huh?"
Ree's heart broke.
"Tatum...please...don't say that. And I always used protection with her, that's why it's so hard for me to believe."
She covered her face in shame with her hands. She didn't know why, but she felt stupid, embarrassed, and dumb... dumb for thinking they could be some fairytale. Now, the next bitch would have his family. It hurt like hell, it hurt worse than that.
She could feel him walk closer to her. She could feel his arms around her. She could feel his lips kissing her on the top of her head, repeatedly. But she couldn't look at him. He was jaded, her perfect man, was now, flawed.

"Tatum, I need to know if we can get through this...," he whispered deeply. "I know what we have is deep enough... but I also know that it's a difficult thing I am asking of you."

It took her a few minutes to open her eyes and look up at him, and when she did, she stared into his sincere eyes, and truly didn't know what to do. Yes, this was a very difficult situation, but wasn't he worth it? Tatum knew finding another man like Ree was impossible, but she wasn't sure if she could deal with this even if she wanted to. He would have a bond with Trinity and that child that she couldn't offer him, and she feared that. But she also feared losing him. He could see the hesitation in her face.

"I told Trinity that I want a blood test."

Tatum remained quiet, but was pleased to hear it. She could tell by the whole naked in the office scene that the girl was extreme as hell. Tatum exhaled loudly and ran her left hand through her hair, fingering through her curls with a pitiful look on her face.

"I ...I need to think."

She turned and walked slowly toward the door and Ree watched her regretfully, not wanting her to leave. He was relieved when she made a detour for the bathroom and closed the door behind her.

He walked over to the bathroom door, and could hear her in there, sniffling, and it tore him up inside. He leaned his forehead against the door and closed his eyes, praying that she'd emerge and say that they could get through this. He had come too far to lose her again.

It would be another hour before Tatum would emerge. And when she did, Ree would be right there, sitting by the door, waiting. And she would know exactly what she had to do.

"No...no. Please don't tell me that."

The whole mood of the hospital room was melancholy at the latest news.

"Not E...oh my god," Sasha whimpered in shock. This was turning into the worst series of events ever.

She was lying in the hospital bed, her arm wrapped around a resting and sedated Aubrey, and Chauncey was seated in a chair, blank faced, his hands tented under his chin. It was after 5 am, and the hospital was dead quiet. Mike had left a few minutes before; he was called in for surgery, so they were there alone.

Jayde and Bleek had just come in, sneaking past security, and relayed the news, after dropping the body in an alley near the hospital. They didn't want to bring him to the hospital, knowing that it would be a ton of questions, especially being that Bleek was sure that he had hit at least one of the gunmen. And they didn't want to get rid of it, because they would want his family to find out and give the proper burial.

Chauncey understood the logic, but it didn't feel right. His man, his right hand man, was laying in an alley shot up, dead. Gone. And Chauncey felt responsible.

"Who did it?" He asked, voice dripping with vengeance.

"I think it was one of Father's people," Bleek figured. "That's all I can come up with."

Jayde butted in.

"It was Capo... I seen him."

Chauncey and Bleek's eyes fell on her and Bleek furrowed his eyebrows. This was the first time he had heard of this sighting.

"Capo?" Chauncey asked, surprised. Not only was Capo cool as hell when Chauncey had met with him to cop, he was also E's man. E had set up the deal. "Why would Capo do that shit?"

Jayde rolled her eyes like 'duh'.

"Because...ever since you and I have partnered and taken all of this new territory, Capo is the only person who remains a sole proprietor, and no one wants to cop from him anymore. Everyone knows they can see me, or you, and get the same deal, and our shit won't be as stepped on as Capo's."

Chauncey looked up at her baffled.

"But I thought we weren't selling to Capo's people...and we giving him a sweeter deal than everyone else, right?"

Jayde remained quiet and Chauncey knew she was hiding something.

"Right?" He repeated, growing more upset, as Sasha looked on trying to follow.

"Look," Jayde started. "Capo and I…may have exchanged some words last week. I mean, he's the only one who won't come onboard and just work for us. It makes no sense, his little blocks that he's holding onto…they're dead smack in the middle of our-"

"So!" Chauncey barked, standing up and becoming angry. "So the fuck what J? Let him keep those measly blocks!"

Chauncey understood a man wanting to make his own moves, he could respect it. Capo wasn't taking anything out of their mouths, and now he could see how greedy Jayde actually was.

He ran his hands over his face and shook his head.

"Oh my god…oh my fucking god. Do you realize you just started a war… got my man killed, over a couple of half ass blocks?"

Jayde looked down and shrugged.

"I'm sorry about E…but it's a respect thing, Chauncey."

Chauncey paced the floor and continued to shake his head. It didn't matter how angry he was, Jayde was on his team. If her and Capo bumped heads, and especially if Capo killed E, then war was established.

Chauncey was not concerned with that, they were huge, so Capo could not win. It only was unfortunate that the pretenses on which the beef was built was bullshit, not worth it.

Sasha kept her mouth shut and held a sleeping Aubrey closer, but she knew that Jayde had started some shit. Although she was sure Chauncey was not concerned, she thought of E being shot down and she quickly feared for Chauncey.

Bleek also knew it was about to be some shit, but he was ready. He had a personal bullet with Capo's name on it, but it would probably not beat Chauncey's.

Chauncey looked over at his daughter and couldn't believe he had went from one extreme of being happy of Aubrey's recuperation and now in sorrow from the loss of E.

He looked at Jayde and could almost hear E's voice.
Not a female Chaunc, a bitch... Chauncey nodded to himself and took his seat again. *A bitch.*

Ree heard the faucet turn on and then seconds later, shut off. About a minute after that, the knob turned and Tatum emerged from the bathroom. He stood up and looked at her, trying to read her but she just made her way to the bed, blank-faced. However, she remained standing.

Finally after a few torturous minutes, she laughed lightly and looked up at the ceiling.

"I just can't believe this, Ree."

She turned and looked at him in disappointment.

"I love you, Ree...but...I don't know. I'm not sure if I can live with someone else starting your family. That means, this woman..." Tatum didn't even feel right calling her a bitch if she was potentially carrying his child, and she really didn't know why, because she couldn't stand Trinity. "This woman, will be in your...our, lives forever. I don't know if I can handle that."

Ree dropped his head and nodded, but felt like someone was taking his air from him. He regretted ever fucking with Trinity. Had he known that Tatum would come back into his life, he would have waited forever and a day.

Tatum walked closer to him and grabbed his hands, pressing her body to his.

"But I'm gonna try."

He looked up and stared at her, stunned. He searched her eyes for certainty.

"I'm gonna try to handle it...because I love you, Sean Knights. I love you so much, and I know that what we have...it's the real thing. That's why..." Tatum paused, never being this upfront about her emotions in her entire life. "That's why I know we can get through anything...even if I have to take the backseat."

Ree shook his head and cupped her face in his hands.

"No, never. You will never have to take a backseat."

"Yes I will, Ree. She's gonna be the mother of your child. *Possibly*...be the mother of your child," Tatum corrected. "And what will I be?"

Ree pulled away and placed his hands in his pockets, sighing. He shrugged and Tatum stared at him.

"Well...," he started. "I guess you'll just have to be..."

He pulled a tiny box out of his pocket and gently flipped it open, while he slowly sunk down to one knee.

Tatum's heart skipped a beat and she shook her head, not believing it.

"...My wife," he finished, looking into her eyes sincerely.

Tatum gasped, her vision clouding with tears. She couldn't even think straight. Every part of her wanted to say yes, but she had to know...

"Are...is this... just...because of...Trinity?" She asked between breaths. "Because you don't have to..."

"And what...I ran out and bought the ring while you were in the bathroom?" He asked playfully.

"Come on, Tatum. I've had this...I knew this...you, was what I wanted, for a long time. Now you gonna leave me down here on my knees... or you gonna give me an answer?" He took the ring out of the box and slipped it onto her finger, its beauty completely captivating her. It was an enormous Russian Alexandrite, because he knew Tatum did not wear diamonds. The Russian Alexandrite was one of, if not arguably the most, rare and expensive stone. To Ree it represented everything that Tatum was – beautiful, inimitable, rare.

"Will you marry me...Miss Lady?"

She took a deep breath and looked at him, overflowing with emotion. Finally...finally love had arrived.

"Yes," she whispered. "Yes Sean. I'll marry you."

He smiled wide and stood up.

"That's what I'm talking 'bout. Come 'ere."

He pulled her close into a secure embrace and kissed her deeply, and Tatum felt like she was floating. If it was a dream she didn't want to wake up.

She had the man, the man any woman would desire, and he wanted her to be his wife. She knew their love would conquer anything. The situation with Trinity drifted further and further from her mind.

Finally...love had arrived.

Ding Dong.

The old rusty bell, which hung from the doorway, sounded, as the door swung open in the old shop.

"How may I help you?" The overweight redneck man asked, looking skeptically at the figure dressed in oversized sweats and a black hoodie.

The person stood and fidgeted with a picture in their hands, causing the man to look down at it. The picture was of a beautiful young black woman who appeared to be, from where he could see, naked.

He looked up at the mysterious individual that had just entered his shop, who was just standing there, looking lost.

"Look, I think you may be in the wrong place here," he figured, squinting to get another glance at the picture.

As if on cue, they folded the picture and stuffed it into their pocket hastily, stepping up to the counter.

"No, I'm not lost. Not at all."

The fat white man folded his arms across his big chest, as his huge belly hung from under his too short gray t-shirt. He didn't have time for small talk. He looked on blankly and shrugged.

"Well, like I said then...how may I help you?"

The mystery person looked around at the many things the shop had to offer and then their eyes landed on it. It was perfect, so perfect, it should have had Sasha's name written on it.

I…I need a gun," they finally stammered. They pointed to the compact Ruger .38 with the pearl handle and smiled sinisterly, the nervousness seeming to vanish with each second. "I need *that* gun."

Chapter 20 - Wrath

"Oh my god," Tatum murmured, covering her mouth with her right hand, her left hand still on her phone that she couldn't even think to hang up. She woke up the next morning and had called Sasha to tell her the good news, and Sasha had hit her with this before Tatum had even gotten the chance to tell her.

She turned and looked down at Ree, who had woken up and was looking at her perplexed.

"What's up...everything okay?" He asked, his voice raspy.

"E...E died... he was shot..."

Ree stared at her for a few seconds in silence. Although he looked at death a little more differently than average people, and with more understanding and less emotion towards it, he definitely regretted the news. E was someone who he had worked with, he knew that he was a good person, and was very loyal to Chauncey.

"Damn." That was all Ree could reply with.

"Yeah, Sasha said Chauncey's really fucked up about it, and I know he is...I just can't believe it."

Ree nodded solemnly.

"Yeah, it's a fucked up situation. E was good people... But it's all apart of the game baby."

Ree rubbed her back and kissed her on her bare shoulder, which was only decorated by the strap of her silk nightgown.

"I'm so glad that you're out of *that* game," Tatum said with a content sigh. "I don't know what I would do if anything ever happened to you."

Ree remained silent in contemplation, but then stood up and slipped on his boxers, his perfectly sculpted and tattooed body making him appear as an Adonis god.

"Yeah well, you wouldn't have to worry about that anyway."
Tatum didn't like that response, and it showed all in her expression. She tilted her head at him.
"I wouldn't have to worry about *that,* because you're out of the game... for good, right?"
Ree stared into her eyes in an assuring way. Yes, his body was physically out, but his mentality, his way of being, would always be...street.
"Yeah, I'm out," he affirmed.
And then he turned and walked away, before Tatum could see any hesitation in his face.

As if the day could get any worse, Sasha walked out of the hospital cafeteria and sucked her teeth when she noticed the woman from Child Services approaching.
"Hello Mrs. Bernstein," the woman greeted neither warm nor testing. "Your husband told me that I could find you down here."
Sasha chuckled and placed her hand on her hip.
"You mean my daughter's father."
The woman snapped her fingers as if remembering something.
"Dammit, that's right, I'm so absentminded...I have to remember that.
Husband...daughter's father...husband...daughter's father...two separate people..."
"What do you want lady?" Sasha demanded with more than a little attitude. "You don't like me or something?"
The woman's face turned serious.
"No, Mrs. Bernstein I like you fine...It's just that I like Aubrey, a little bit more. And I'll tell you, one thing I don't like, is liars."
Sasha furrowed her eyebrows and jerked her head back.
"Liars?"
"Liars," the woman repeated. "You said you didn't leave your daughter at home alone, Mrs. Bernstein. You said you left her in fact, with an Amanda Bernstein."

Sasha nodded matter of factly and the woman shook her head in disappointment.

"You're still lying... Listen, I know for a fact that you did not leave your daughter with a babysitter, and in fact you left her alone, and this was not the first time that you did so."

Sasha cut her off in anger and felt herself about to explode.

"That's bullshit! You *don't* know that because I would never do that...there are no facts! I would never leave my baby. Never!"

"Yes you would. And I have several witnesses that will attest to it."

Sasha shook her head as if this was a terrible nightmare, as Chauncey made his way up to them.

"Who?" Sasha screamed.

"I don't have to reveal that."

"What's going on?" He asked, feeling the emotion in the hallway filled with tension.

"Your *daughter's mother*, made a big mistake...and until I get to the bottom of everything...Aubrey can not return home with her."

Sasha felt her heart drop to her stomach and could simultaneously taste the egg sandwich she'd just eaten about to come up. Her body began to shake.

"What! Why are you doing this? You can't do this! I don't even know what's going on? Chauncey...don't let her do this...she can't do this!"

Sasha began to cry hysterically, placing her hands over her face.

"Nah, fuck that, you can't do that shit!" Chauncey challenged.

The woman rolled her neck.

"I can and I will...Several sworn statements from incredibly reliable sources saying that you, Sasha Bernstein, left Aubrey alone, a one year old who was poisoned, while her mother shows up to the hospital dressed for the nightclub, smelling like champagne, who openly admits to leaving a half open bottle of pine cleaner in the kitchen..."

Sasha lunged at her wildly and Chauncey had to restrain her.

"You fucking bitch!"

239

"Mrs. Bernstein! You better get a hold of yourself before I have you arrested and you'll be in jail throughout this entire investigation."

"You stupid ass bitch!" Chauncey barked. "Get the fuck outta here on ya power trip, yo!"

"Mr. Mills, I advise you to calm down before you make things worse." She pulled out a packet of paper from her briefcase.

"This here is a court order that allows Aubrey Mills to reside at the premises of her biological father, Chauncey Mills, from the time of her release from the hospital, until the investigation is complete and the decision is made on whether the mother is fit to have the child returned to her."

Sasha stood, a little more calm, with her arms folded and her lip quivering as tears rolled down her face. Chauncey put his arm around her and assured her, "It's gonna be okay princess."

"This is only based upon the assumption that Mr. Mills abides by all of his rules and regulations in regard to the Parole Board and his parole. In the event that you don't Mr. Mills... well I guess you can just assume what would happen."

She turned on her heels with a smirk and made her way back down the hall.

"Have a great day," she added, and Sasha and Chauncey stood there wondering what the hell was going on.

Two Days Later

With all that was happening, Tatum convinced Ree to extend their stay for a little while longer. It actually didn't take much convincing being that Ree totally understood – between Aubrey being hospitalized, then her recovering, E being killed, and then the whole Child Services thing; he knew that Tatum wanted to be there for Sasha.

And then in addition to all of that happening, he still had the news that Trinity had thrown on him weighing heavy on his mind, and he was in no rush to get back and face that situation. All in all, making this a twisted series of events.

Tatum had been traveling back and forth between the hotel and the hospital, Ree's big bodyguard friend by her side every step of the way. She had managed to calm Sasha down a little, letting her know that it would all work out and convincing her to be thankful that they had allowed Aubrey to stay with Chauncey when she was released. Jayde also assured Sasha that she would get to the bottom of things. Jayde knew too many people in high places to not be able to find out who these supposed witnesses of these blatant lies were. She would find them, and then, they would be sorry.

Sasha rested assured more, knowing that Jayde would get some answers, and knowing that Aubrey would be safe with Chauncey, but more than anything, glad to have her best friend, Tatum, there with her. Regardless of how many times she was questioned, Aubrey seemed to have no recollection of anything that had occurred, and while the doctor said that was perfectly normal, it made it difficult to figure out what happened. Sasha believed in her faith though, that everything would work out, it just had to. Mike was still worried about what had happened to Amanda and the whole event seemed to be a big mystery.

Regardless of the circumstances however, when Tatum had revealed the news of her and Ree's engagement, Sasha was thrilled for her. It was hard for her to be as happy as she normally would have been, but either way, she was definitely happy for her. She was actually upset that Tatum's joyful event was overshadowed by all of the horrible occurrences. And she promised herself that when it all worked out, she would throw Tatum a proper celebration. Tatum held off about the news of Trinity being pregnant, she felt that could definitely wait.

Meanwhile, Chauncey was trying to simultaneously figure out what exactly had happened with his daughter and what exactly had happened with E.

He went over the night with Sasha a million times, and he went over the details of the shooting, with Jayde, about the same

241

amount. He knew his friend was gone, and he knew a problem was coming, but apart of him couldn't help but be thankful that his little girl had survived. Today was the day that he would bring her home.

"So don't feed her anything with too much sugar, oh and don't let her drink late at night, Chauncey...make sure she has her Pedialyte every night, the doctor says it'll help, oh, and try to read to her, it helps her sleep... and the doctor said she may be a little traumatized so keep the night light on, or maybe, sleep with her. Rub her ointment on before you put on her pull-up at night...and oh, she really likes those cookies, with the strawberry flavor..." Sasha began to tear up thinking about not having her baby home with her and she stopped. "Why is this happening? This is torture," she painfully admitted.

Chauncey stood there, with a solemn look. They were upstairs in his house, and Mike was outside, waiting on Sasha so that they could go to a lawyer and try to fight this whole thing. They wanted to find out some information, and try to get Aubrey back home.

"You wanna take her?" Chauncey offered. "How would they know she wasn't here?" He hated seeing Sasha so miserable.

"I can't risk losing her, Chauncey. We need to follow the rules..."

"Then, stay here with me... move here with me...be here with me, Sash."

She looked into his sad eyes and she didn't know what to do. She didn't know if she could ever forget the pain Chauncey had caused her, but something inside told her that he was a changed man. A street man still, but a changed man.

Just then the horn blew, and she knew Mike was waiting. They had to be on time.

"I need to think, Chau-"

He cut her off by pressing his lips to hers and holding the back of her head firmly, as he kissed her with enough passion to try and prove a point. She squirmed in objection, but then, submitted.

He pulled away and stared at her and she ran her fingers over the tattoo of her and Aubrey on his arm. *He loves us.*

"Again. Kiss again," Aubrey laughed, sitting up in her bed.

Sasha walked over with a smile and hugged her tight, and then kissed her repeatedly.

"I love you baby girl. And mommy will be back, okay?"

Aubrey smiled and hugged Sasha, laying her head on Sasha's chest.

"No Mommy, stay."

Sasha closed her eyes tight and kissed the top of her head.

"I…I will be really close, okay? And I'll be right back."

Her voice cracked and she had to force herself away before Aubrey saw her cry. Then she knew Aubrey would get worried and probably cry too.

"I love you Bri-Bri," she added, at the doorway, her heart breaking into a million pieces.

"I love you Mommy."

Chauncey stood there and watched his girls with love, and as Sasha was almost out of sight he heard her whisper something.

"I love you, Chauncey."

A few seconds later he heard her make her way down the stairs and close the front door.

"I love you too, Princess…I love you, too."

And then he heard the car pull off.

Trinity lay in her bed sobbing, a box of Kleenex as her only companion. She thought of how dismissive Ree had been with her, even after learning she was pregnant. She had figured that when he realized that she was carrying his child, she would have surely won him by default.

More than the obvious however, she thought of how she would pull off this whole scam.

A blood test?

The most apparent thing had completely gone over her head.

How could I have missed that?

It was the one part of the plan that she had not went over, probably because she hadn't expected him to request one. As far as she was concerned, she and Ree had been an item, and he had to know that there was no one else.

She didn't worry about Rodney saying anything to anyone; she knew that his fear of losing his job and his fear of Ree would keep him hushed. Plus, if he were to say anything, he would have done so by now. She had repeated their raw sex escapades thrice since the first time.

There was a possibility that the child would have come out looking nothing like Ree, but that was a common situation, and she'd assumed that after nine months of him catering to her, seeing her belly grow, sonogram pictures, baby names, and showers, he'd be too excited to question the paternity. But now she was not so sure.

No matter how much she tried, she couldn't get Tatum out of her mind. The way she looked, her demeanor, her confidence, everything about her proved exactly why Ree was in love with her. Trinity knew that she could not compete with her on any level, until now.

Oh my god, this is it. Once he starts to see me showing and with my pregnant glow, he'll have no choice but to send that bitch back to the States where she belongs.

Dreams of family moments with Ree thrilled and excited Trinity. The only thing she knew that she had to do, was to use these nine months to convince Ree to change his mind about the blood test.

Once she did that, she knew she would be in the clear.

She briefly thought of the rumors she'd heard of Ree, how deadly and cold he could be, but she tried to place those thoughts far in the back of her mind.

But still, when all of her other thoughts were used up; she couldn't help but to wonder…

What if he finds out the truth?

"The lawyer said the investigation is procedural…he thinks we can have Aubrey home in no time."

"We?" Chauncey asked, his jaw flinching in anger as he threw his fork down into his spaghetti.

Sasha had come back to his house that night, telling Mike that Aubrey couldn't sleep without seeing her. But really she couldn't sleep without seeing Aubrey…or Chauncey. Sasha had made them dinner, and now they were sitting there eating, while Aubrey was enthralled in her cartoons.

Sasha looked down into her lap, not wanting to look at Chauncey.

"Believe it or not Chaunc, Mike cares about Bri-Bri too. He wants her home."

"And what do you want, Sasha?" Chauncey questioned, sounding annoyed and becoming angry. "Home with him? Or home with me? Because if it's honestly…honestly him…then you gotta let me know, ma."

His voice was filled with a sincerity that Sasha felt she had to match, or she would cheapen the mood.

Chauncey had broken her heart, indeed. But he had managed to keep a firm hold on it that Sasha could not deny. So she figured, why try to.

"I want…" She paused and blinked away tears, her slender, manicured hands shaking lightly. "I want a home with you, not him…but I don't want you to break my heart…again."

"Never," Chauncey responded quickly, looking her dead in the eyes.

He reached over and grabbed her hand, and she sighed and shook her head.

Was she ready to do this? Was she ready to forgive him?

'My princess," Aubrey whined, interrupting the deep moment.

Sasha faced her.

"Baby girl, mommy packed your princess. She's upstairs."

Aubrey calmed briefly and then pouted, as if remembering something.

"My Pinky."

Sasha rolled her eyes, thinking of the scraggily pink teddy bear that she had been meaning to get rid of.

"Bri-Bri, do you really need that tonight? Can't mommy bring it tomorrow?"

Aubrey poked out her lip and scrunched her face up in sadness, and Sasha frowned. She knew her baby had been through a lot and she wanted to make her happy. Chauncey was an even bigger sucker for what he referred to as 'the face'.

"I'll go," he volunteered, standing up.

Sasha jumped up and put her hand to his chest.

"Whoa, not so fast buddy. I'll go."

She knew Chauncey, and the last thing she wanted was him going to her home, and he and Mike getting into it, and Chauncey blowing up her spot and telling Mike that she was leaving him.

If she would decide to leave Mike, she would have the decency to tell him, and deep down inside, she knew she would leave soon.

She reached for her purse, fishing for her keys when her cell phone began to ring.

She answered on the third ring.

"Hey Jayde, I'll call you back, I'm on my way to the house."

Sasha waved bye and blew a kiss to Aubrey, as Chauncey assured her that her mommy would be right back, with Pinky.

"Where are you?" Jayde asked, sounding a little concerned.

"Oh, I was at Chauncey's," Sasha told her, reaching her car and jumping behind the wheel. It was dark and quiet on Chauncey's street.

"Well, you'll have to drive and talk because I have something interesting to tell you."

As Sasha pulled off and listened to Jayde, her confusion grew by the second. Most of what Jayde was saying didn't make sense.

"So wait," Sasha asked mystified, finally pulling onto her street after Jayde's long tirade. "There is no Amanda Bernstein…is that what you're telling me?"

Jayde sighed.

"Well, there *is* an Amanda Bernstein…but she died two years ago in a car crash."

Sasha furrowed her eyebrows as Jayde continued.

"There is a woman who was caught using the name as an alias on several occasions, her name is Liz Preston."

Sasha was stunned.

"And you know what, Mike did say that before we moved down here, he hadn't seen Amanda since she was younger," Sasha recalled, as if it were making sense to her. She couldn't believe that they had left her baby with a stranger. "She was playing us like she was Amanda the whole time I bet!"

Jayde stammered in deliberation.

"But even still, you think Mike wouldn't recognize his own cousin, I mean, even if it had been years?"

Sasha shrugged as if Jayde could see her.

"I don't know, but I'm gonna let him know what's going on. I'll call you back."

Sasha was sitting in front of her house, and Jayde's line had started going in and out.

"O-k…le – know – im – al – record – sh – be- safe."

"Huh? Girl, let me call you back, your phone is breaking up."

"Hello. Sasha? Hello. Can you hear me?"

Jayde moved closer to her bedroom window and spoke again.

"Sasha, I said let me know what he says because this girl has a crazy criminal record, and I want to make sure you guys will be safe!"

"Hello!" Jayde repeated.

"Hello!"

But Sasha had already ended the call.

"Mike!" She screamed, busting in the house. "Mike!"

All of the lights were off, besides the one illuminating from the kitchen.

Sasha's chest heaved in anger and in confusion, and she wanted them to get to the bottom of what was going on.

"Mike!" She called again, walking toward the kitchen, a small feeling of fear coming over her.

Where is he?

All of her nervous feelings of Mike's whereabouts vanished when she noticed his huge 35 millimeter camera sitting on the counter, the back opened as if the film had been taken out.

He's here.

She breathed a sigh of relief and knew that meant one thing, that he was in his small studio in his mini shed out back.

Under normal circumstances she was not allowed back there, but these were excruciating circumstances.

She placed her purse down on the counter and stormed toward the deck, sliding the glass doors open and making her way to the shed.

"Mike," she called, as she knocked. "Mike."

She softly pushed the door open and squinted through the darkness. She knew there was a hand built light switch in there because Mike had bragged about it when he had first installed it.

"Where is that switch? Where is it?" Sasha asked out loud, feeling around for it.

Finally, her fingertips lightly touched something that felt familiar, like a switch. She clicked it up, and the sight before her instantly frightened her into stillness.

"No...," she whispered, not believing it. She continued to stare on and became more and more horrified as she took in the scene. "Oh god no, please...don't let this be happening."

Sasha looked straight ahead and tears welled in her eyes, the sight being so terrifying.

There were pictures, everywhere.

Pictures plastered all around, completely covering the walls and the ceilings... even the floor.

Pictures of Sasha, doing everything... everywhere.

The most intimate and private moments of her life, robbed.

Pictures of her eating...sleeping...cooking...playing with Aubrey. Pictures of her showering...masturbating late nights...pictures of her jogging...even some pictures of her at Tatum's in Jersey before

Christmas…pictures of her coming and leaving the jail while visiting Chauncey…pictures of her…

"Oh my god."

Sasha's eyes fell on the pictures of her and Chauncey making love, on his counter, at his home, even the time in Sasha and Mike's bed. She closed her eyes and reopened them as if it were a dream.

There were even pictures of Sasha from when she lived in New Jersey, way before she was with Mike, back when she was still with Chauncey.

Pictures of her at the hospital. Some pictures of just her mouth, just her eyes, pictures of her at her desk, talking on the phone. Pictures of her at her old Elizabeth apartment, pictures of her at Kim's funeral…pictures, pictures, pictures.

"Oh my god," she could barely whisper.

She felt a presence behind her.

"You like?"

Sasha turned abruptly and found Mike standing there, a sinister smile on his face. Sasha held onto the wooden table to maintain her balance as she shook her head at him.

"What the fuck is going on, Mike?" She asked, her voice trembling. "What the hell is all of this?"

He stretched his neck out to each side, enjoying the sound of the bones cracking, and he stepped closer to her.

"Oh, this is nothing. This…is you. It's you, babe…aren't you beautiful?"

He looked around at all of the pictures, as if he was seeing them for the first time, and his eyes twinkled. Sasha swallowed hard, and began inching closer to the door.

"You're a real sick fuck, huh Mike?" She couldn't help but ask. "You've been stalking me?"

He snapped his neck in her direction and his eyes turned ice blue cold.

"Me? Sick?" He shook his head. "No…not me. You see, Sasha. I'm not the one who had the perfect man, the perfect life…but had to ruin it for some lowlife street thug."

He reached over and gently picked up a picture of Sasha sucking Chauncey's dick at his home not long ago.

"I loved you, Sasha! I loved you since the very beginning, before I had you. I would have taken care of you!" He screamed, his face reddening.

Sasha's eyes were wide as saucers and her breathing quickened. The way that he was referring to his love for her in the past tense caused the goose bumps on Sasha's arms to rise.

"I love you too, Mike," she proclaimed sweetly, with fear in her voice. As she continued to inch toward the door, he inched closer to her and further inside the shed.

"You love me?" He asked sarcastically. "I… bet… you… do."

He pulled out a recorder out of his pocket and pressed play, staring at her blankly.

"I bet you love me so much, that you can't even stand to be with me anymore," he said as Sasha's voice came into play.

'I want a home with you, not him', she admitted on the tape, which was less than thirty minutes ago at Chauncey's.

Sasha shook her head, truly terrified. *Who was this man?* She didn't even know him.

"I…I didn't mean it. I love you. I was just trying to spare his feelings."

Mike raised his eyebrows and smiled.

"You did a good job. But I guess you couldn't spare mine, huh?"

She shook her head with tears in her eyes, truly frightened and looked toward the door of the shed. At the angle that she was standing, and the way Mike was positioned, she knew if she could ever make a break for it, it would be now.

Now or never Sasha.

She took a deep breath and dashed sharply and quickly, reaching the doorway and tasting the sweet night air before a pair of strong hands yanked her back inside and threw her down to the ground forcefully.

"Get your ass back in here," he demanded.

Her body hit the man-made concrete floor with a thud and her head banged hard against the wall. Sasha felt pain throughout and her head pounded. She placed her hand to her forehead and closed her eyes, trying to fight the dizziness.

"Why...why are you doing this?" She mumbled.

"Why?" He asked. "Why!"

He stormed over to her and knelt down, looking at her angrily.

"Why did *you* do this? Huh?"

A thought went through Sasha as she stared into his deranged face. She swallowed hard.

"Who's Liz Preston?"

A glare flickered in Mike's eyes and then he stood and put his hands in his pockets, looking away.

"I don't know what you're talking about?"

The way he said it, sent chills down Sasha's spine. Just thinking of him having something to do with what happened to Aubrey turned Sasha's fear to anger. She repeated her question.

"Who the *fuck* is Liz Preston...and what happened to your cousin Amanda?"

Mike grimaced and glared down at Sasha like a madman.

"You know... I didn't want to hurt anyone...but *you* Sasha. You just pushed me. And if that fucking *brat* weren't around...then Chauncey wouldn't even be in the picture! I...I...I had to do it, you know? But Liz, she didn't finish...She was supposed to give her the drink...make sure she was dead, and then leave...but...but she fucked up. She had to go. She just had to go."

Mike was talking like a lunatic but Sasha didn't care. She was seeing red. He continued.

"Amanda's dead. She's been dead. That time when you thought you met her, you actually were meeting Liz. Oh, and I almost forgot... since I'm on a roll. The witnesses, the ones that spoke to Child Services about you...yeah, I took care of that too. I figure, if the brat wouldn't die, at least she wouldn't be here with us. No now, it's just me and you... babe."

Sasha jumped up, against her banging head and thumping body's will, and swung her arms wildly at him.

"You fucking bastard! I fucking hate you!"

But Mike simply laughed and in a brisk motion, grabbed Sasha's arm and twisted it around her back, placing the cold steel Ruger .38, to her cheek. It was the same Ruger with the pearl handle that he had purchased from the small shop outside of town.

"No bitch, I fucking hate *you*."

He stared at her, the instant terror in her eyes, her beautiful face frozen in pain and horror. He leaned closer and licked her tears that were running down her cheek.

"Mmm," he moaned. "But I love you, too."

With the gun still to her face, he let go of her arm and grabbed the back of her head, pulling her close to him and kissing her sloppily and deeply.

Sasha did not kiss him back as her insides shuddered, she couldn't believe this mothafucka had tried to kill her baby.

He covered her face with kisses and closed his eyes, pressing his mouth to her face and holding her tightly.

"God, I love you."

Sasha shut her eyes, her expression not changing. She was no longer scared of Mike hurting her as long as she went along with his flow, but she was concocting her plan of getting free, and what she would do when she was.

"Come on babe, let's go inside. We have a long day ahead of us tomorrow."

Sasha looked at him, alarmed. She needed to stay around the people who would rescue her. Tatum, Jayde, Chauncey, she knew they would eventually come looking for her.

"Wha-what?" She asked, shakily.

Mike put his arm around her, and began walking her slowly out of the shed, as he held the gun to her side.

"Yes, tomorrow morning. First thing. Me, and my beautiful wife...that's you by the way," he whispered. "We're going on a trip...a romantic getaway so to say."

They reached the glass patio doors and Sasha's legs felt like spaghetti as she contemplated making a run for it. *But would he shoot her? Did she want to chance that?*

"But first," Mike continued, leading her inside and closing the door behind him. "We're gonna spend this night...our last night here...doing what I've wanted for so long."

Sasha looked up at him as he ran his free hand up and down her curvy figure covered up in her tight jeans and sweater. Her long hair was wild and loose, but to Mike, she was perfect. Perfect enough that he needed a piece of her, even after she was gone.

"We're gonna make a baby...*baby*."

Sasha felt vomit rush to her mouth and she reluctantly swallowed it back down. She couldn't believe this was happening and she wondered if anyone would come to her aid tonight. Chauncey and Jayde both knew where she was, but to them, she was just...home. Sasha tried to think quickly on her feet.

"I...I'm on my period," she lied.

Mike chuckled.

"No you're not. You're ovulating," he corrected.

Sasha fixed her face in disgust and glowered at him, as he pushed her to the stairs. He was truly obsessed.

"Now get...go. We got work to do," he ordered.

He waved the gun, commanding her to walk, and all she could do was hope that someone would save her. *Please, save me.*

Chapter 21 - Vengeance

Jayde was in the driver's seat of her brand new Range Rover, her left leg cocked up on the dashboard. She picked up her cell phone and checked it again, wondering what was taking Sasha so long to return her call.

She threw it back down as she felt herself really getting into the work Bleek was putting on her, as his head stirred in between her thighs.

"Oh shit," she whispered, feeling her nut rise.

Bleek licked her faster, determined to make her bust quick and run up in her. She had gotten her shit off the first time, but this time, he was determined to feel her insides.

As her body tensed and her face contorted in that sweet pleasurable ache, Bleek glanced up at her and enjoyed it. It was the only time that she would be submissive to him, and now, he was about to take advantage of that.

He massaged her ass while her orgasm came to a blissful end, and as he lifted up with a smirk, ready to slide on a condom, something caught his attention in the parking lot that they were parked in.

Jayde panted, ready to feel Bleek's dick, she had made up her mind that she would give him some, but his facial expression alerted her.

"What's wrong?" She asked, noticing him staring out of her driver's window.

He didn't answer; he just reached into his waist and pulled out his gun, his eyes falling low into slits. *Damn, once again...no pussy!*

Jayde sat up and pulled her skirt down and then turned and followed his gaze, her eyes falling on Capo who was walking briskly across the parking lot, completely unsuspecting.

Her heartbeat quickened, and she knew what time it was. She sat up, turned on the ignition, and began to slowly creep in his direction.

Capo continued to walk across the parking lot, his face looking as if he were deep in thought, and it looked as if he were heading toward the bar across the street.

As they got closer to him, Bleek rolled down the window and hung out of the car.

"Yo! What up, Capo?" He asked blasé.

Capo turned and grinned.

"What up, Bleek. What you doing on this side-" His words were cut short by the sight of Bleek's .45. "What the fu-"

Pop! Pop! Pop!

Bleek fired off rounds at Capo, as Capo reached in his waist for his gun and simultaneously tried to run. Jayde rested her foot on the gas, keeping up with his chase.

Pop! Bleek caught him once in the leg. Pop! Pop! He continued to fire, but not before an unknown old Chevy pulled up out of nowhere, and started firing back at them.

Capo had also located his gun by now and was banging back as well, and when Bleek's gun jammed, he turned to Jayde.

"Go J! Go!"

She skidded off, out of the lot and looked in her rearview, making sure the Chevy wasn't giving chase.

The other car had stayed behind, probably to tend to the wounded Capo and she wondered how she had gotten herself into this. Her status, and at her level, she was not supposed to be getting her hands this dirty. But she knew with her and Chauncey's takeover, problems were to come.

"Yo, you sure it was Capo you seen?" Bleek asked seriously, turning to her once they were in the clear.

She paused and focused on the road, and then she turned to him.

"Yeah…why?"

Bleek leaned back, breathing hard and looked at her out of the corner of his eye. He couldn't get out of his mind the look on Capo's face when he noticed the gun in Bleek's hand.

It was a look of pure shock and surprise, a look that was odd for someone to give if they had blazed at you first *and* hit someone on your team.

The more he thought about it, Capo had greeted him warmly, as if nothing had occurred. And what guy, street dude at that, blazes at someone and then walks on the late night, by himself, not prepared for retaliation.

He continued to look at Jayde as she looked over at him, her chest heaving.

"Why?" She repeated, reading his mind.

"Nothing..." Bleek licked his lips, still tasting Jayde. "He just seemed...surprised."

There was a silence as they both thought to themselves, and then Jayde attempted to put any thoughts he may have had to rest.

"He shot E, Bleek. I saw him...He started it...and now we have to finish it."

She looked over and slowly traced her top lip with the tip of her tongue, letting out a smirk.

"But first...we have some unfinished business of our own."

Bleek looked over at her and Jayde took the exit heading to her condo.

Yeah she was a bitch, Bleek thought. *But she was a sexy ass bitch!*

The phone rang constantly and Sasha could see from where she was positioned on the bed, that the calls fluctuated from Chauncey to Tatum back to Chauncey.

She bit the skin on her lip and Mike stayed seated in a chair at the end of the bed, gun in his hand, his gaze locked on her.

"Mike...we should answer," she whimpered.

"Shut up," he ordered.

Suddenly a thought went through Sasha and she was glad that they didn't answer. She knew after a while, Chauncey would get worried, and come looking for her. It seemed as if Mike had simultaneously shared the same vision because he suddenly stood up from the chair, walked over to the phone, while still aiming the gun at Sasha, and picked it up off of the charger.

Shit, she thought.

Before he pressed the talk button, he pointed the gun at Sasha.

"You tell him you're tired, tell him we just made love, you hear me?" He spoke in a harsh whisper. "Tell him that, tell him you wanted to make love to your husband, and you better convince him…or I swear to god, you'll be dead by the time he gets here."

Sasha's body shook terribly and tears began to form in her eyes as Mike kept his cold glare. He pushed the talk button and handed the phone to her and Sasha hesitantly took it.

"He-hello," her voice quivered.

"What's going on? I thought you were coming back?" Chauncey shot at her, finally getting a hold of her.

"I was…" She looked over at Mike who held the gun steady. "Did…did Aubrey fall asleep without Pinky?"

"Yeah…yeah she alright," Chauncey answered, calming down a little. "But that's it…you not coming back then?"

Sasha remained silent, trying to send some mind signals through the phone. Mike raised the gun and pressed it hard to her head as she began to breathe quickly, terrified.

"Um…Uh…I…I'm tired." She looked at Mike hoping that was it, but he leaned closer and whispered.

"Tell him!"

A tear fell from her eye as she closed them and continued.

"I…I wanted to…" Mike pressed the gun forcefully against her temple urging her. "I wanted to...make love…to my husband," she managed to get out.

Chauncey was stunned into silence and then he retorted.

"What? What did you just say to me?"

Mike grabbed her hard by the hair, getting angry by her stalling and her difficultly in telling Chauncey this. Sasha knew he meant business and was becoming angry by the look in his eye.

"Get him off the fucking phone," he hissed.

"I said…Chauncey. That I wanted to make love to him," she said louder. "He's…he's my husband…and I love him."

Chauncey ran his tongue on the inside of his cheek in anger and in hurt. He couldn't believe this shit.

"Word?" Chauncey asked, shocked. "You love him, huh?"

Mike didn't even give her the chance to answer, he simply took the phone and ended the call.

"You did good, babe," he complimented her. Sasha cried hard as she tucked her knees up to her chest. She knew now that her chances of Chauncey rescuing her were now cut in half. She looked up at Mike who stared at her in a demented way.

"Now, take off all of your clothes," he ordered. And Sasha knew now, the torture had just begun.

The next morning, Sasha awoke to Mike positioning himself on top of her and in between her legs.

"No," she moaned, waking up from her coma like sleep. "Mike please, I'm sore…it hurts."

He ignored her protests and used his right arm to cock her leg up on his shoulder, his left hand, pressing the gun to her face.

"Please…," she cried, as he rammed deep in her and she whimpered.

Mike had fucked her a total of twenty times last night, and now this would be twenty-one. Lucky twenty-one she figured he thought.

She blacked out in her mind, envisioning her baby, wondering if she would hold her again. She should've never left. She should have stayed with her and Chauncey, forever. Now she feared she may never have the chance.

The good thing about this morning was that it was quick; she figured last night he must have been on some type of drug or Viagra or something.

After he came in her, he made her get up, get showered and dressed. She limped the whole way in pain and he watched her every move.

After she dressed in a sweat suit and sneakers, Mike locked her in the closet while he dressed and when he let her out, he had her breakfast waiting and she noticed bags packed at the front door.

"Where are we going?" She asked nervously, but he didn't respond. He just sipped his coffee, with one hand of course, the other one holding his new permanent accessory, the .38.

Just then, the doorbell rang and broke the intensity and fear in the room. Mike jumped up and looked at Sasha as if she had done something wrong, but she just shook her head.

"Who is that?" He barked.

She shrugged.

"I don't know...I swear."

Mike grabbed her forcefully by her hair, pulling her out of the chair and dragging her to the front door.

Once they approached, Mike looked out of the peephole and sucked his teeth.

"Fuck!" He whispered, stomping his foot and waving the weapon. Out of nowhere, he threw Sasha against the wall roughly and pressed the gun to her face.

"One fucking wrong move, and I swear, even if I go...I'm taking that baby with me, you hear me?"

Sasha could tell by his words that it was Chauncey at the door. She swallowed hard at the thought of something happening to Aubrey.

Mike pushed Sasha up to the door, and stood close behind her, appearing to have his arm lovingly draped around her but really had the gun pressed to her back.

"Don't fuck it up for your precious Bri-Bri, Sasha," Mike warned as Sasha took a deep breath and slowly opened the door.

"Hey," she said lightly looking at Chauncey standing there. His face wore a blank expression.

"Hey baby girl," she addressed Aubrey, a little void of her normal cheer.

Mike stayed close to her and smiled at them both and then kissed Sasha softly on the top of her head.

Chauncey furrowed his eyebrows at Sasha and Mike's sudden display of affection. He shook his head and wouldn't look her in the eye. He didn't know what kind of game she was playing.

"Bri need some shit from the house," he coldly stated. "Bring me down some more clothes, her DVDs, and her pink bear."

Sasha flinched to go, but Mike held her firm and pressed the gun into her back. She pressed her lips together in dread and tried to look at Chauncey, but he would not look at her.

"Actually, you can go and grab it, Chauncey," Mike said, opening the door further and positioning their bodies so that he couldn't see the gun.

Chauncey looked at him strangely and then slowly made his way inside. He studied Sasha, who just looked down at the ground.

Chauncey shook his head in confusion and handed Aubrey to Sasha, and then began to make his way up the stairs.

"Hi Mommy, I miss you," Aubrey said sweetly, wrapping her arms around Sasha's neck.

As soon as he was up the stairs, Mike grabbed Aubrey from Sasha, with her much resistance and then moved the gun to Sasha's stomach.

"Stop acting so fucking strange," he hissed. "When he comes down here, act like your regular ditzy self and tell him we're going away for a few days, you understand me?"

She didn't answer, and he began to lift the gun to Aubrey, who just rested her head on Mike trustingly, not knowing what was going on.

"Mommy, you go bye-bye?" She asked.

Aubrey didn't miss a beat.

Chauncey began to make his way back down the stairs, and Mike passed Aubrey quickly back to Sasha, and stood behind her back again, gun out, cocked, and ready.

Chauncey had overheard Aubrey and then noticed the bags by the door. As he took Aubrey from Sasha, he used his head to point to the luggage.

"Going somewhere?" He asked sarcastically.

Sasha feigned a smile through her desperation.

"Yea…yea, we are. We're going away…for a few days."

Chauncey chuckled and ran his hand over his face, not knowing where this was coming from.

"Where you going? And what about the investigation thing, with Bri?"

Sasha hadn't expected that question, but Mike was prepared.

"We'll be back shortly…we just need some time away. We'll probably go out camping and hiking, something like that."

Chauncey squinted, locking eyes with Mike, and then he turned his attention to Sasha. Her face looked void, null, and lost.

He didn't get it. Was she really feeling guilty, and wanted to get away with Mike?

He shrugged his shoulders and made his way out of the door.

"Your call kid," he said behind him, letting her know just what he felt, and his words had more than one meaning. And after he made Bri say goodbye to Sasha, he made his way out of the door.

Sasha screamed on the inside, screamed for him to stop and to turn around, screamed to tell him that she was in danger, but he was gone. The only good thing about it was that Aubrey had made it away safely. She knew that Mike originally wanted to hurt her baby, so getting her safely away from him was a plus to her.

Mike grabbed up the bags with haste, and grabbed up his wife, and then led them to his car. And by the time Chauncey had a realization that something wasn't right, Mike and Sasha were already on their way to his cabin deep in the Chicopee Woods.

Tatum, Ree, and even Jayde were on their way to Chauncey's after he had called them and let them know the urgency of them needing to be there.

After Chauncey and Aubrey had left, Aubrey had went on and on about Mike's toy. Chauncey, too occupied with his deliberation over his situation with Sasha, only half listened. But as they pulled up to the house and he turned around to unhook her car seat, he seen that her fingers were in the shape of a gun.

"He put it to mommy, his toy…pow pow," she described.

Chauncey furrowed his eyebrows and it clicked to him.

Deep down inside he knew something was wrong. Sasha would never leave Aubrey for days at a time like this, she barely wanted to leave her for a night. She also hated camping and bullshit like that.

He had let his anger by her saying that she had fucked Mike the night before, cloud his judgment, and now, he was vexed.

"Thanks for staying with Aubrey Tay," Chauncey said, standing at the door and waiting for Jayde to pull up. He couldn't leave until she got there with the info.

"No problem," she said desolately. "Just bring my girl home."

She made her way inside after giving him a somber look.

Ree approached the door, not too far behind her and Chauncey extended his hand. They did the hood handshake and then hugged.

"It's good seeing you," Ree said to Chauncey.

"Nah, it's good seeing *you*, boss," Chauncey responded. "I got some things I wanna talk to you about, but as you know, I gotta handle something first."

Ree nodded.

"Of course…of course. You go handle that, and handle it well," he instructed, letting him know to be careful and get it done. "I know you said you got this alone, so I'll be here."

Chauncey nodded, and then he saw Jayde pulling up. He jogged to meet her halfway, as Ree made his way inside.

"You got it?" He asked.

"Yeah, I got it," she said running up with a paper in her hand. When Chauncey had told her that Mike suggested that they were going camping and hiking, Jayde remembered that Sasha had said that he owned a cabin in the woods. She did her research and came up with an address. "This has to be it."

"Okay good looking," he said, hopping swiftly in his Bentley and speeding out of the driveway. Jayde stood there and watched him leave and she whispered to herself.

"Kill his ass, Chauncey. Kill him."

Chapter 22 - Death

Tatum and Jayde were upstairs with Aubrey, while Ree was in Chauncey's basement making a few phone calls.

'I can't believe this shit," Tatum muttered. "I'm going crazy trying to figure out what the hell is going on."

Jayde sighed.

"I know…it's like from what Chauncey says, and from what I found out about this chick that was watching Aubrey, it all points to Mike being shady as hell. I hope Chauncey kills that mothafucka," Jayde added through clenched teeth.

Tatum just looked at her. She wasn't one to talk venomous but for once, she had to agree with Jayde.

Tatum looked down at Chauncey's suede bedspread and all she could think of was Sasha. *Please let her be okay.*

But she trusted Chauncey, and she trusted his love for Sasha, so she knew that he would bring her back safely.

She felt Jayde's fingers in her hair and she looked up at her.

"You have the prettiest hair…you're fucking gorgeous, bitch," Jayde laughed.

Tatum chuckled and Jayde plopped back on the bed.

"Oh my god, I have the biggest headache. It's like a fucking migraine…all of this crazy shit happening."

Between Sasha and E and Capo and Bleek, Jayde was feeling the pressure.

"I need my IB profin," she proclaimed, searching for her Prada alligator purse.

"Where is it?" Tatum asked, breaking her trance.

"Shit! I left it in the car."

Jayde started to get up, holding her head in agony, but Tatum stood.

"Don't worry, I'll get it. You stay with Bri... is your door open?" Tatum wanted to check on Ree anyway.

"Yeah, it's open. Thanks Tatum."

Meanwhile, Capo was riding in the passenger seat of one of his chick's cars. They were coming from her crib, when he spotted Jayde's Range Rover.

Still with the cast on his leg, it was easy for him to remember the mini shootout they had recently exchanged.

"Drive slow, shawty," he drawled to her as he took out his nine and finessed it in his hand. "I'm 'bout to dead this bitch."

He recognized the missing side mirror that she had failed to get fixed since they had shot it out, and to his luck, he noticed her, with her back to the street, leaning into the car with the back door opened.

"Yeah bitch...got you now."

He slowly lifted his gun out of the passenger window as they cruised by, and once he squinted and had the perfect aim, which was too close to miss, his finger found the hairpin trigger.

Pow!

One bullet was all it took.

The girl in the driver's seat screamed at the sound of the shot, but floored the gas to pull off.

She looked over at Capo, who fell back against the seat, a hollow bullet hole smoking in his forehead.

"Aaaaaahhhhhh!!!" She shrieked in terror, but her cries were cut short instantaneously by a shot that exploded the back of her head like a watermelon.

The car continued to cruise way down the street but then reached the end of the block, swerved and crashed hard into a pole. It was pure madness.

Tatum was frozen in the street, trembling, as Ree stood by the doorway, his smoking gun in hand, only two precise and direct shots fired.

She looked over at him, tears in her eyes. Her mouth was opened but no words would come out as he made his way quickly to her and wrapped his arms around her.

"It's okay…It's alright."

Her body continued to shake as he walked her inside, where Jayde was now standing at the doorway in complete shock.

Ree continued to console her as he kissed the top of her head. He was fuming at the fact that someone had raised a gun to her and he knew that she was traumatized.

But little did he know, Tatum was not only shocked by someone attempting to shoot her, she was also surprised, almost alarmed, by Ree's primal, in fact natural, killer instincts.

If she didn't know it, or if she had ever doubted it, she now had no choice but to accept it…

She was sleeping with a killer.

"Why are you doing this?" Sasha cried, sitting in the middle of the bed in the cold and desolate cabin. "I said I was sorry…we can work it out."

Mike looked at her lovingly but then his face changed to one of anguish. She had ripped his heart from his chest. He had finally gotten her, he had finally won, and then she had humiliated him.

It was just like every other moment of his life when he had lost. He had always been… a loser.

"I want to believe that baby, I really do. But for now, my mind is set."

He twirled a pair of handcuffs in his hand, his other gripping the gun.

"Maybe when the baby comes, I will change my mind. But for now…in nine months, you die."

Sasha cried hard, terrified, and she looked around the barren room for some type of escape, some type of weapon, some type of sign. And then she saw one, and she knew she would be fine.

Mike neared her with the handcuffs.

"Okay, you have to put these on. Please, don't try to fight me."

He moved closer to her and grabbed her wrist.

"That won't be necessary."

Before he could even turn around, Mike felt the cold, hard steel against the back of his head and he knew it was all over.

He took a deep breath, and before he could lift up his gun, Chauncey struck him hard with the butt of his own, knocking Mike down. He grabbed Mike's .38 and tossed it to Sasha, who was still on the bed.

"Go wait in the car."

She looked down at Mike, her breathing heavy. She couldn't believe that she had actually married this man.

"Now, Sasha. Move," Chauncey demanded. He lifted his gun, ready to blast Mike as soon as Sasha was safe and away. He didn't want her in the room, he knew the effects of watching someone die, even someone you hated.

She jumped up and started for the door, but then she thought of Aubrey and what he had done to her, and she turned around.

She walked up to Mike and sneered down at him and then she hog spit right in his pathetic face.

"Burn in hell mothafucka," she hissed, knowing Chauncey was about to send him to his maker.

Mike weakly wiped away the spit while laughing, and then with it dripping from his fingers, he licked it away.

"I… love… you-"

Boom!

The single shot caught Mike square in the neck, his eyes bulged wide open. After a few seconds of gargling on his blood, his body twitched, and then lay lifelessly.

Chauncey slowly turned his head toward Sasha and her face was blank, her hand still shaking with the smoking .38 in it. After a few seconds of silence, she finally realized what had just happened.

"I…I killed him. Is he dead?" She whispered.

Chauncey with his mouth open in shock, walked over to her and gently took the gun from her as she stood stunned, in disbelief.

"I …I killed…I killed Mike," she repeated.

She finally looked at Chauncey with panic in her face. She couldn't believe that she, Sasha, had killed someone.

"Oh my god…I'm going to jail," she panicked.

Chauncey took her face into his hands.

"Ssshhh, no one's going to jail. It's okay…It's gonna be alright. I'll take care of it."

She shook her head.

"I did it Chauncey…I killed him… I killed Mike," she continued to cry.

He hugged her tight and rubbed her head. He knew that she was distressed and scared to death.

"No you didn't, I did…. I killed him."

She hugged him back for dear life, knowing that he would always protect her. This would forever be their secret.

"You hear me? Don't ever say that again. Not to your family, not to Tatum, no one. *I* killed him," Chauncey repeated, not ever wanting her to get into any trouble. "You were already in the car."

Sasha nodded understandingly but still knowing the truth, and as they hugged again, she looked down at Mike's corpse, who seemed to be staring back at her.

Without another word, Chauncey grabbed her bags and walked her outside, and then he called Bleek and told him to come and clean up the mess. *His* mess.

Tatum ran downstairs to where Ree was with a look of relief on her face.

"That was Chauncey…he has Sasha. Everything is okay."

Ree nodded, glad to hear the news and also glad that Tatum had calmed down and was now distracted from the earlier incident.

The police had come and questioned everyone on the block, and no one knew anything, especially not Jayde, who pretended to be there alone with her daughter. The car had also mysteriously caught on fire making it even harder, almost impossible, for the police to find out exactly what had occurred.

Jayde came down the stairs, from out of the restroom, and overheard the good news.

"That's great," she said, grabbing her coat.

Tatum turned to her, confused.

"You not waiting here for them?"

Jayde shook her head.

"No, but I'll be back. I have an important meeting with someone, it won't take long."

Tatum raised her eyebrows, surprised, but said her goodbyes.

"See ya later," Jayde said casually, and then she headed out of the door.

As she hopped in her now twice shot at new truck, she thought over the past days' events.

"That's it for me and Range Rovers," she mused.

She drove in contemplation and in deep thought for about twenty minutes. She was glad that Bleek was able to set that car on fire before the police had arrived. Finally, she reached the restaurant.

After parking in her reserved spot, she stepped out of the truck, put on her alarm, and strutted to the door in her black alligator stiletto heeled boots. A large bodyguard opened the door for her and she continued inside, never slowing her walk.

"Has my guest already arrived?" She asked, approaching another henchman.

"Yes, right this way Big-J," he based.

They made their way throughout the empty restaurant. Jayde had ordered it be cleared out for her meeting.

As she approached the table, dead in the center, she smirked at her visitor.

Takerra Allen

"Hello, long time…no see," she humored, taking a seat.

Jayde sat her purse down and stared with poise.

Neli sat up and folded her hands on the table, her face stern.

"Yeah well, you've been a hard person to catch up to Miss Jayde Dupree."

Jayde laughed lightly and took a sip from the water that was already on the table.

"What can I say, places to see…people to do…" She smiled sinisterly and her green eyes twinkled. "But I'm sure you can understand that…Miss Neli."

Neli rolled her eyes and reached into her purse swiftly, but two henchmen nearby pulled their guns and she froze.

"Whoa, whoa guys…cool out," Jayde told them giggling. "Me and her go *way* back."

Neli glared at them all, but then continued into her bag cautiously. She pulled out a manila envelope wrapped in a rubber band and threw it dead smack in the middle of the table, hard.

Jayde's face gradually became serious and she just looked at her.

"What's that for?"

Neli kept her intense stare.

"You *know* what it's for…it's the money."

Jayde chuckled and leaned back in her seat, slightly amused with Neli.

"I don't need the money, love. It's fine."

Neli's blood began to simmer.

"No it's not!" She looked around at the henchmen who were getting antsy, and then she lowered her voice. "It's not fine, Jayde…It's over. Just take the money, and leave it alone."

Jayde started to laugh hysterically at Neli's seriousness.

"Take the money Jayde, leave it alone," she mocked.

"Neli, Neli, Neli…when will you learn? I'm the one that calls the shots. What's wrong…you having a revelation now? The looney bin took all of your big, bad, problems away and now you want Jayde to change her ways, too? You must have forgotten… you started this love."

270

"Yeah, and now I'm ending it. It was a mistake," Neli sassed back.
"Oh so *now* it was a mistake? You tracked me down, and you paid me to finish what you started…you wanted me to make sure that Sasha wasn't done suffering when you found out that she was moving down here, you paid me to finish ruining her life since you couldn't do it, because you were locked in the looney bin. This was your crazy ass obsession with her, baby doll."
"I was sick!" Neli yelled. "I was wrong…and now I'm paying you to stop…so just stop."
Jayde shook her head at Neli as if she were clueless.
"Stop what? I'm not doing anything…" Jayde popped an altoid and then looked at Neli sincerely. "Oh wait…you thought that was *me* the whole time? Poisoning the kid, all of that bullshit? No sweetie, that's not my forte. Besides, I wouldn't have fucked that up." Jayde took another sip and leaned into Neli, her bad bitch aura overpowering Neli's pathetic attempt at confidence. "No see, that was her little weak ass husband, Mike. In fact, he's a lot like you. Well, *was* like you, I'm sure Chauncey has killed him by now. But anyway, he was ridiculously obsessed with the broad, just like you, to the point where he couldn't see her happy with anyone else… Oh, and for the record, you can't pay me to leave anything alone, because I never did it for the money."
Neli looked on in resentment, while Jayde continued.
"I'm a queen bee sweetie, I make more money than your little nutty ass can count... I did this, well, because ever since I was a little girl, Sasha always had the silver spoon in her mouth. And at the time, when you offered it to me, I thought it would be fun to take that spoon out, shake her shit up a bit, and maybe get a glimpse of this man… and this dick… that had you going crazy…literally. But now, I'm over it. I like Sasha…she's become… more real, since the last time I've seen her. And being that I'm not the least bit interested in Chauncey, I'll let them two have their happily ever after," Jayde concluded with a shrug.

Neli still felt a twinge of jealousy at the thought and mention of Sasha and Chauncey's happily ever after, but she knew she had to let that go. She furrowed her eyebrows.

"So that wasn't you?" She asked, surprised.

Jayde shook her head.

"No, it wasn't."

Neli didn't understand one thing though.

"Sooo...if you're not trying to hurt Sasha, then why are you still around them? I know the ever so self-sufficient Jayde is not pressed for girlfriends," Neli humored.

Jayde shot her a slick smirk and she drummed her manicured fingers onto the table rhythmically.

"Let's just say...something, or better yet...*someone*, has caught my attention."

Neli didn't respond and Jayde looked up with a smile before continuing.

"You know, Neli. I don't get you. You spend all of this time, chasing behind a nigga like Chauncey...trying to ruin Sasha's life, all for a man that is clearly in love with someone else..." Jayde spoke slowly. "I mean yeah, he's sexy. He's got that tall, dark, rugged thing going...but he's not the king. How could you even focus on him, when you have a man, like Respect, in your same proximity?"

Jayde's eyes filled with lust and she bit her lip as she thought of Ree. Ever since she laid eyes on him, she knew that she had to have him. Neli shook her head, and now she understood.

"You mean *Tatum's* Respect."

Jayde sucked her teeth.

"Oh please. A man like that belongs to no one, but himself. He's a god Neli, out of this world. They don't make his kind anymore...and I...will...have...my...piece."

Now it was Neli's turn to laugh, and she did.

"Not...gonna...happen. Do you see the way he looks at her? He loves Tatum... not to mention, Tatum's smarter than Sasha. She'll sniff you out like the trash that you are Jayde."

Jayde jerked her head back and grinned.

"Ooh, testy. I think you're forgetting one thing as well, Neli. I'm... smarter... than... you. And I won't try to fuck my way to Ree, like a whore." That was a clear stab at Neli because that was her M.O. with Chauncey. "Well, not literally... I will mind fuck him. Plus, I've got something that he wants, very badly. He just doesn't know it yet."

Neli lowered her eyes, truly feeling bad for bringing Jayde into the mix. She loved Tatum and she knew Tatum had been through a lot, she didn't deserve this. She looked up at Jayde with courage.

"I'll tell her. I'll stop you, Jayde. I owe her that much."

Jayde shook her head dismissively, and grabbed her purse to leave.

"They hate you. They won't even listen to you. Remember last time you tried to warn Sasha about me, don't you?"

Neli fumed, still determined.

"I'll get through to Tatum...she'll listen. And then Ree won't even come near your evil ass!"

Jayde looked up at Neli venomously and scowled. This meeting was over.

"You know Neli," she said standing up. "I think we're done here. And I'm feeling a little like... it's judgment day or something."

Jayde pulled out the .32 from her purse and promptly aimed it at Neli, who gasped in shock.

"Your wicked ways have finally caught up to you, mama."

Pop! Pop! Pop! Pop! Pop!

Jayde looked down at the bloody and limp Neli and shook her head in arrogance.

"How dare she threaten me...clean her up!"

She stormed out of the restaurant, her alligator shoes clicking across the floor, as Neli lay dying in her pool of blood.

"Mommy, I want to be beautiful like you," a young Neli had sung to her mother. She stared at her mother's reflection in the mirror, her long hair, and striking features, her designer labels, and sweet perfume. Her mother was glamorous, fabulous, high class, and Neli admired her so.

"Aw sweetie, I can help you," her mother had responded.

Neli remembered feeling instantly hurt. Her mother hadn't said that she was beautiful herself, or anything of that nature. She only said she could help her.

She remembered her father coming into the room, completely ignoring Neli and wrapping his arms around her mother.

Her father was tall and dark, just like Chauncey.

"Your mother's beauty is a rare one," he had said. "No one can be as beautiful as her."

Tears had welled in Neli's eyes as she watched her parents interact so lovingly, as if she weren't there. And this was what everyday was like for Neli growing up in her house. Attention deprived, and lonely.

Years later, she would be watching Sasha putting on her makeup in the mirror, and she would find herself uttering to her glamorous and fabulous friend.

"God I wish I were beautiful like you."

Sasha had turned around and smiled, and then she said.

"Aw Neli…I can help you, girl."

Neli had an instant déjàvu, and it worsened when Chauncey had come and wrapped his arms around her, as if Neli weren't even there.

Something inside of Neli snapped at that moment like a broken twig.

These were the memories that played in Neli's mind as she lay there on the restaurant floor. But at this moment, none of that mattered.

She was off of Sasha, off of Chauncey, off of her parents, and off of herself. She had made a promise from the moment the bullets riddled through her body and she was determined to keep it.

If I make it through this…I have to do one thing, and one thing only…

I have to… Stop Jayde…

Chapter 23 - Rebirth

Two Days Later

"Well, it's been an eventful week, to say the least," Sasha acknowledged, sitting on Chauncey's lap while Aubrey played with her toys on the living room floor. "I don't know how I got through all of this...but I'm glad I have you all here."
She smiled kindly at everyone, who were all seated on the couches, and her and Tatum locked eyes.
"Aw shut up girl, you know we love you..."
Everyone laughed and Tatum looked over at Ree and grinned wide.
"And I love *you*," she whispered. He kissed her softly.
"Alright, alright, enough of that," Jayde interrupted, rolling her eyes. "There is still *one* single person here," she joked. "Y'all mothafuckas are too lovey dovey for me."
"Aw, y'all...we gotta get Jayde a man... new project," Sasha declared.
Jayde shot her a middle finger playfully. Tatum, lost in her thoughts, sighed, still not believing everything that had happened.
"What's wrong...you okay, Tay?" Chauncey asked, noticing her solemn look. Ree looked at her seriously.
"It's just...I don't know. Between this shit with Mike, and Kim dying, and E... and even my brother...I just hope this is it, you know?"
Sasha nodded understandably and Chauncey looked down in reflection of everything that had occurred. Ree grabbed her hand and brought it to his lips.
"It is...," he assured her. "Excuse me for a minute."

He stood and dismissed himself, unable to really look at her at that moment. He had never really heard her talk about the effects of her brother dying.

He made his way downstairs to the bar in the basement and Jayde stood up as well.

"I think I'm gonna grab a drink, too."

Ree stood at the bar, sipping on a glass of Hennessy, deep in thought. He heard the footsteps coming down the stairs and he saw the red heels and jeans before he saw Jayde's face.

"Can you pour a lady one," she suggested, finally reaching the floor and walking in his direction. Her long hair was down and she looked flawless, but Ree was unaffected.

He grabbed another glass and filled it halfway, and then he handed it to her.

"So…Mickel Dupree's daughter." Ree looked at her acutely and she matched his gaze.

"Figured it out, huh?"

Ree took another sip and shrugged.

"Not much to figure…"

Jayde swallowed hard and took him all in, her head becoming light. Being in his presence was so electric, it was so arousing, she could hardly contain herself. Once Tatum had revealed that the bellhop was really her long lost love Ree, Jayde had known at that moment that he was the infamous Respect. From then on, his appeal had multiplied. It was something with her, but powerful and dangerous men turned her on. It was like playing with fire.

"My father told me a lot about you…he really had a lot of love for you," she disclosed.

Ree nodded.

"Your father was a really good man. He was…a friend."

Ree got lost in a memory.

"My condolences," he added.

Mickel Dupree was something like a teacher to Ree when he had first come to New York from the states. And Ree remembered when he was murdered.

"My father said you were a natural...a natural at this," Jayde spoke. "He said you were smart...and calculated...and that you knew how to make a lot of money. He said you were...a born gangster."

Jayde's voice was breathy as she spoke, she had been infatuated with Ree before she had even laid eyes on him.

The reflection caused Ree to look at her. And then he shrugged.

"Yeah well, that's flattering. But I'm a little more than that now."

Jayde looked at him incredulously.

"Really? Like what else?"

"Like somebody's potential husband," he stated matter of factly. He didn't even mention the possibility of being a father to Trinity's baby.

Ree knew the game should be over for him, but for some reason it kept calling him from all angles.

The statement annoyed Jayde, although she had already seen Tatum's ring. It would be hard to miss that big ass thing.

"Oh, so that's it. Back to Jamaica now?" She questioned.

"That's it," he nodded.

Jayde smiled and there was silence as they both sipped their drinks. And then...

"It's a shame," she finally admitted.

Ree looked at her firmly, wanting to know her angle, and she could tell by his expression that she'd better explain.

"It's just...I don't know. You're so good at what you do. And plus, I mean there's money here. Me and Chauncey we're doing well. But with someone like you in charge. Your ideas...your plans...the sky's the limit, you know?"

Ree was quiet as he let her words penetrate his mind.

"Plus the guy you killed, he was the last obstacle to us completely taking over."

"Chauncey said he killed E," Ree added, feeling as if he had killed two birds with one stone, or with one bullet for that matter.

Jayde pursed her lips.

"Well...now that I think about it, my vision is getting a little foggy... I don't think it was Capo that I saw shoot E. I must have been mistaken. But it *is* a damn shame what happened to E, huh?"

Ree stared at her and the growing smirk on her face read that she had done it, she had played a part in E's murder, and more importantly, she wanted him to know that she had done it.

"Why?" Ree asked, showing no change in emotion. People rarely shocked him, especially people like Jayde.

She sighed before answering and then leaned against the bar.

"E wouldn't respect me... and I know you of all people know the value of *respect*. Plus, I found out he was into some shady dealings...he was planning on linking up with Capo and doing some side business."

"So set E up and then say it was Capo, to eliminate them both."

She nodded and pointed at him as if to say, 'bingo!'

Ree put his drink down on the bar and took a step toward her.

"You know I should kill you, right?" The intensity of his words shook and excited her. "That was my dude's right hand," Ree reminded her with a somber look.

Jayde swallowed hard, briefly frightened by the potential she knew that Ree had, but then her regular swagger returned.

"You should...maybe. But I know you won't."

Ree raised an eyebrow and rubbed his goatee, anticipating her analysis as Jayde stepped closer.

"For one," she reasoned. "You know I was right. Regardless of who he was, he was apart of my team, and he broke the code of the game...just like Chris did."

She could tell by Ree's tenseness in his face that she may have crossed a boundary mentioning what she knew about the Chris situation.

"And two," she continued, wanting to put the mood back at ease. "You wouldn't...because..." But she didn't say it out loud, she just stepped closer to him, close enough to where she could smell the faint and tantalizing scent of him, and then she whispered something softly into his ear.

That something, caused Ree to reconsider and Jayde knew she had sealed the deal.

As she pulled away, and Ree stared straight ahead in deliberation, her heart pounded, and not because she was afraid of what he would do. She was like a bitch in heat for Ree, only moments away from howling and jumping all over him.

"You think about it," she said, forcing herself to reluctantly turn and head for the steps.

Ree began to soak up the conversation, especially the end of it, as he heard her make her way up the stairs. Moments later, he heard footsteps return and he wondered if it was Jayde.

"Hey you."

It wasn't. It was his queen.

Tatum smiled lightly and walked over to him.

"I was wondering when you were gonna come back upstairs, we're about to eat."

He wrapped his arms around her waist and pulled her close.

"I was just down here having a drink."

"And talking to Jayde?" Tatum tried to hide her discomfort.

"Yeah, *Jayde*," Ree repeated as if Jayde were a joke. "She was doing most of the talking, though."

Tatum wrapped her arms around his neck and looked at him sassily.

"About whattt?" She questioned and Ree chuckled at her jealousy.

"About some business proposals."

Tatum knew what kind of business Jayde was into and she didn't want Ree back in any of that business. Before she could say anything else, Ree kissed her tenderly on her mouth and then pulled away and used the tip of his tongue to trace her lips, causing her pussy lips to quiver.

He put his mouth to her ear and whispered deeply.

"You're the most beautiful woman in the world."

And then kissed her earlobe and made a trail of kisses down her neck.

"Ree," she panted in bliss, as her head fell back in ecstasy.

In one swift motion, he picked Tatum up strongly and sat her on the barstool and then he slid one leg out of her velor sweatpants.

"Ree…," she whined. "What if someone comes?"

"Well, let's just make sure we come first," he joked, pushing her panties to the side and steadily gliding all of him deep into her.

"Oh!" Tatum had to cry out. It felt so good.

She grabbed tight onto him, holding his dreads, and he began to move swiftly in and out of her.

"Oh god," she moaned. "Oh yes! Oh, I love you!"

He held her ass while the little barstool rocked back and forth in mercy, and Ree continued to hit her with a vicious stroke.

"Shit," he grunted, feeling his dick twitch.

They continued to go at it heavily, completely insatiable for one another.

Unbeknownst to them, Jayde stood at the top of the steps, her fingers inside of her jeans rubbing vigorously on her clit.

Just the sounds of the two beautiful people getting off were bringing her to orgasm.

"Oh!" She heard Tatum scream again. "Oh, Ree I love you…I love you!"

And Jayde rubbed faster imagining how good it must be.

They kept going, and she kept going, and finally they all reached their peaks at the same time.

Jayde hoped that it wouldn't be long until she had the real thing.

After the episode, Ree and Tatum got themselves together, and rejoined everyone else upstairs for dinner as if nothing had gone down.

Jayde chattered as if everything was normal, and she even had a warm glow on her face.

Sasha and Chauncey were in their own little world, and very affectionate. To everyone, it was clear that she was giving him another chance. Aubrey sat picking at her food and when the topic turned to the recent events that they had all just gone through, Sasha couldn't help but say…

"My baby is really a little soldier, despite those crazy ass folks, she really pulled through." She stroked Aubrey's pretty hair, thinking of Mike, and Tatum smiled.

"Well, god looks out for his little angels," she added.

Just then, Aubrey looked up at the table and giggled.

"Kim," she said clearly. Everyone was shocked and silent. "Kim give me kiss and hug and told me wake up."

The statements gave a warm and peculiar feeling as Tatum and Sasha both had tears in their eyes. It took a few minutes for everyone to get over the astonishment of what Aubrey had said.

Everyone else tried to shake it but the girls knew in their hearts there was truth to the revelation, and it was sentimental to them.

Everything was festive not too long after, the mood was just right and then Chauncey remembered something.

"Aw shit, I forgot to tell you…congratulations. Mr. and Mrs. Knights, huh?" He joked.

Ree smirked and Tatum thanked him laughing.

"I just feel so bad," Sasha started with her lip poked out. "All of this bad stuff happening, you guys didn't even have your moment."

Ree waved his hand in dismissal.

"It's fine, Sasha." He looked at Tatum and continued. "It's not about that, you know? It's about me…and this gorgeous girl right here, spending our lives together. Plus, we already had our moment." And then he winked at Tatum.

She smiled wide, thinking of their episode that had just occurred and Sasha looked on in admiration. She was so happy for them.

"So, when are you guys going back to Jamaica?" She added, a tinge of sadness if her voice.

Everyone looked at them for the answer.

Ree glanced around the table at the waiting faces, including Tatum's and then his gaze fell briefly on Jayde. He thought of what she had mentioned to him, and he considered all of the opportunities. Yes, he was out and he was at peace, but he knew the magnitude of what was possible, for everyone. It wouldn't take long at all, and it was the one master plan, that hustler's final score

281

that he had always wanted to put into motion before he left the game for good. Mickel had invented it, Ree had perfected it, and Jayde and Chauncey, seemed to be putting it into gear.

Ree still had some thinking to do, because he knew that his life was in Jamaica, and he also knew that he couldn't think just for himself...but he had a good idea where he would be doing his thinking at.

He ran his hand over his mouth before speaking and he looked at Tatum affectionately. He knew she would enjoy being around Sasha more. He also knew he'd have to lay low, but that was nothing new to him, so he proceeded with the well anticipated response...

"I think," he answered, choosing his words wisely. "I think we may… stick around for a little while."

And everyone smiled, glad to hear it. Everyone… especially Jayde.

A Few Minutes Later…

"Hello."

"Hey Sasha, it's your mother."

"Nooo…really?" Sasha shot back sarcastically. Her mother's silence let Sasha know the seriousness of her call. "Ma? What's going on?"

"I have to talk to you, are you busy?"

"We're having dinner. What's it about?" Sasha asked nervously.

"It's about Mickel."

"Who?" Sasha asked, confused.

"Mickel Dupree. Jayde's father."

TTW 3: The Last Installment…Coming Soon!

A Note from Jayde

I know you guys hate me, and for the most part, simply, I can really give a fuck.
But come on, don't tell me you expected me to let this end on some, happily ever after shit. Not happening!
Look, seriously people, I'm not trying to be the villain, or get bad girl of the year award, no. I'm just trying to get a piece of that fine ass, god of a man, Respect.
*And not for nothing, half, nah, fuck that, **most** of y'all know that if you had the chance to get next to him, you would take it.*
So, I'm not asking for you to root for me or anything, I know that would be crazy. You guys probably want to see that dream wedding between him and Tatum and all of that bullshit. So no, I'm not asking for you to be on my side.
All I'm saying is, don't be alarmed with the shit you'll be reading in the conclusion to this saga.
Because I promise you darling, Neli was an amateur compared to me. I'm about to turn up the heat in this bitch!
So, for all of my rare, really bad bitches out there, who all know there's a drought on fly ass niggas like Ree, I know you guys are with me.
Make sure you tune in, and as they always say…May the best bitch win.
Team Jayde Bitch!

Takerra Allen

Heaven Inc. Urban Entertainment &

Angelic Script Publishing

Order Form

Angelic Script Publishing

PO BOX 5873

New Brunswick, NJ 08903

Name: _____

Address: _____

City/State: _____

Zip: _____

Email: _____

Titles	Price	Quantity	Total
Thicker Than Water	$15.00	_____	_____
Heaven's Hell	$15.00	_____	_____
Still Thicker Than Water	$15.00	_____	
Total		_____	_____

Prison Orders Are $10.00 per title.

Shipping & Handling costs are $3.95 for first book and an additional $2.00 for every book added.
Please ensure that proper payment is enclosed in your order.
We accept checks or money order payments.
You can also order online – www.hiue.blogspot.com

Thank you for your Business! Reading is Sexy!

Still Thicker Than Water